Once Upon A Time

Mr. Greenan's Flying Stories

James Carroll Greenan

iUniverse, Inc.
New York   Bloomington

Once Upon A Time

Mr. Greenan's Flying Stories

iUniverse books may be ordered through booksellers or by contacting:

iUniverse
1663 Liberty Drive
Bloomington, IN 47403
www.iuniverse.com
1-800-Authors (1-800-288-4677)

Because of the dynamic nature of the Internet, any Web addresses or links contained in this book may have changed since publication and may no longer be valid. The views expressed in this work are solely those of the author and do not necessarily reflect the views of the publisher, and the publisher hereby disclaims any responsibility for them.

ISBN: 978-1-440-10552-4 (pbk)
ISBN: 978-1-440-10553-1 (ebk)

Printed in the United States of America
iUniverse rev. date: 10/21/08

Acknowledgements

I would like to thank all the members of the Writing Group, past and present, for their friendship and support during the writing of this memoir: Joan Condon, Tom Condon, William Drake, George Hahn, Joyce Hahn, Mary Krainik, Helen Parker, Beverly Paik and Evelyn Smart.

--James Greenan

Mahalo also to the many people who assisted in getting this book made; The entire Greenan Clan for all their love support and encouragement. To Margret LeMasurier and Sandra Odgen for their typing and organizational skills. To Jim's many friends, past and present, Butch, Doc and Kiwala to name a few, who kept him laughing and inspired.

Prologue

Solo

A first solo in an airplane is private and intense. The day your instructor climbs out of the airplane, pats you on the head and says: "Take it up!" will only happen this one time.

"Wait a second!" your mind says. "Hang on a minute! What makes you think I'm ready?" but you don't say anything, you just sit there, a little numb, but exhilarated.

Your instructor ambles away from your airplane, turns and smiles reassuringly. Your mind is very keen and you can see beyond his confident smile. Turning a new pilot loose is a tough judgment call for him and even with what you're going through, you can appreciate his feelings.

Well, you can't sit there forever. You move the hand on the throttle, release the brakes and, with a roar, you taxi to the far end of the field.

You are alone in the aircraft, alone on the field. The past hours have been spent in the company of dozens of other planes, dozens of other instructors and their cadets like you. Not this day. A first solo is away at another field, a practice runway, far from other potentially damageable planes and people.

The big radial engine ticks over quietly, waiting for you. Your aircraft is called a AT-6. It is the only aircraft you have ever flown.

It is a full-blown powerful aircraft, not much different from the frontline fighter of the Japanese Empire in World War II, the fighter-pursuit plane called a Zero. The AT-6 is a low-winged monoplane with a 450 horsepower engine.

You've had 15 hours or so with your instructor in the AT-6, 15 hours of loops, spins, rolls, take-offs and many, many landings.

This day, this hour, this minute is the start of it all.

You're lined up straight at the far end of the runway, ready.

Taking off is not a problem. You've done it many times. You will get torque and need a lot of left rudder, then the tail will lift as you feel the airplane want to fly. Ease back on the stick, keep the wings level and you will be up, up in the sky. No problem.

You push the throttle forward and you and your airplane begin the take-off roll.

You're up. This is it. You're committed. You and this powerful airplane are alone in the sky. The feeling washes over you like love and you very nearly take your hand off the throttle to pat the instrument panel.

Aloft, the primary difference between all your previous life and solo flight occurs to you. Once in the air, a brand new, never before experienced thing happens. You are in three dimensions, alone, unable to pull off to the side of the road to get your bearings, to collect yourself, call home to mother, wire for emergency funds.

No, no. Up here, it's all your show, no one that you ever counted on can do it for you. You can fly around for as long as your fuel holds out, but the fact remains: eventually, sooner or later, you must land. You and you alone.

The numbness has passed. You feel nothing but exhilaration. Your canopy is open and you hear the rush of air, the deep roar of the engine. You and this beautiful aircraft are one in the sky and there is nothing the two of you cannot do.

At 1,000 feet you bank to the left to see the airfield and the tiny figure of your instructor on the ground, earthbound while you are here free in the sky. You roll to the right in a steep bank, wanting very much to keep it rolling, to do a slow roll, a victory roll. The urge to fly for a time is nearly overpowering. But you don't. Your job on this flight is to take it off and land.

The landing procedures memorized over the weeks are there. Prop full pitch. Mixture full rich. Check your gauges for altitude, fuel, your instrument panel in a brief sweep. Turn base and move the lever to lower the landing gear as you slow your aircraft down. Half flaps and your final turn, that long glide slope to the runway and a reuniting with earth.

The reality of the landing is here and now. Too slow on this final glide path and you stall. Too fast and you overshoot.

You are over the beginning of the runway now and you know you are too hot, too much airspeed and will be long. You feed the throttle on smooth and strong and your engine responds as you take it up again for another try. Gear and flaps up and you feel the cool prickle of sweat. You could have made it that time, you think. Never mind, do it this time.

On final approach again. You are set. Gear down, flaps down. Slow it to landing speed, your eyes making a quick sweep of the instruments, then back on the job.

Flare it out, ease the throttle off. Feel the airplane settle, grope for the tarmac, then find it and you are down.

You're soloed.

Cadets

In The Beginning: Missouri

We were a sort of United Nations of flying cadets in primary flight school: Sven Anders from Scandinavia, Fabrice Nichol from France, Bobby Logan from Texas and myself from California. We were here to begin flying training, to see whether we had the right stuff, but surviving the heat seemed to be becoming just as important.

It was hot in Missouri that summer and Sven Anders suffered the most. During the days, the temperature would be up around 100 degrees or a bit more, but it was in the night that it became nearly insufferable. The thermometer never changed its reading and the humidity seemed to actually rise, although how it could from its 90 degree daytime range was questionable.

Shortly after we found ourselves quartered together, Anders began taking his nightly walks to the shower. There were four of us in a small room, steel bunk beds stacked neatly two to a corner, two bureaus, two small closets and an attached bathroom.

None of us was sleeping well, lying atop our bunks in shorts, panting in soft cadences as we tried to get in the brief six hours rest until formation at 5:15 a.m., but Sven couldn't take it. His eyes became more sunken by the day, ringed with dark circles. Out for a breath of hopefully less sodden air one night, he remarked gloomily that he found it impossible to imagine anyone living in a place like this.

"It's crazy!" he said. "Like living in a sauna. I must sleep!" and that night he started it. It was around midnight and he dropped quietly to

3

the floor and pulled the top sheet off his bed with him. He padded into the shower and we heard the cooling rush of water. Then he was back in the room, wrapped as tightly as an Egyptian mummy in the soaking wet sheet. He stood by the side of the stacked bunk and with an extraordinary twisting leap, flung himself onto the top.

"I can get about an hour-and-a-half," he confided later, "and then I must re-wet myself. Once you cross some heat threshold, you begin to cook like a potato. I set my wristwatch alarm. You should try it!" he urged.

The next morning I looked with suspicion at his hand holding a coffee cup as we waited for our next flight. "Sven, look at your skin! It's all puckered as if you had slept in a tub. God only knows what tuberculosis danger you are flirting with!"

"Perhaps," Sven replied, "but I must sleep!"

Fabrice was another strange one in our group. He was from Paris and very French. He was quiet and stern, with big, broad shoulders and a strong face, full of character. He was a fantastic pilot, easily the best in the squadron. He soloed first, after a mere 11 hours in our primary trainer, the surprisingly complicated and tricky AT-6. He endured the solo ceremony, which consisted of being heaved into the swimming pool by fellow cadets. Back in our quarters, we congratulated him as the first to solo and predicted a fine career as a military aviator.

"Listen!" Fabrice spoke deliberately and slowly, enunciating each word, "I would rather sell newspapers on the streets of Paris for the rest of my life than be in the military!"

He had a point. Whatever ideas we all had about flying training, none of us knew what we were in for on the military side. Patterned after West Point, we ate three square meals, sitting on the final two inches of chairs, hit a brace whenever any upperclassman spoke to us, drill marched in the damnable heat and ran to the flight line and classes.

But the flying made it all worthwhile. It was wonderful. It was hard to get Sven out of the air. "My God!" he exclaimed. "You can breathe up there!" He tried to be the first off in a flight period and almost always the dead last to land.

We had all soloed by 20 hours and were into the syllabus: take-offs, landings and more landings, emergency procedures and acrobatics. Acrobatics were what it was all about, we felt, and tried to top each other with stories of occasional perfect barrel rolls, loops, lazy eights and Cuban eights, chandelles, spin and stall recoveries. We did spin recoveries by the dozens and Bobby Logan became spin king.

"God!" he would moan to us in the soup of the Missouri night as we waited for Taps. "All my instructor will do is damned spins!" Our instructors who stayed with us throughout primary were all civilian contract pilots and he had drawn an introverted, small guy with a spin hang-up.

Putting any aircraft into a spin is an unsettling and unnatural experience. You have to keep the nose high until the airplane begins to mush and shudder, stalling out as you start not to fly. Then, in the AT-6, you dump the stick back in your lap and wait for the bottom to fall out. When this happens with a sickening here-we-go feeling, you kick in hard left rudder and the airplane whips around nose down and you begin a spin around your axis.

You need to know why you got there as well as how to get out of it. No question about that. But Bobby had drawn this guy with a fixation, a spin neurosis.

"I asked him why so many spins," Bobby told us, "and he said some day I would thank him. He couldn't get out of a spin once and had to bail out, he said."

"Oh?" Fabrice questioned, mildly interested. "Did he injure himself?"

"No," Bobby answered. "He landed easily in a wheat field."

"What was the problem then?"

"It was in Germany and he spent the next two years in a prison camp." Bobby laughed, and Fabrice said something that sounded rude to him in French.

Fabrice didn't seem as bothered as the rest of us by the oppressive heat and humidity. He was too consumed by his dislike of the military to have much patience with any other problem. Except for food. This was the final indignity for him.

Sitting bolt upright on the edge of his chair in the mess, eating the required square meal, he took these affronts with a severeness that intimidated even the watchful eyes of upperclassmen. While they snapped and growled at the rest of us during meals, a procedure supposed to have some bearing on encouraging our abilities to perform under stress, he was pretty much left alone.

In the heat, his eyes and bearing were fixed on the soggy carrots, the wilting salad, the breaded veal chop congealing in sauce and his whole attitude seemed to say, "I have to live, so I eat. I have to fly, so I endure the military. But there is nothing on earth that says I have to like it!" Any attempt to ask him about the food of France brought a silence, a misty look of recollection and a shrug of his Gallic shoulders. Apparently, it was too much of a leap to speak of in our present circumstances.

When all of us remaining in the squadron after the predicted 25 percent washout rate had soloed, we had flying periods where 10 or 15 of us would fly our bright yellow monoplanes to a field where we would spend the next hour-and-a-half shooting landings. The favorite place for this training was a short grass strip in the Missouri countryside.

The instructors would land first and stripe a white line across the grass and then watch and score our abilities to land on or near the line.

By this time we had perhaps 40 or 50 hours in the AT-6, not much time in an aircraft with many sophisticated features. The AT-6 was very much like the Japanese Zero of World War II and to say we were neophytes to it and flying would be putting it mildly.

At any given time there would be five or six of us waiting to take off, five in the air and five in the approach for landing, all in a small space. Making a good landing score was important, of course, but equally as pressing for 15 brand-new pilots was not running into one another in the process.

Fabrice was still the ace, always with the best scoring. Sitting in our separate planes on the grass with our engines ticking over, he motioned to me. In dumb show, in mime, he pointed to the white stripe on the grass, then at me. As I watched, he let his flaps down, then up. It took a minute to understand what he was attempting to show as he repeated his movements. He was trying to teach me how to land on the stripe, how to make a good score. Over the marker, inches off the ground, but floating long, he would pull up his flaps, causing lack of lift and his plane to settle in and nail the line. Sven and Bobby got the word and the four of us had the top scores in landing accuracy thanks to Fabrice.

We would scout out the countryside when we eventually were given weekend passes. We were not wildly popular with the local gentry. Too many of us had tried a practice strafing run down the river or a forced landing in some field scaring the cows out of their milk for us to be liked. We were tolerated at best.

It didn't bother us. Flying is an all-engrossing business and all we cared to talk about was that. We would find a tavern on the banks of the river and drink and talk.

Bobby Logan and I were beer drinkers, quantities of lager. Fabrice would go through his usual futile attempt to find a quality glass of wine, finally settling for whatever they had, while Sven would lie in the river, everything but his nose submerged in the life-giving, cool water.

The heat broke in our sixth week. It was like a miracle. Sven looked stunned, unbelieving and pathetically grateful. He abandoned his wet sheet. There was new life in the squadron and we marched, drilled and flew with zest.

We became upperclassmen, given cadet rank and privileges. I became squadron cadet major, Fabrice squadron cadet lieutenant, while Bobby Logan and Sven brought up the rear as cadet sergeants.

It was a fine time for the following six weeks. We growled and snapped at new cadets, hauling them up short in stiff braces while they repeated the forced landing procedure at top speed. We shook hands and agreed to remember each other when we got our orders to different bases for the next training phase, but we all knew that this was only the beginning of a long road and we only hoped to remember.

Well, my hope is that somewhere today Sven is sitting in a cool breeze, Bobby Logan has a beer in hand in Texas and Fabrice holds a glass of excellent wine while savoring some superior pate de foie gras in Paris.

Most of all, I hope they all made it.

He Wouldn't Come Down

He wouldn't come down. Or he couldn't come down. Nobody knew because he wouldn't talk.

The word got around the airfield like smoke, through the same strange osmosis process as when there had been a crash. You would see a look of concern, a quietness, something, and asking about it, you would get the word from a friendly instructor.

This time it was our meteorology officer. "A guy in the second flight, up on his first solo and they can't get him to land. They don't know what's going on. He won't reply, won't speak on the mike. What we hear is he just keeps flying around in big lazy circles." Our minds kicked into gear, thinking of how it went when we soloed, putting ourselves up there with him.

It was a time of first solos, a period when we cadets were between 15 and 20 hours and were being sent into the sky alone. This guy was one of the last in the squadron to solo. And now it had happened. He wouldn't come down.

Of the four of us sitting in the briefing room: Sven Anders from Scandinavia, Fabrice Nichol from France, Bobby Logan out of Texas and myself from California, Anders was the first to speak.

"That's the problem. Taking off isn't the problem with soloing. It's the getting down, back to terra firma, that is what it is all about."

Bobby Logan nodded his head in agreement, looking thoughtful. "It was the first time I realized something about flight, about being a pilot, that I had never looked at before."

Fabrice, closer to Bobby than anyone, asked what he meant.

Bobby smiled at him. "For the first time, I knew I was in a place I had never been before, a place that was unique." He had our attention and went on, explaining: "Remember when we all went water skiing? Well, I'd never done it before and I remember thinking what would happen if I fell, maybe hit my head on the ski and got into trouble." He grinned at Fabrice, the rest of us. "No problem. One of the three of you would jump in and save my bacon."

"So?" Sven asked, "what does that have to do with soloing?"

"Everything!" Bobby answered. "I realized on the first flight, my solo, that nobody could help me. Getting it back on the ground was up to me. All the friends in the world couldn't land it for me. Only I could!"

Fabrice, our resident ace pilot cadet and wise man, nodded his head. "You are right, Bobby. A moment of truth for all of us."

Outside on the tarmac most of the cadet squadron and instructors were standing, gathered in little groups. Up over the field at about 2,000 feet was the yellow monoplane looking cheerful and bright in the blue Missouri sky, turning in slow circles over the airfield, its big radial engine throttled down to a slow cruise. It sounded lonely, the usual drone of dozens of airplanes of this primary flight school absent from the air.

A cadet from another flight came up to us briefly and filled us in. "They pulled all the planes down. He came back here from the auxiliary field a few minutes ago. They're sending up the chief instructor to see if they can get him on his wing, get him to follow him down and land. They still don't know what's going on. He won't talk."

I glanced at my watch. "How much fuel does he have? How long before he has to come down?"

The cadet was quick to answer. "An hour, they figure, more or less."

Sven took his eyes off the circling airplane. "Christ! It makes it worse! It's like standing too long on the end of a high diving board. The longer you wait, the more you freeze!"

Fabrice was solemn. "He has no ladder to go back down. Eventually, he either has to land it, or," and he paused for a moment, "or he can jump, bail out, use his parachute." We all looked at him in astonishment, not having thought of this one possible option.

"My God!" Bobby exclaimed, "That would be worse, a thousand times worse!"

"Maybe," Fabrice said. "Maybe not. It all depends on how badly he is frozen."

The time seemed to pass slowly as we sat under the wing of an airplane. We had gone from watching the sky and the hypnotic easy circling of the airplane, to sitting and listening with a part of our minds while we talked quietly.

"I don't remember a time when I wasn't interested in airplanes," Bobby murmured. "My father was in the oil supply business, and Texas being as big as it is, we flew everywhere. I had my first ride when I was three and I remember it like it was yesterday. I loved it. He was letting me hold the wheel by the time I was seven."

Sven nodded his head. "Like me, only for me it was model airplanes, hundreds of them."

"I used to go out to the airfield and watch them take-off and land for hours," I said. "Even after dark. I'd be sitting there on my bike freezing my ass off, watching just one more land."

Fabrice laughed softly. He was so French even his laughter seemed to have a French accent. "For me, airplanes were like women. We lived outside Paris in the countryside, not far from a small private flying field. I would go to the parked planes and find one with an open door, sit in it and imagine flight. I love even the touch of an airplane. I would marry one and have children, if it were possible!" Our quiet laughter was complete and understanding.

We were watching the sky again. The chief instructor had gone up and was flying off the circling airplane's wing. We had turned on the radio of the parked airplane next to us and, like cadets all over the parking area, were listening. The chief pilot had tried to speak calmly to the cadet, but had gotten no response. He was trying another tack now, the voice of command, telling the cadet to land and to be quick about it. There was no reply and, with a burst of power, the cadet took his airplane up a thousand feet. The instructor followed him up after a minute, telling him to be calm, that it would all work out.

He asked if the cadet would fly off his wing, just watch and imitate him. If he slowed down, dropped his landing gear and flaps, would the cadet try that? There was no reply, but the airplane flew closer to the instructor and, after a short time with the instructor telling him they were beginning, they started down.

It looked good to all of us as we stood and watched, our fingers crossed. They came down with the cadet aimed by the instructor for the runway, while he flew off to the side. For a moment or two it looked good. Then we heard the deep roar of the cadet's engine as he pulled up his gear and flaps and went back up. There was still no sound from him. His silence was eerie, unsettling; it was like a ghost airplane.

Fabrice was looking at his watch. "He's getting close to the time, the fuel problem." We all watched as the plane circled higher, up to four or five thousand feet.

"Lord!" Bobby breathed, his head cocked back to the sky. "Wouldn't it be awful to love airplanes, want to fly, yet to have it be unnatural, to be frightened of it?"

Sven had binoculars he had gotten somewhere fixed on the plane. "He has the canopy pushed back. Fabrice! Maybe he is going to jump!"

Fabrice shook his head firmly. "No. He has shown too much control so far to parachute over the field. He will know the airplane would have to come down and he would fly it away from the field, from us, if he were going to jump." It was just then we heard the sound of the two engines stop. The cadet's engine was off.

"That's it!" Sven whispered. "He's out of fuel! He has to either bail out now or land without power!" With the rest of the cadets, instructors and mechanics, we watched while the silent ghostly airplane circled lower and lower, to finally make a near perfect, powerless, dead-stick landing on the runway and roll to a stop.

Well, life went on, flying went on. It was sometime later we heard what had happened.

The cadet, a bright-faced, eager, dean's list student and varsity athlete, stood by the side of his quiet airplane on the runway until the officers and instructors got to him.

With the biggest smile you can imagine, we were told, he said with simplicity, "I quit!" and was happily escorted off the field to become a nameless legend in the cadet corps.

Terry

All of us in the Malden, Missouri flight school knew Tom Terry, or at least knew of him. A genuinely funny person, Terry was an independent spirit, one of those rare people not awed by military authority. He was a cadet and would 'Yes Sir, No Sir" as we did, but there was a tone in his voice that seemed on the verge of laughter. We appreciated Terry. The military is tough on non-conformists and one quiet rebel like Terry was worth his weight in gold for our morale.

Normally, guys like Terry aren't around for long. The military has little patience and no humor. But Terry happened to be a natural pilot, underneath it all was very bright and, perhaps above all, had drawn an instructor pilot who found him challenging.

Terry's instructor was Lieutenant Lacy, at most two or three years older than Terry, a short muscular man with a gorgeous young wife whom he obviously adored. She was the cause of the first confrontation between the two.

Wives of our instructors were rarely seen around the flight school at Malden. It was an unspoken rule and helped us retain our 'men only' sense of purpose, but Lieutenant Lacy's wife ignored it. Only a week into training, she drove her little blue convertible up to the fence guarding the parked airplanes and waved to Terry's instructor.

After talking to her, Lacy turned back to Terry, standing wide-eyed in appreciation.

"My wife," Lieutenant Lacy finally said, red of face.

"Outstanding!" Terry said fervently, eyes in his handsome, guileless face fixed on the departing convertible.

"What?" Lacy nearly shouted, back into full military posture.

Terry didn't back down an inch. With a hint of a smile and firm voice, he repeated, "Your wife, Sir! She's outstanding!"

Well, there wasn't really much Lacy could do as she was unquestionably exactly that and it was the beginning of their contest. It was an unfair contest as our instructors held all the cards, mainly because they were able to 'pink slip' us. Three pinks and you were due for a check ride that could wash you out.

But Terry received no pinks; he was an exceptional cadet, one of the first to solo. We had to give Lacy points for a sense of fairness, even humor, as he continued to fly with Terry, undoubtedly knowing a character like him couldn't change. Their relationship evolved into a continuing battle for supremacy, to the delight of our cadet corps, and new Terry/Lacy stories ran through the squadron almost daily.

Terry was tall, at least six inches taller than Lacy, and he never lost an opportunity to sit tall, stand tall when with Lacy, peering down from the bill of his cap in earnest attention. Or entering a low doorway, Terry would duck his six-foot-three inches and look solicitously at Lacy to make sure he also cleared it. There was nothing really for Lacy to complain about and, to his credit, he didn't.

Off the end of the runway at Malden was a large wooded and swampy area known locally as The Bogs. We were all aware of The Bogs, an unfriendly locale, full of trees and vines, a good-size swamp and animals. The local legend had it that The Bogs was the home place of bears and big cats, but worst of all, it undoubtedly had snakes. Fat and deadly or long and mean, we had no idea. They were there and that was enough. Positioned as it was off the end of the runway, it had an unsavory reputation as a place for a forced landing. We all had a tendency to come in for a landing high and hot, willing to overshoot rather than risk putting it down in snake and animal country.

The problem didn't end with keeping our planes and ourselves out of The Bogs. The runway would heat up during the hot Missouri days and at night heat-seeking reptiles would slither onto the warm tarmac for comfort. We were warned of this, at any rate, and always made a careful inspection of the cockpits of our airplanes before climbing in for a flight.

The report of a BOAC airliner taking off from Karachi and the pilot discovering a fer-de-lance wrapped around the control column was part of the local lore. The story was accepted as gospel in our cadet corps and the thought of this horror along with the normal stress of taking off was unacceptable. We made an extremely close inspection each time. A funny scene, when you think about it, dozens of cadets with penlights grasped firmly in teeth peering anxiously into cockpits for intruders. If any of us had ever discovered one, a major heart attack would not be out of the question, notwithstanding our young and healthy bodies. Naturally, it was Terry who gave substance to the rumor.

Terry and Lacy had one of their entertaining pre-flight briefings this particular night and, listening from all over the room, we enjoyed the one advantage we had in these seriously tilted instructor/cadet, master/slave relationships we had with our instructors. Lacy was alert as he briefed Terry, watchful as Terry listened. You could almost see him thinking, "What is this goofball going to pull now?"

Little did he know that Terry had gone to the trouble to find and buy a rubber snake, one of those novelty items that stores sell for children to play with. Terry had, in his inimitable way, opened his flight jacket for a second as he walked into the room, showing us a flash of his rubber reptile. You could see by our expressions many of us thought he had gone beyond the bounds of reasonable humor, yet there was not one of us who could wait to see the outcome.

We found various reasons to hang around his airplane as we went out to pre-flight our planes. With Terry up on the wing, leaning by turn into both cockpits, we had no idea what he was going to do. Our best guess was he would place the snake in Lacy's cockpit during this inspection and then deny any involvement if Lacy lived through the shock. But a passing cadet gave us a whispered new theory. The word was that Terry planned to have an airborne struggle, holding the snake up with one hand in flight while shaking it, then throwing it over the side. That is not the way it went.

Lacy walked up to the airplane, glancing quizzically at the large group of us nearby. Then, ignoring us, he demanded to know if Terry had made the visual inspection. When Terry hit a brace and responded that he had done so, Lacy hopped up on the wing and began to climb in the cockpit. He just as quickly shot out and back onto the ground.

"There's a damned snake in there!" he shouted.

Without hesitation, Terry scrambled up on the wing. He reached in the cockpit and then held the snake aloft triumphantly, shaking it realistically while we watched in admiration. Then he let out a horrifying scream and stood stock still as the snake continued to wiggle in his hand. It was the real thing, we realized, as Terry came to the same conclusion and fainted, falling first onto the wing and then the tarmac. Lacy had switched the snakes, Terry's fake rubber one for the real thing.

"Gotcha!" Lacy screamed. "I finally gotcha, Terry!"

The harmless garter snake slithered off, scattering us, while Lacy yelled his victory, holding aloft Terry's rubber toy, laughing his revenge. Terry, conscious again, lay prone on the tarmac and, showing his character, gave Lacy a weak smile of congratulations.

Well, it didn't change Terry, but he seemed to have aged. He continued to fly with Lacy; in fact, they seemed to have become friends. Terry graduated with the rest of us to the next phase and a nice thing happened the day before we were to leave.

Lacy joined all of us in our final briefing where we accepted the good wishes of the men who started us on the long road to wings. He shook Terry's hand and handed him the rubber snake with a pink bow around its neck.

"Easy on the next guy, Terry," he grinned, "And keep this to remember!"

Big Springs

Jack Burrell had become a sort of good luck piece for the four of us. As cadets, the transition from piston airplanes to jets was enormous. We were all experiencing the same skill and emotional shock in going from our piston-powered AT-6 to the near speed-of-sound jet T-33 and Jack Burrell showed it most of all. Jack was a talisman for us, for sure, and, we thought, if he could make it, well, perhaps we all could.

The four of us—Sven Anders from Scandinavia, Fabrice Nichol from France, Bobby Logan from Texas and myself from California— had, through the luck of the draw, remained intact after soloing in primary, through basic and now at advanced training at Big Springs, Texas.

Shaky Jack Burrell was what we called him. This was after Fabrice and Bobby Logan had helped him into the jet for his first solo in that wholly different aircraft. They had come back to the flight ready-room after strapping him in the cockpit and patting him reassuringly on the helmet.

"Man!" Bobby Logan exclaimed to us, "You should have seen him shake!" He looked to Fabrice for confirmation. Fabrice nodded soberly in agreement.

"It's true," he said. "But I think Jack Burrell is perhaps the bravest man I know!" He didn't say bravest, he said courageous with a French spin on it. As usual, he left us to think about what he had said and what it meant.

We sat for a time thinking and then Sven spoke. "I believe I understand Fabrice," he said in his textbook English and we listened intently.

"Jack is frightened," he continued, voicing what none of us in the squadron ever mentioned, that fear was a part of what we were doing. "He is too intelligent to miss academically, too capable to fail in the flying and has too much pride to sign the fear-of-flying statement."

That was it. Shaky Jack was an unnatural pilot, a guy who shouldn't be flying and who wouldn't get out the only way they allowed you out. You had to sign a written statement that we all knew about and called the 'fear-of-flying' paper, a cursed document that added up to admitting you feared flying.

We had them around the squadron, perfectly brave enough guys who just weren't aviators and had signed. They stayed around for a week or two waiting for transfer orders, still going to academic classes with us, but they were like ghosts, avoided for the pity we all felt for them.

Shaky Jack couldn't wash-out, wouldn't sign and the four of us rooted for him. In a way, he epitomized what we felt to some degree or other: fright and fear from the ever escalating, steep demands of becoming a fighter pilot. They pushed us hard.

We had barely soloed and they had us doing loops. While still trying to master the basics of flight, they had us chasing experienced pilots while they went through wild acrobatic maneuvers. We tried to keep on their tails as sometimes we came dangerously close or at other times fell too far back, always at the limit of our abilities.

It worked. Push us beyond what we thought we could do and, somehow, we did it. Well, mostly, but not always. It wasn't rare that we would see a column of black smoke and hear the sirens of the airstrip crash trucks, or hear the emergency helicopters lift off.

We talked of Shaky Jack that night in our quarters. Fabrice was the same age as the rest of us, twenty-two or three, but he seemed much older. He was part of our sessions, but spoke seldom; when he did it was usually with great impact and wisdom. He was a natural leader, the acknowledged best cadet pilot in the squadron and his opinions were sought.

We asked him if we were right about Shaky Jack.

"Shaky Jack," Fabrice repeated and smiled at the name. Then he was serious. "We must watch out for him, help him." This from Fabrice who was constantly helping us in many ways. Of course we would.

We had the chance sooner than we expected on our first cross-country night flight.

The Texas sky was filled with stars, a clear moonlit darkness and, as we marched to the flight line, we heard again the unique wail of jet engines starting up. They were eerier than usual in the night. This was in an era before jet flight, and the banshee cry of the jet engine was just beginning to be heard by us and not at all by most.

We were each to take off in five-minute intervals, fly from Big Springs to Amarillo, then to Lubbock and return to Big Springs, careful to report in over each town. We were to conduct ourselves as military aviators, disciplined and competent, to have no unnecessary chatter on the microphones in flight, just strap the aircraft on and do this night mission!

Bobby Logan was one aircraft ahead of me, Fabrice and Sven two behind and no sooner were we in the air than we began hearing it. Abrupt urgent calls on our frequency from our airborne instructor-officer. On this clear night, there was an unexpected cumulonimbus, a thunderhead, between Lubbock and Big Springs.

Each of us alone in our cockpits over the barren moonlit plains of Texas, scanning the glow of our instruments in the soft whisper of our jets, understood what it meant. A thunderhead. Your compass and instruments go haywire near one, pointing to the electricity housed in the rising billowing cloud. A thunderhead. Terrific updrafts and downdrafts, rain, hail and ice.

The decision was made by the officer-instructors. We were to keep to the course. The thought of rerouting a squadron of wet-behind-the-ears cadets, brand new to jets, to avoid the cumulonimbus, was worse than letting us fight our way through.

The thunderhead was real and there, we realized, as we turned at Lubbock. From our flight level at 35,000 feet we could see a long way and there was no mistaking it.

Each of us could see it awaiting us. It rose alone and huge in the bright moonlight. It seemed solid, a great mass rising fifty, sixty thousand feet high into the sky. Within it, lightning bursts flashed every few seconds as if someone inside was playing with a light switch.

Was it big enough to fly around, assuming our instruments didn't give faulty readings causing us to screw up and get lost? Was it possible to go over? Could we fly through it? Cadets ahead were trying all these things and we tried to measure what success they were having.

The trouble was we were at the tail end of the line and things kept changing. The thunderhead kept rising and broadening, growing while we neared it.

We ruled out going over when we heard a shaken cadet call in. "Negative, negative," he breathed into the microphone. "It's at 55,000 and rising. No go on top!"

Then we heard Shaky Jack ahead of us. He sounded preternaturally calm. "Big Springs base," he called in, "understand no go on top. Circling east at 40,000. Please advise." That's when Fabrice took over, obviously saying to hell with military no chatter. He called in the clear.

"Logan, go to altitude and pick him up. Burrell, click your mike button if you hear." We heard the click. Then Fabrice continued, "Burrell, circle left at 40,000 and join on Logan."

Minutes later Bobby Logan called in that he had Shaky on his wing. And here was Fabrice again. "Bien!" he said. Then "Go under," he ordered. "Stay at about 200 feet. Stay together. All go under!" With that we heard two mike clicks, then three, then four. We all had heard and we all went down.

Well, heck, we all made it. How Shaky Jack stayed on Bobby's wing that night was hard to figure. First the two of them and then one by one we flew fast and low under that monster in a driving rain, buffeted hard, slammed every few seconds as if we had gone through a wall, hail rattling off the Plexiglas canopy like gunfire, fleeing over blessedly low hills and strung fences, the world lit up now and then with brilliant lightning. Then we were through and ahead was the field at Big Springs.

Fabrice was called into the instructor's office with all the brass as soon as we landed and he was in there for a time while we waited for him.

Personally, we thought they might as well give him a medal and from the set of his shoulders and the look in his eyes when he came out, I don't think we were far wrong.

Shaky Jack gave him a hell of a handshake and asked if he could get him coffee. He did and Bobby Logan got him some sugar while Sven and I got the cream.

That about wrapped it up. Shaky Jack stood proudly in formation with the rest of us a month later as we got our wings and commissions.

Afterwards, we all went out the gate to receive our first salutes. We considered champagne for celebration, but in the end found a cantina on the south side of Big Springs for a bunch of beers.

Bobby Logan made the first toast. It was to France and Fabrice. It felt exactly right to all of us and Shaky Jack bought the round.

Fighter Training

Buzz Casino

There was some talk of shooting him down. The word on the field, on the base of this premier Air Force fighter-weapons training station outside Las Vegas, was that he had lost a great deal of money at the casinos of the nearby gambling spa and was either angry or despondent enough to make them pay. He was up in a Sabre now, working over the hotels, golf courses and casinos as if they were an enemy headquarters.

The trouble was not so much his buzzing of the golf courses and hotels, bad as that was. The real trouble was the knowledge that his fighter had full 50 caliber loads in its six machine guns and nobody knew how crazy he might be. Four instructors, the best on the base, each who had shot down five or more MIGs in a combat tour of Korea, had been hastily sent airborne while the brass tried to figure out what to do as the trainee continued to beat up the town.

It was already on television, picked up by a local station that had been filming the arrival of a group of movie stars checking into a major casino and hotel. It had terrific entertainment value to the group of us watching on the officer's club television.

All of us, at one time or another, had paid our dues over the green felt tables of the casinos playing cards or trying to make eight the hard way rolling dice. All of us had experienced the incongruity of our dangerous, sweaty daily job of learning how to shoot up the enemy, shoot down the enemy, then to mix at night in anonymity among the beautiful show girls and cigar-smoking high rollers. We were part of a

23

country at war in Korea, but to the visitors and owners on the glittering strip of casinos, in the show rooms with Sinatra singing, there was no sign of war. The only thing we represented was second lieutenants with a few dollars of flight pay in our pockets. This guy, whoever he was, was doing what many of us limping back to the base with empty wallets had dreamed of doing.

"Look! Look!" Darrell Hadly yelled as we clutched our beers, watching the TV. The camera had shown a foursome of golfers scrambling out of golf carts and jumping into a water hazard as the Sabre made a grass-cutting, zero-altitude pass down the fairway.

"Oh, God, look at those swan dives," Hadly breathed ecstatically as the camera stayed tight on the golfing foursome, now floundering in the little lake.

Hadly pulled at my arm. "Jesus, this is beautiful, but they are going to hang him when he gets down."

"If he gets down," I corrected. "The word is there are four aces right over him in fully armed Sabres. If he is truly crazy and decides to shoot up the golf course, or anything else, he's a dead man."

Hadly looked thoughtful. "I wonder what happened to him in the casinos?"

Captain Roger Shorn, our combat flight instructor standing nearby, motioned for us to bring our beers to a table. Steve Brown and Joey Mann, the other two in our training cadre, came with us. We sat for a moment, still glued to the TV over the bar as the nearly incoherent television announcer tried to provide commentary as the trainee zoomed down the highway beneath the casinos' huge and brilliant neon signs.

"You guys are shooting your mouths off a little too loudly," Shorn advised us as we sat at the table. "You are looking and talking too damned happily if any of the brass happens to be around. This is serious business. I believe they've always had nightmares of this happening with this base right next to the biggest gambling, entertainment city in the world. Sooner or later, some fool trainee would lose his entire bankroll and decide to do something about it."

"Is that what happened?" Brown asked.

"Worse, from what I hear," Shorn answered grimly. "His best friend here, another trainee, says he lost it all a week ago."

"You mean he waited for a week before he decided to go whacko?" I asked.

"I said worse," Shorn repeated. "He lost everything a week ago all right, but then the stupid bastard got his poor old dad in Missouri to hock his farm and lost that too!"

"Terrible," Brown said. "You're right. It is worse."

"I said worse," Shorn spoke again, not through yet. "He was going to get married as soon as he finished here. His girl told him to forget her and left. Today."

"My God! That it?" Hadly asked guardedly.

"Just about," Shorn said, signaling the bartender for another round. "Maybe one more thing. He found out he was going to Korea as soon as he finished here."

Darrell was fighting a smile. "Isn't there a joke that goes that way?" he asked. "You know, I ask if she left because he lost all his money, the farm, going to Korea, and you say no, she left because she found out he's a Democrat."

Darrell lost control and laughed. We all started to laugh. We really couldn't help it. It was so pitiful, so too damn much, and except for the guy maybe getting shot down if he didn't quit pretty soon, it was god-awful funny if you thought about it.

You really had to put our reaction into context. Hadly, Brown, Mann and I were not the same people who had signed up for flying cadets. Whatever we were then, we were different now. If you spend over a year doing something every day that can get you real dead at any moment, you change. The context of living changes. Things you used to worry about, things you used to think important, all fade away. Things you would have taken seriously before now just seem funny. The business of living on the edge is very engrossing. All you really do is stay involved in each day. It's not a bad way to be.

How worried could we be that some fat golfer would sprain an ankle leaping out of harm's way? How worried could we be that a hotel-casino owner might lose a few dollars with customers checking out because they had been frightened, or people, who had no idea that some other people were fighting a war, might experience a little fear themselves?

Hell, we didn't talk about it, but in the process of learning to be fighter pilots, being frightened fairly often was something we had shaken hands with a long time ago. Deep down, we might even appreciate that some other citizens were getting a little scare. It's kind of good for you, really. Shoots a bunch of adrenaline into you, cleans out the pipes for a time. I think we were all of a mind and only worried about one thing: what would happen to the poor guy who was up there? It might be better if they had to shoot him down.

"I did it once." It was quiet when Brown suddenly started talking as our laughter subsided.

"You did what once?" Shorn hadn't laughed along with us.

"Buzzed a town," Brown said.

"Me, too," Hadly echoed, looking surprised at his confession.

I grinned at him, at them. "That makes all of us," I said and even Shorn had to smile.

"How about you, Captain?" Hadly asked. "You ever break the rules, fly under a bridge, beat up a town?"

Shorn shook his head. "Enough of this. Making one pass over your hometown doesn't equal what this maniac is doing."

Hadly looked serious. He was a thoughtful guy, a little older than the rest of us, smart and resourceful. "You know, Captain Shorn, the Air Force has rules and rules, all reasonable and pretty much followed. But in fighter training, it's a little different. I believe the brass expects some outlaw behavior. The fighter pilot mystique. Look at the motto you see everywhere on this base: 'Every man a tiger.' It's not as if we are training to fly passengers around sweet and safe, not even close."

Shorn nodded his head. "To a point. But don't get caught. This guy," and he looked back at the bar TV where the announcer was excitedly bringing the story up to date, "this guy is finished. Kaput. Dog meat."

We all looked at the TV. The four combat aces up to stop the raider had apparently caught him the announcer, somewhat distractedly, was saying. Two on each side of his Sabre, they were forcing him back to the base, or so the announcer had been informed.

"What happens when he lands?" Brown asked.

"God only knows," Shorn sighed. "One thing for sure. It's the last landing that pilot will ever make. Court martial, for sure. If they don't shoot him, which I'm sure everyone from the commanding general on down would dearly love to do. Talk about bad public relations. Fighter pilots have a tough enough image to begin with. We're kind of a necessary evil, like a sheriff with a bunch of trigger-happy deputies. The town loves them when they take on the bad guys, but in quiet times, they are a bunch of hotdogs hanging around with pistols on their hips."

"Maybe so," Hadly agreed. "But one thing I have to like. The next time I go into a casino and get a poor relation look from the fat cats in the blue suits, I'm going to just grin, then swoop my hand down real low and fast, remind them."

Quiet Brown smiled softly. "And they just might remember there's a thing going on in Korea. That would be nice."

Highfly

The look of the world from above in a Sabre jet is breathtaking. You'd think the views from the edge of a cliff or from a tall building would give you some idea of the excitement and exhilaration, but you are still bound to earth. Even an airline flight with a chance to get the feel of it out the cabin window doesn't give you more than an insight. To really look from above, you have to be alone and arrived there by your own hand, in control of your own destiny. To be alone in this, to not have any others with you, no co-pilots, no attendants, no passengers, is critical. The experience is for you and you alone.

You finally understand the word dimension, as in two dimensions, three dimensions, fourth dimension. You have been living in a world of two dimensions, you realize, a world fixed to earth, to the surface upon which you have eaten, slept and walked. Up here in the sky, the magic of leaving the bounds of earth comes to you, not necessarily on the first time or even after many times, but finally it comes with a rush. It happens particularly at night.

At 48,000 feet, you are more than nine miles above the earth, some 10,000 feet higher than the summit of Mt. Everest, the tallest mountain on earth. It's cold outside the thin invisible shield of your Plexiglas canopy, minus 60 degrees Fahrenheit a scant eighteen inches from your head. You sit high and forward on the fuselage of your aircraft, only eight feet back from the air intake of your jet, so that all sound of your passage is behind you and unheard. It is no place for agoraphobia with the sides of the cockpit ending at chest level and the 180 degrees of the bubble canopy curving overhead from one side to another.

From this altitude, the cities below are one gigantic light source, visible as far as a hundred miles, sometimes beyond the horizon. The light from a city is a different light, a light modified by altitude and all the millions of particles in the air into a single white-gold light that could be an entity in itself. It's a friendly light to you scudding along so many miles above the planet earth.

Down lower, the aspect changes. Now as you bank quietly and gently in the dark over the city's streets and avenues, you can see the individual headlights from the automobiles inching along in single file. There are so many things to go to down there, so many things to come from, so many tasks. There are larger lights of businesses and centers, with still more tiny lights coming and going. You feel a great sympathy for these ant-like movements, all the human interlocking of tasks, errands, work and play and at the same time you feel a flush of luck that you are up here, the observer, the eyes in the sky.

Over Texas at night you see something that startles you, something that no one ever thought to mention before. On the vast plains below you are gigantic streamers of fires, rising high into the night. There are too many to count and you have no idea what their source could be. It reminds you of a day flight over Arizona when your attention was suddenly fixed on a huge figure mark on the ground below, a flat figure a half mile long made by rolling very large boulders one after another into place to construct a man figure understood and visible only from the sky. There is no answer to this man-warrior drawn on the desert floor, unlike the fires of Texas which turn out to be lit gas escaping from oil wells.

There are hallucinations at night. Flying accidentally into an airspace filled with cadets up over a flying training field, you become convinced that you have stumbled into a mass of huge bombers improbably circling. You know that you are seeing the wing and tail lights of individual airplanes, but you cannot help banking hard, climbing and diving, dodging and turning to avoid the phantom bombers seeming to exist between lights.

St. Elmo's Fires is something you hoped never to experience. The leading edge of your wings are lit with an ultimately eerie green light, the greenish glow surrounds your cockpit and encircles your air intake, staying in place effortlessly as you fly along at over 600 miles an hour.

There is a disconnecting and a connecting, a take-off and a landing. The take-off is a leap free and you feel the two dimensions caused by the gravity of earth leave you. You recall the statement made by a thoughtful and drunken pilot one night when you complained that you had never understood the concept of original sin. Looking like a wise and intoxicated owl, he intoned that original sin was indeed nothing but gravity. Maybe he is right.

Connecting, landing, is putting on again the constraints of two dimensions. It doesn't occur suddenly when you touch your wheels down on the landing strip, it starts earlier when you descend to the landing pattern.

As you slow your aircraft down for the landing and the jet engine slows to a muted murmur, you can feel the process begin like a sigh of regret. The clunk of your wheels coming down and locking into place along with a shudder as the configuration of your aircraft changes to meet the drag of the wheels is the next step in the change of this free, three-dimensional bird into a land-held, two-dimensional piece of machinery called an aircraft.

Down, you are just another ant and your magic craft just another thing made by smart ants.

Flame-out

Peter Lauder was an unusual pilot. Unlike the rest of us with engineering school backgrounds, he had taken his degree in philosophy from a liberal arts college when his love of flying and the urgent request of our government to participate in the service had overtaken him. He had just made a forced landing at our field.

He was shaken by the time our commanding officer had gotten through with him. He had called for emergency landing clearance at temporary training base just up the coast from San Francisco some minutes before. With the tower clearing out all incoming aircraft, he had made a power-off, flame-out landing in his Sabre.

We had all witnessed the landing from the roof of the operation's building after the sirens from the fire trucks and ambulances had alerted us. In his favor, it was a textbook landing, smooth and professional. Still, he had called for an emergency landing and that required an explanation.

There seemed no reason for it. The weather had been perfect for weeks and the purpose of our Air Defense Squadron, intercepting Russian bombers should they decide to annihilate the restaurants of San Francisco or the hot tubs of Marin County, had never seemed less likely. The only scrambles we had had in 10 days were two foreign cargo carriers off course, allowing us to shake them up with a diving, frontal pass before moving alongside for their identification numbers.

Peter had gone up on a proficiency flight, a euphemism for going up and having fun. You just took off and did whatever appealed to you. The only limitations were range, about 250 miles out and back, San Luis Obispo to the south and near the Oregon border to the north. Except for the airspace around San Francisco with its heavy concentration of airliners going and coming, we had the skies pretty much to ourselves. About the only workout we would get was an instrument let-down and landing if the fog rolled in from the sea. This day had none of that and what had caused Peter's problem was interesting to us. We hung around the squadron ready room, waiting for Peter to come out of the CO's office. When he did, he moved quickly, striding away and shaking off our questions.

"Meet you in quarters," he muttered out of the side of his mouth, taking the stairs two at a time down to the engineering office.

We had been back in our bachelor officer's quarters for a half hour before he showed.

"Shut the damned door," he ordered the three of us and took a long drink from the beer we handed him. We shut the damned door and, beers in hand, waited for the story.

Dick Casper, the senior lieutenant among us, asked the central question, "What happened?" Then, quickly, amended it. "What did you tell the CO?"

We all understood the difference in the questions. No matter what happened in an emergency, if you lived through it, it was always something mysterious that happened to the machinery. It was never that you did something outside the textbook, the rules, something that might cause you to eject out of the million-dollar aircraft abandoning it to make its final flight without your guiding hand. The basic paradox in pilots for fighter aircraft was that to be of the breed made indulging in outlaw stunts part of the person. It was what they looked for in a fighter pilot; risk takers with a jaundiced eye for rules. At the same time, they created heavy strictures and penalties for rule breaking.

No buzzing, for example, yet there was no fighter pilot who didn't yearn for the chance to show his girlfriend, his hometown, what a hotdog he was. Long-distance truck drivers coming near lonely desert training bases found this out at first hand. Tooling comfortably down Route 66 on the straight highway through Nevada, many saw the unusual sight of a world-class jet fighter coming the opposite way ten feet off the road at near Mach one.

But you didn't want to get caught. They tended to make an example out of you, court-martial and grounding at the least. When you had an escapade in mind, you made sure it was during a time with many aircraft airborne in the area. When you came off your escapade target, the trick was to point straight up and roll your wings fast until out of sight, preventing angry eyes from getting your identification numbers.

When something happened and you had to answer the CO's question, the unspoken rule was to keep it simple. "I'll be darned if I know, Sir," you might say, "All the instruments were okay and then there was a clunk, sort of, and I got all the red lights lit up. It was going to blow, Sir, so I punched out. Damndest thing!" What actually happened was you got into an inverted spin trying some fool maneuver and couldn't pull it out.

Peter took his time answering. "I ran out of fuel," he said succinctly. "The gauge must have malfunctioned. It showed plenty of fuel, three hundred pounds, three fifty, until I was over the field. Suddenly it showed zero and the engine flamed. Damndest thing!"

We all were quiet for a time, admiring the simplicity of his answer. The fuel gauges on the Sabres were somewhat suspect and had been documented to be off as much as that in the past. The technical manuals had written of the frustration in finding the cause or even to get a consistent bad reading. It happened sometimes.

"Too bad," Dick said admiringly, "Now cut the bullshit and tell us."

Peter grinned happily. "It was the damnedest thing," he said. "You know what a superior day it was, big, fat cumulus clouds rising to forty-five, fifty thousand, ocean out over the Faralones as clear and blue as the sky?" We all nodded, having been up on flights earlier.

"I flew out to sea, maybe 80 miles off the coast. I tuned in an FM jazz station and started flying the clouds to the music. It was fantastic, the clouds as real as peaks in the Rockies, like skiing forever up and down mountains of snow." We were all there having done much the same thing on proficiency flights.

It was a unique experience. You had no sound from the jet, no sound at all except the music you picked. The aircraft flew itself with no thought from you as to up, down, right or left. You had merely to think of rolling through that hole in a cloud, leveling off to take a downhill run on a bank of white that stretched for miles and your aircraft did what you thought. All you had was the pure music in your head and the oneness of you and your aircraft. The ocean and the sky became the same, any notion of whether you were upside down or right side up gone, the gravity holding you in your cockpit seat the only reality. There was a blissful hypnosis to it all that could get you low on fuel.

"What I didn't realize," Peter continued, "was the station had a special program going, a 40-minute tape without a break. The first thing I knew, I had flamed out."

"But you didn't call emergency until you were over the field," Dick protested.

"True, but I flamed past the Faralones," Peter said, "I knew they wouldn't buy that. I flamed out at 45,000 at the top of a loop. Talk about coming back to reality! I didn't know which way was up or down, tell you the truth, didn't know how far out I had gotten. I must have glided 70 miles before I called emergency over the field at 8,000 feet."

"You must have felt like an idiot, running out that way," Dick remarked with a grin.

"I did," Peter said, "and a little nervous about getting back. But more than that, I kept thinking about what a zone I had been in, how spaced, how unaware I was of everything but the flying. And I kept thinking what an incredible thing flying is, as free as we can get in this world." He paused for a second, then continued with a stubborn look on his face. "I thought of something else on that long glide. We fly the best aircraft in the world, the fastest, the most maneuverable, beautiful things that can take us into another world. And the way we use them, they're nothing but gun platforms."

Dick looked uncomfortable. We all did. "Peter, that's what we do. We're an Air Defense Fighter Squadron. We fly fighters."

"I know," Peter agreed. "Still, I kept thinking about dolphins."

"Dolphins? What are you talking about?" Dick asked, thoroughly confused as we all were.

Peter was embarrassed, but not willing to back down. "Coming in over the sea, I was thinking about dolphins, the way the Navy is suspected of training them to carry weapons, to intercept enemy divers and frogmen, eliminate them."

"And our aircraft are dolphins, something like that?" Dick asked after a considerable silence.

"No," Peter said, "not alone. But with us with them, when we get together, yeah, sure, like dolphins."

Dick got to his feet. He was in for the long haul in the military, 30 years and out a colonel, maybe a general. He wasn't too patient with Peter. "Pretty thought," he said, "but not much good in the military." He turned and walked to the door. With his hand on the doorknob, he stopped. "Well, glad you got down okay." He paused for a moment, then, smiling, asked, "Peter, you planning to stay in once your tour is over?"

"I've been trying to decide," Peter said with an answering smile.

"And?" Dick asked.

"I think out," Peter replied.

"Going to be a dolphin, something like that?"

Peter was smiling broadly now at Dick. "Sounds just about right."

They were both laughing. "Do dolphins drink?" Dick asked and when Peter allowed that they did, we all headed for the club and the daily happy hours drinks.

Dogfight at Nellis

It made you wonder if you had any idea what a brawl was really like. You may have thought you had a notion, like something out of a John Wayne western where someone takes a swing at someone else and the next thing chairs and bottles fly and 40 or 50 stuntmen cowboys begin slugging, crashing through railings, knocking the living hell out of each other.

Maybe you had even been in a brawl or two in your time. Something at school, perhaps on the football field, when one of your teammates got his legs clipped out from under him in an illegal block and a fight started with the benches emptying. But whatever you might have thought gave you some insight into a real donnybrook, nothing prepared you for this.

Seventy of the world's best fighter aircraft to meet high over a lonely peak in the Nevada desert, to join for one purpose: a massive dog-fight, a supreme hassle, one huge practice combat shoot-down. In the incredible melee there would be instructor pilots and student pilots and in the instructor group, a dozen aces out of combat in Korea, the best combat pilots in the world.

This was quasi-graduation from 11 weeks at the fighter weapons combat training base at Nellis Air Force Base outside Las Vegas, and it came without warning. Toward the end of the course on a bright and sunny day, we noticed unusual activity and when our instructor briefed us on the day's flight, we saw the grin on his face as he told us the plan.

It's 120 degrees Fahrenheit out on the runway in the middle of a Nevada summer, but it's much, much more as you sit under the bubble Plexiglas canopy of the shining silver metal Sabre jet. This giant exercise has every flyable Sabre on the base taxiing for take-off, lined up in twos, waiting to get airborne and the line is long. The air conditioning in the Sabre doesn't cut in until you begin the take-off roll. It starts to blow around 60 miles an hour and is at full blast at around 160, near lift-off speed.

While you wait under the merciless sun in helmet, oxygen mask, flight suit, G-suit, boots and gloves, you rain perspiration. In minutes you are soaking wet through the flight suit, the sweat coursing down your face. The temperature in the cockpit has to be better than 130 Fahrenheit, and you feel like your brain is frying.

Finally you are on the runway, supposed to count ten seconds after the two Sabres ahead of you go before releasing your brakes and beginning your roll. You are so hot you feel you may burst into flame and the sweat pools in your eyes. You count ten in about three seconds and release your brakes, thinking to hell with jet wash, you have to move.

At 100 miles an hour you feel a faint rush of cold air, then in another few seconds, an arctic blast. The air conditioner you had turned to full cold, even knowing what would happen, kicks in hard and suddenly it's throwing quarter-sized snowballs at your face mask that make you dodge and wince while you become airborne, gear and flaps up. At 250 miles an hour you roll severely to the right to join on wing and the G forces wring water from your eyebrows into your eyes, blinding you for an instant. The temperature has dropped from around 130 degrees to somewhere around 50 in half a minute and whatever your quivering liver might think inside your soaked flight suit, you're too busy flying to do much except give the air dial a quick modifying twist.

You have never seen so many aircraft in one place. Even in cadets, with as many as 25 or 30 student pilots trying to land at the end of a flying period, you never have seen anything like this before.

Over the lonely peak in the middle of desert, 50 miles from base are the 70 swept-winged Sabres at 40,000 feet, circling to wait for the last to join. They arrive and with a single command from our airborne commander, the battle is joined and all hell breaks loose.

You're flying in elements of two, one Sabre is lead while the other covers his tail, then you switch positions. It is utter chaos, the radio crackling with warnings.

"Break right, Red Dog, break hard!"

"Scissor, Blue Lead, now!"

"Pull it up, Angel Two, now, now, now!"

And all the while you are attempting to weave a protective tail cover back of your lead as he pulls diving, turning, five and six G turns to get in position for his gun cameras. The prospect of a mid-air collision is forefront in your mind as you pull your aircraft through violent maneuvers; there are aircraft everywhere, coming at you, diving, climbing, looping. You see a Sabre coming straight at you, between your airspeed and his, you have a closing speed of over 1,000 miles an hour. You just have time to have this register and you roll over and under, diving away from collision. You call your lead that you have lost him, to watch his own ass as you set sail for a Sabre below you and slip down to fix him in your sights.

He doesn't see you. At one hundred percent power and the advantage of altitude on him, you ease up on his tailpipe and press your gun camera trigger to a full burst. Your head swivels even as you do this and you catch sight of a Sabre sliding to your tail. Without conscious thought you roll right into a diving 90-degree bank pulling as many Gs as you can stand, greying out partially, your head turned accepting the gravity force on your spine and neck, trying to see if you have lost him. You haven't. He is in the turn with you.

He's good, very good. It flashes through your mind that you are tangling with an instructor ace, like what you have heard of flying in Korea if you were unlucky enough to mix it with a Chinese combat pilot instead of a usually briefly-trained North Korean. You flip your aircraft over from a full right turn to left, as fast as you can roll, always pulling as many Gs as you can stand. If he can stand more, he will get the angle on you, and that, as they say, will be all she wrote. He stays with you, not pulling more, but glued behind you. You suck oxygen greedily, always in partial grey-out from the G forces, having forgotten the other fighting aircraft, the possibility of collision. You and this tenacious bastard are locked in your own private war.

You both lose altitude as you make the turns, as you try for what is known as a scissors. Into a right bank and pull five, six and seven Gs, then slam it over 180 degrees into a left bank and more of the same. If you can out-pull him, you will gradually fall even in the turns to finally fall behind him, reversing your positions and he will be the chased. But it isn't happening, he stays with you, not gaining, but not losing.

Even in the effort and stress of the fight, you remember in a flash a conversation, one of the many nights when groups of you met and ignored everything but the drinks and the flying talk, always with hands as aircraft to show what happened good and what bad. You remember someone saying it was possible to roll under in a scissors, to not flip it over into an opposite bank, but to go under to the opposite bank, pulling Gs all the way. You and this tough guy are down low, down to 8,000 feet over the mountain peak. It is time to try something.

You pull it right as hard as you can, near blacking out, and suddenly complete the roll by going under and immediately into a left turn with as much pull as you can bear.

It works! He no longer has you and breaks off! You bring your wings level as he flies the same way off your wing. He slowly brings his Sabre close until you can see him clearly in the cockpit. He motions back to the field and then draws his hand across his throat to show low fuel. He gives you a thumbs-up sign, circles his thumb and index finger in approval and turns for the field.

As he grows small in the distance, you turn toward the field as well, wondering if he was one of the combat ace instructors. You'll never know if he was. But if he wasn't, you never want to meet anyone better.

Korea

Formation Flight

A line squadron is made up of four flights. That means 16 aviators, 16 Sabre fighter jets, each flight made up of two elements of two aircraft. Our fighter squadron was the 325th, our four flights Tango, Zulu, Bravo and Red One, our home base Korea. Our squadron insignia was a fighting cock and that was pretty much our attitude. That wasn't unusual. If you flew single-seat jet fighter interceptors you pretty much had to have an attitude or you were in the wrong business.

Jimmy Conlin was flight leader of Tango, the best flight in the squadron, in our opinion. Bobby Summer (Bobby One), flew off Jimmy's left wing as number two, I flew off Jimmy's right wing at number three as assistant flight leader and Bobby Harms, (Bobby Two), flew off my right wing at number four.

You have to get your mind around the relationship of the four pilots in a flight. It's hard to find an analogy in life to compare it to.

We three in Tango flight, number two, three and four are highly skilled, very professional fighter aircraft aviators who individually take a back seat to no one on earth or in the sky in the art and skill of flying fighter jet aircraft. Yet in the normal four-ship formation, flying with wings overlapping, we in Tango—or Zulu, Bravo or Red One for that matter—would fly into a mountain if our leaders had a mind for that maneuver that day. Unhesitatingly. Without a quiver.

In a flight formation from the ground up at around 200 knots to 45,000 feet at 400, 500 or 600 knots, numbers two, three and four stop independent flying. It becomes another type of flying for which there is no name. You give up any of the usual thoughts and maneuvers of your aircraft. You simply stay on your position tight on your leader's wing. You have your left hand on your throttle, your right hand on the magic control column. Your head is turned to the leader's wing and the fuselage of his aircraft on which you are flying wing.

It doesn't make any difference what the leader does, your two hands—without conscious thought—move the throttle forward or backward in coordination with your right hand moving the control column in combinations of left, right, backward, forward. It's a matter of extreme and total concentration as you maintain your position.

Once in awhile in your peripheral vision you might see rising cumulus clouds or, for that matter, a sight of earth or mountains above or below and for a fleeting instant have the thought that you are inverted. It makes no difference, as long as your lead maintains positive gravity force so that you always feel your seat firmly seated in your cockpit whether upside down, vertical or level.

The four-ship formation flight is standard on a scramble and most vectors until the I. P., the Initial Point, is reached and an engagement is imminent. Then the four-ship flight breaks down into elements of two.

Number one and number three become the attack aircraft, the gun ships, with two and four respectively covering one and three's backs in wide swinging, protective arcs while the gun ships bore in without worry of an enemy coming up on their tails.

By the time you've flown wing at positions two and four for months, it's a relief if you're good enough and experienced enough to become lead. All you need at lead is flying skill, very good judgment and the nature allowing you to handle the large responsibility. Some guys are terrific as wingmen but no good on the lead. It happens more often than you might think.

Jimmy Conlin was quite something as Tango lead. He looked like what you would expect of a Division 1A state college tight end, a bit over 6 foot 1 and big. What fooled you about Jimmy beyond his skill as an aviator and his unfailing excellent judgment was his sensitivity to the guys in his flight.

On a hot scramble one day out over the Yellow Sea in a bad marginal cumulus weather pattern ground control was consistently unable to give us a climb-out vector. We were forced down to not more than a couple hundred feet over the white-capped sea, banging and slamming through the narrowing gap between the bottom of the squall and the sea when Jimmy called control and advised them we were climbing out on 270-degree vector and to let us know when they got their acts together, in so many words.

As we found out later, survived and shaken, Jimmy lost all his weather flight instruments the moment we hit the soup. He had nothing but primitive needle, ball and airspeed as well as altimeter and rate of climb. It is near impossible in instrument flight conditions with extreme turbulence to maintain any reasonable flight altitude and to climb up through such weather.

On top finally, above the weather and after what seemed forever, Jimmy immediately called for me to take the lead. I did so and when ground control finally checked in and called the intercept off, I led Tango back home down through the now simply normal cloud cover weather in as smooth a let-down as is possible.

Once we were on the ground, Jimmy walked over to me in his sweat-stained flight suit just as my wingman, Bobby Harms, soaking wet, came at me on the dead run, practically screaming.

He was in a rage, close to tears, this guy who was my very close friend and had flown my wing since he joined us in Korea. This guy who with a skin full of liquor one night at O'Rourke's stood on a chair and announced to the roomful of pilots and nurses that he loved me and would fly my wing straight into hell if I cared to go.

Bobby was shaking, shouting, "I'll never, never fly your goddamn wing again! You hear me? That let-down was the worst ever!" and with a few snarling curses, stormed off.

Jimmy restrained me with a hand on my shoulder.

"Jesus, Jimmy, that's bullshit!" I said. "I've never made a smoother let-down! What the hell's the matter with him?"

Jimmy patted my shoulder. "Listen," he said, "go relax, have a beer. I'll talk to Bobby."

"Okay, okay," I muttered. "Goddammit Jimmy, I was as smooth as silk coming down."

Jimmy spoke again. "I'll straighten him out." He looked at me quizzically. "Don't you know what happened? That flight up with me on practically no instruments was as bad as it gets. Only reason I didn't call for you to take the lead on the way up, was because I never knew for sure what our altitude was from second to second. I swear we may have been upside down a time or two. And it was worse for Bobby way out at number four. That raving just now was because he hadn't quit fighting to stay on wing, not ram you, from the trip up. Hell," Jimmy finished, "I even felt it and I wasn't flying anyone's wing."

He grinned at me and went off after Bobby. The two of them joined me in O'Rourke's an hour later.

Bobby was contrite, sheepish. "Hey," he said. "I'm sorry about that sounding off. Jimmy explained it all to me."

I gave him a grin. "Okay," I said. "We're all okay again. Still," I couldn't resist asking, "do you still love me?"

Bobby laughed with a huge grin. "Sure, you asshole. Always have, always will!"

And we Tango guys drank well into the evening.

O'Rourke's

Inside the barbed-wire surrounded perimeter of the flight line of our Korean airbase was a special place called O'Rourke's. It was a bar, pure and simple, and what made it special was that it was for fighter pilots only.

Our base was made up of two fighter squadrons of 16 of the world's best fighter aircraft, the new swept-winged, speed-of-sound Sabre jet and so we had 32 pilots, young, randy and all convinced that we, individually, were also the world's best aviators. Nothing suited any of us better than a drinking establishment that acknowledged our position at the top of the flying world.

It was for fighter pilots only in a narrow sense, however. Women, any woman, long, short, young or less than young, civilian or military, it made no difference, they were all happily welcomed. When a somewhat rare instance occurred and a planeload of nurses was on base, or a troupe of USO ladies passed through, they were more than acceptable. In fact, drinks were cheap for them or, to be exact, cost nothing at all. But arrival in O'Rourke's for any male non-fighter pilot was short-lived. Rank made no difference and the sight of a first lieutenant ushering a transport pilot bird colonel to the door was balm to our enlarged egos.

First Lieutenant Michael Doud was in charge of O'Rourke's. Mike was a 25 year-old flight leader by reason of his four months head start on us on our year's tour of duty. He was also an excellent pilot and an innate leader, a slow-spoken, humorous guy, short and muscular, who seemed to have something about him that warned you not to stare too challengingly into his blue eyes.

We all had extra assignments in addition to our flying. They were mostly meaningless with titles like assistant fire marshal, morale officer, and the like, but the brass had taken one look at Michael Doud from Boston and asked if he had any knowledge of bars, of taverns. Mike had just grinned and nodded and with that, a new head of O'Rourke's was commissioned.

"Well," Mike had mused later, looking around the shabbily comfortable interior of O'Rourke's with its long varnished bar, ranks of bottles and glasses shelved conveniently behind, a brass foot rail and wooden tables holding up candles in old wine bottles, pictures on the walls of various vintage fighter airplanes and a battered upright piano. "Consider this your home away from home!" he finished with satisfaction and bought drinks for all of us. That was not as expansive a gesture as it might seem, given the price of a full bottle of good cognac was two dollars and twenty-five cents, a quart of the best scotch two dollars.

In fact, what we paid for a single drink was a mystery. Mike had his Korean barmen simply mark chits, one drink, one mark, four marks and a line went through the four to count five. At no particular time in an evening's dice rolling and drinking, sometime during the course of a month, Mike would push a chit along the bar in your general direction. It would have a simple heading, a first name and perhaps another identifier, like the single world 'tall' or perhaps a hair color. Sometimes it would have no marks at all, just a price, twelve dollars, for example, firmly underlined. Mike also had a rubber stamp made that said 'service compris' and he would stamp the chit so we would realize that we'd had ten dollars of liquor in the last period of time and a two-dollar add-on for the barmen. It was a hell of a good system, one we would all regret and miss.

Mike's best friend was a tall Texan named Joey Browner, a sleepy, quiet guy who spent most of his hours at the bar of O'Rourke's drinking beer and reading letters from his fiancée or, if not that, bent over writing back to her. He had a wallet full of pictures of his Texas girl who bore a remarkable resemblance to a movie star named Susan Hayward. This same Susan Hayward's full-length, three-panel magazine pullout was tacked to the wall opposite the bar by some former fan and in-residence pilot. When Joey first walked into the bar and saw it, he stopped dead in his tracks and seemed to stop breathing.

"My sweet Lord," he finally got out. "Look!" and out came the pictures of his girl for us to see. She was sensational. She was close, close enough to be Hayward's twin, making us all look twice and then congratulate him.

It was well into the end of November and cold that year, and Korea in winter is a bleak place. The cease-fire had finally been signed up in Panmoonjon and things had quieted down considerably. It didn't make that much difference in our operations as, for some time the North Koreans had showed a nearly complete reluctance to engage in air war and we kept up our flight operations, air sweeps, air-to-ground firing and aerial tactics. The only real difference was we flew against each other and took gun camera movies, rather than against the MiG-15 and 20-millimeter cannon fire.

It was for the ground troops finally able to stand down that made the difference. Flying is a whole different role from ground troops in a conflict. No matter how difficult or dangerous an operational flight might be, due to fuel limitations, the flight would be back on the ground in an hour or so. Even with several operational flights a day, at the end we had showers, fresh khakis, a drink or two and a hot meal. It didn't work that way for ground troops. Joey Browner knew the difference better than most as he had spent two weeks before the cease-fire forward from our base as a ground spotter for air strikes. It was during this time that he got the letter.

He got back in mid-December and Mike Doud had handed him his mail. Mike knew something was wrong as Joey's routine daily mail from his Texas girl had ended abruptly two days after Joey left. One letter and then nothing. All of us in the Quonset hut we shared with Joey were apprehensive. The one single letter on his bed didn't look good at all.

It wasn't. Mike filled us in after a time. Joey had gotten a classic Dear John letter.

"She married another guy," Mike told us somberly. "Friend of Joey's. They all went to school together. Perfect. Just like in the movies."

"Painful," one of the guys at our table murmured. "Lousy," someone else said and we looked from our table at Joey standing at the bar with the straight cognac he had taken to. "He's not the same," a third guy said.

"Would you be, asshole?" Mike inquired in a friendly voice.

Christmas was in two days and Mike had had his barmen fix O'Rourke's up. It looked great with lots of tinsel and holly, a tree over by the pot-bellied stove and over the bar a large cloth-covered frame that Mike said he planned to unveil Christmas Eve.

Our squadrons were told to stand down for Christmas and with the arrival of a troupe of USO women musicians and performers along with a half dozen en route nurses, we expected a peak evening at O'Rourke's. That was exactly what we got. The upright piano was taken over by a strawberry blonde who knew what she was doing and, along with her, a bass and guitar. By ten o'clock, O'Rourke's was roaring and with all of it, the winter, Korea, the whole works, I doubt if any one of us would rather be anyplace else.

At eleven, Mike jumped up on the bar and yelled for quiet. He wished us all a Merry Christmas and then demanded our attention for the unveiling of the covered frame over the middle of the bar.

"Do any of you ladies and guys know why this fine bar is called O'Rourke's?" he asked to a general raucous denial. "Well," Mike continued, "I do. Long before we got here, a South African fighter squadron flew out of here in P-51s. This," and he turned to the frame and grasped the edge of the cloth, "is O'Rourke, the first South African killed in action." And he pulled the cloth away. In the frame was a photograph of a P-51 in flight, clouds fleecy behind it. Underneath was a brass plaque with the name O'Rourke on it, and Mike raised his glass in a toast.

As we stood there with our glasses raised with him in a suddenly quiet room, Joey Browner moved from the bar with his glass.

"To O'Rourke!" he said loudly with a slight smile on his face and threw his glass across the room at the pullout of Susan Hayward. There was a moment of absolute quiet following the shattering of the glass and then Mike grinned at Joey and repeated, "O'Rourke!" and threw his glass at the photograph of Susan Hayward as well. With that we all crashed our glasses at the wall, against the base of the wall, shouting the name "O'Rourke!" Mike leaned over to Joey in the mayhem and spoke briefly to him and then as Joey smiled and shrugged his shoulders, they both grinned, shaking hands.

We broke every glass in the place that Christmas Eve and spent the rest of that memorable night drinking champagne and whiskey from bottles. The next day the battle scarred picture of Susan Hayward was gone from O'Rourke's forever.

Tactics

You could always tell when a guy had been in a fight. The 50-caliber gun ports on each side of the silver fuselage of his Sabre would be streak-blackened by powder burns from the firing of his six machine guns.

Still, this didn't necessarily mean he'd been in a real hassle against the very good Russian MiG-15 jets flown by the North Koreans and occasionally by the very dangerous Red Chinese. Sometimes a flight leader would be a little nervy or even anticipate seeing something and order his flight to spread out and fire off a two-or-three second burst. After all, you'd want the damned things to work if you needed them.

But sometimes maybe in the sharp clear air of early dawn near the sinuous run of the Yalu far below, the radio would crackle in the soft hum of your helmet. A quiet voice would warn: "Heads up. Bandits at twelve o'clock low," and your heart would pound for a second or two with the surge of adrenaline.

The voice in your helmet would be pure Chuck Yeager in style and content. Yeager was the fighter pilot's pilot and his style was always low-keyed, slightly country, a murmur, pretty near just audible. Yeager could announce the end of the world to come in fifteen seconds and you would feel he had trouble holding back a yawn. Every fighter pilot worth a damn tried to speak the same way.

* * * * *

51

You're in a swept-winged supersonic jet nine miles up and so is the other guy. The other guy flies a MiG-15 and you an F-86 Sabre. The two are the best in the world as high-altitude interceptors. You've never met but shortly the two of you are going to do your best to kill each other. It's a pretty amazing thing, when you think about it, impersonal, just two gleaming silver aircraft miles up in the thin air over earth, determined to kill.

The voice in your helmet again, "Heads up, twelve o'clock level, engage."

At 100-percent power you roll over, dive, level out and at close to Mach 1 head straight for the speck in the far distance.

You're closing on each other at well over 1,200 miles per hour. In the quickest blink of an eye he's there, here and gone as you both claw straight up for altitude advantage after the pass. It's rare this head-on pass but, by God, there's that word amazing again.

You bore straight up, the altimeter hand sweeping fast through 40,000 feet, your airspeed unwinding fast, 600 hundred, 500 hundred, 400 hundred. You level your aircraft, your head swiveling to find him. You bank vertically left, right, checking the most dangerous spot right behind you. Nothing. He's gone. You turn south checking, checking, your head swiveling, then vertically up and down. Empty sky except for you. You power back and start a descent for home.

Back on the base, debriefed and relaxing with a beer, Tim Jaans, Zulu flight leader, is holding forth on the subject of flying, always the central subject. We are in O'Rourke's, the flight line bar and unofficial operations room. We are a half dozen pilots around the table, not counting the two base nurses.

Tim was good and we listened respectfully. He had two confirmed kills and was a flight leader well into his tour in Korea. He was flying with his hands to make his points. Anytime you saw two or more fighter jocks talking, you could bet 90 percent of their talk would be of flying and tactics. And their hands would be airborne the better to illustrate.

Tim was saying, "In the end, remember this: the better aviator will win. If I know my aircraft better, if I know the maximum of my capabilities, I will shoot the enemy down."

Captain Jack Slayton, lean, saturnine, kicked back in his chair, one hand on the beer bottle resting on the table, the other arm draped over nurse 1ˢᵗ Lieutenant Sue's shoulder, objected. Everybody listened, heads turning. You never knew when you just might hear something that would save your ass sometime.

"True, Tim, true. But not the absolute truth." The barroom was quiet, everyone listening. An absolute truth? Something at the heart, the core of this game. Moses at the mountain was not listened to more intently.

"Here it is, for Christ's sake!" he leaned forward releasing Sue but holding tight to the beer. Sue's mouth was slightly agape, her body slack, her eyes fast on Jack.

"Always get altitude," he ticked off the commandments on his long index finger as he talked.

"Always see him first!" he continued and he folded the rest of his fingers triumphantly in his fist with satisfaction and sat back in his chair.

Sue couldn't stand it. Her eyes were wide. "That's all, Jack? That's it?"

Jack was grinning at Tim who was grinning just as fiercely back at him.

Tim answered Sue, for Jack, for all of us.

"Well," he drawled, "that's the important part sure enough. The rest is easy. Slide down out of the sky, out of the sun if you can, sneak up behind him until you almost fly up his tailpipe. Then blow the bastard out of the damned sky!"

There were reflective smiles around the table, satisfaction. We all knew this truth, but it was always good to hear it again.

Hitman

Every pilot in our fighter squadron in Korea was assigned an F-86 jet fighter. This didn't mean he would fly that particular Sabre. If it was available and on line, fine, that would be his aircraft. But more often than not he would fly whatever 86 happened to be available.

Still, he had his aircraft and was allowed to name it. He did this in consultation with his crew chief, whose primary job was that particular aircraft.

Buck Sergeant Zane Hitter and Zulu flight's Second Lieutenant Eddie Mann ran instantly into trouble when their 86 showed up one day with the legend HIT MAN painted in bright red on the silver metal fuselage above the gun ports of their Sabre. The brass took one look and ordered the name removed.

Eddie was different than most of the pilots in the squadron. He was young and, unlike most of the pilots, had come to Korea straight out of cadets and fighter-weapons training. He was the junior member of the squadron.

He was shocked by our commander's order. "With respect, sir, what's wrong with HIT MAN?" he asked, standing at attention in front of Lieutenant Colonel Nevin, a veteran World War II fighter pilot now commanding our squadron.

"As you may know, sir," he continued, "my crew chief's name is Sergeant Hitter, and mine of course, is Mann, with a double n. HIT MAN, from our names, sir, you see?"

"I see, Lieutenant," Nevin said. "Clever, but it won't work." He sighed and looked long at Eddie's bright, fresh young face.

"How old are you, Lieutenant?"

"Twenty-three, sir, twenty-four in a month, sir." Eddie replied uncertainly.

Nevin sighed again. "You were about eleven or twelve, give or take, Lieutenant, when a B-25 bomber got hit over Japan in 1943, in the last war, World War II, which you may have read about. The crew had named their aircraft Murder Inc. That was a bad mistake in judgment. It wasn't a smart name for the crew of the B-25 to put on their aircraft when they had to crash land in Japan. The crew and the plane survived. So did the name they had painted on the fuselage."

"They all made it, sir?" Eddie asked worriedly.

"I'm not sure if they all made it, Lieutenant, but the pilot and co-pilot made it for sure because their pictures were all over the papers. The Japanese called them murderers, criminals, because of the name and beheaded them. You're a fighter pilot, not a Hit Man. I want HIT MAN off your Sabre before it takes another flight. You understand my feeling, Eddie?"

Eddie nodded his head, looking slightly sick. "Beheaded, sir?" he asked unbelievingly.

"Beheaded," Nevin agreed sadly. "Now go put another name on your aircraft. Talk to Sergeant Hitter, the two of you will figure it out."

Zane Hitter and Eddie Mann were very alike. Like Eddie, Zane had taken his degree in a liberal arts college and both had worked on their college newspapers. They had a lot in common. Zane was two years older than Eddie, but like him, looked to be about seventeen, tops. There was no rank business, no enlisted sergeant, second lieutenant officer separation between them. This was more or less true of all the pilot officers and their enlisted crew chiefs, but Zane and Eddie were like brothers from the beginning, argumentative and opinionated, but close friends.

Eddie explained to Zane why they couldn't have HIT MAN on their Sabre, told him Nevin's story of the World War II bomber. Zane was as shocked as Eddie had been.

"Jesus Christ, Eddie, that's the worst thing I've ever heard!" he said in real outrage.

It took them two days to come up with a name that satisfied them, two days of wrangling and trying out names. At one time, Zane, who was a big fan of rock singer Buddy Holly, wanted to name the Sabre PEGGY SUE, a famous song of Holly's, and Eddie came close to agreeing. But in the end they decided on SUEANN, a combination of the names of Zane's girlfriend, Sue and Eddie's wife, Ann. The only reason it was SUEANN without a fight was that even Eddie had to agree ANNSUE didn't make much sense.

They had a picture taken of the two of them standing underneath the name on the Sabre and sent it off to the women. Zane showed up for the photo in a flight suit like Eddie's that he had scrounged somewhere. They looked like brothers, both the same height and build and their features similar enough to be twins. It was about this time that Zane told Eddie his secret.

They had gotten used to visiting an Australian unit's small army infantry post close by the airfield, because enlisted Zane couldn't drink beer in the squadron's officer's bar, while Eddie was uncomfortable in Zane's enlisted mess. Here in the Aussie encampment, no one cared or asked. They were alone one day shortly after the historic picture was taken and Zane turned to Eddie sitting alongside him in the tent that served as the Aussie bar.

"Eddie, I've got to tell you something, something not so good. I've lied to Sue. I don't know why it started. I think it was because she's so beautiful and smart. She's a writer, you know, took her degree in journalism. I guess I was afraid she would think I was a loser because I wasn't an officer. Anyway, she thinks I'm a pilot like you. You know when I ask you how a flight went, how you tell me about it? Well, I write to Sue what you tell me about the flight as if I have done it. She thinks I'm an officer, a pilot like you."

"Holy God!" Eddie gulped. "How in hell did you think you'd get away with a lie like that?"

Zane looked miserable. "I was in cadets like you were, Eddie, when I met Sue. It was out in San Angelo, Texas, about a month before I washed out because of my eyes. Sue had come out with her girlfriend to see another cadet and when we met, I knew there was no one else for me. We started writing each other and when I washed out, I couldn't tell her. I kept writing as if I had gone on to advanced training, graduated and gotten commissioned, the whole works."

Eddie couldn't help it. Sitting in the Aussie bar tent in Korea alongside Zane who looked so thoroughly miserable and downcast with this monstrous lie, he started to laugh.

"It isn't funny, goddammit Eddie."

Eddie choked back his laughter. "Sorry, Zane. Does anyone else think you're a big pilot ace?"

"No," Zane said gloomily, "just Sue. When I saw her after cadets, I wore civilian clothes all the time. I told her I didn't want to show off my officer's uniform, that I liked civilian clothes, which is true. Then I volunteered for Korea."

"As a pilot or a sergeant?" Eddie asked, still tickled beyond measure. "Are you really a sergeant, by the way?"

Zane fixed Eddie with a stern eye, but then he couldn't help himself. He started to smile. "God, Eddie, it was tough sometimes. Did I tell you I graduated at the top of my class out of cadets and fighter-weapons school, considered the number one second lieutenant pilot officer in the Western Command? That I had the highest training score ever made in fighter-weapons?" As Eddie bent over with mirth, he added, "You know the picture of us under the name SUEANN? I wrote Sue you were my wingman, I was training you up and you were coming along nicely. That's why her name comes first."

Eddie sat straight up on his barstool, amazement in his eyes. "You told her all that, you bastard?"

"Oh, all that and more," Zane said with a certain pride. "I figured once I was committed, why not go with it."

"God, I love it!" Eddie said wiping his eyes.

"Yeah," Zane said back into gloom, "but the problem is I really love Sue. I want to marry her when I get back. You can be best man. But how am I ever going to get out of this mess?"

Eddie straightened up, a resolute look on his face. "The solution's obvious, old buddy. You've got to die. Heroically, of course. I'll write the letter to her, how you dove into the target instead of me or how you volunteered for the dangerous mission ahead of all the rest of us appreciative guys because you knew we had wives and stuff. Yep, that's it," he finished, wiping his hands.

"Terrific," Eddie said sourly, "How does that get me married to Sue?"

"I haven't worked that out yet," Eddie said. "Give me time," and he put an arm around Zane's shoulder. "But one other thing, old pal. You have any other little quirks you want to tell me about?"

The time went by after Zane's confession. Eddie flew the SUEANN and Zane made sure it was the most fit and able Sabre in the squadron, but they got no closer to a solution to the problem. In fact, it got worse when Eddie wrote Sue, telling stories of Zane's flying skill. He was unable to resist this, even though Zane protested when he found out about it, claiming it would only make things worse.

"Twin brother!" Eddie exclaimed one day as they sat in the Aussie tent drinking beer, mulling the problem over for the hundredth time. "That's the ticket! Zane has a twin brother, an identical twin who comes to visit after you die. Zane, think about it, it'll work."

But Zane shook his head again. "I told you Eddie, I'm not dying and that's final!"

It was six months later when Zane got another stripe, a promotion to tech sergeant, that Eddie wrote a final letter. Eddie had grown up a lot in the time, as front-line war-zone fighter pilots have a tendency to do, and the humor of Zane's predicament began to wear thin. They were drinking beer in the Aussie tent when Eddie told Zane about it. He had come to believe Zane's devotion to Sue and knew there was only one thing to do.

"Zane," he began, "I don't know if what I've done will work, but it's the only answer. I wrote Sue."

Zane looked with growing suspicion and fear at Eddie. "You told her didn't you?" When Eddie nodded his head, Zane continued. "I had a feeling you would. I'm glad. I should have done it myself. But it's so terrible to tell someone you love that you're a fraud, a liar."

"Jesus Christ, Zane," Eddie exploded, "where do you get this fraud business? You're the best crew chief in the squadron, you know that."

"Maybe," Zane said, "but I'm sure as hell a big-time liar, there's no getting away from that. She'll never talk to me again," he finished in despair.

They spent the next three weeks sweating, waiting for the time for her to get Eddie's letter, whether she would answer and if she did, how bad it was going to be. When it came, it was more than a letter, it was a package and Zane and Eddie retired to the Aussie tent to open it. Eddie was curious and looked at the address on the package.

"It just says to 'Zane Hitter' with the squadron APO number. No rank. How'd you explain that to her, ace?"

"I don't know," Zane said, eyeing the package as if it might be a bomb. "That was so long ago. I probably told her it had something to do with my security clearance."

"Really," Eddie asked, "and what might that be?"

"Top Secret," Zane confessed. "Eddie, you open it, I can't." Eddie cut the string off the package and undid the brown wrapper.

It was more than a letter, it was a box full of typewritten pages. But on the top, there was a letter. Eddie slowly held it up, his eyes widening as he read.

"Holy Mother of God," he breathed, "you're not going to believe this!"

Zane, sitting in agony, could only reply, "Jesus, read it Eddie, my life is flashing before my eyes."

"Here's how it starts," Eddie said. "Dearest Zane, How dumb do you think I am? I've known you washed out from the beginning. Your eyes. Your cadet friend wrote and told me." Eddie paused and glanced with concern at Zane, who had gone white.

"Hold on Zane, there's more," he said and read further.

"I've loved your letters. They're perfect. Read the manuscript, which, by the way, has been accepted for publication. It should buy us a nice honeymoon, hero. I'll write further, but for now, see if you like the title. I love you." Eddie finished and looked at Zane.

"You want the title?"

Zane sat white-faced, petrified. He couldn't answer. He could barely nod his head.

"The title is," Eddie said, trying to control his voice, "LIES FROM THE FRONT."

Their laughter, when it came, was choked and near out of control and soon brought the Aussies who couldn't buy a drink the rest of the long and memorable afternoon.

Harms' Way

It was a little after seven in the light of the rising sun. In the operations shack hard off the flight line an unusual number of pilots were quietly standing drinking coffee, waiting.

We were there for Bobby Harms. Bobby, a new pilot with Tango flight, had become lost on his first night flight in Korea. This could be big trouble. His instruments had failed and he had somehow flown way north over North Korea toward China before getting his bearings and barely making it back to our base safely.

But it wasn't as simple as that. He had declared an emergency, a Mayday, causing a procedure known as Red Fox to be used. Red Fox caused every blacked-out landing field in the south of Korea to be lighted for twenty seconds. Command really did not like this to occur and would want a full explanation at the very least.

With this had come an official protest from the North Koreans who had picked him up on their radar, were thought to have scrambled their MIG 15s and were screaming for blood. The shaky cease-fire of the Korean Police Action had only been in place for a few short weeks and it was felt it could blow at any seam. This incident could do it.

Bobby was in the back with the brass from Wing now, being grilled. In the two weeks he had been with the squadron, this was the third incident in which he figured. He seemed to be one of those guys who are called accident-prone, although, in his case, it should be called incident-prone.

60

On his first flight up with Jimmy Conlin flying chase, Bobby's landing gear wouldn't come down. Not his fault was the verdict when he managed to get it down by diving steeply and snapping up into a vertical climb, as Conlin had advised. But only three days later up over the field on a clear and beautiful day, he had flamed out and had to make an emergency power-off landing. Not his fault again, was the report. It turned out his jet was overdue for overhaul and his fuel feed system had failed. By the time of the night flight he had picked up the nickname of "Harms' Way," for obvious reasons. We were all waiting for the verdict from the brass. This one was going to be hard to explain.

Jimmy Conlin and Tom "Mac" McDonald, flight leaders of Tango and Bravo flights both considered to be the best pilot-leaders in the squadron, were deep in conversation with Zulu flight leader Tim Jaans in the corner of the Ops room. Conlin was shaking his head.

"I know practically nothing. As soon as he got down Ops had him. He's been here most of the night waiting for Wing. The only thing I heard was his instruments went out and he got lost. Apparently his radio compass went out and he didn't know it. But how he flew so far north is anybody's guess."

McDonald grinned at Conlin. The two were friends but, at the same time, they were intense competitors. There was a lot of rivalry between them.

"You ever get lost, Conlin?" he smiled at him from his imposing 6-foot-4 height. "You ever lose your way?"

Conlin pointed his finger at me. I flew number three in his flight, assistant flight lead. As far as I was concerned, I would be content to be assistant flight lead forever behind Jimmy Conlin. He was the best in my opinion and that went for the other two pilots in Tango flight. He had led us through a lot of tight places. He was highly intelligent, a great pilot and, above all, had the ability to make correct judgments without hesitation time after time. Other than skill, this instantaneous decision-making was what made Jimmy Conlin as good as they come.

"Tell him," he instructed me. "Tell this Yale clown whether I've ever been lost." When I didn't answer right away, he added, "Think."

Now I grinned at McDonald. I had been worried. To my knowledge—and Jimmy Conlin and I went back a long way—he had never made a real mistake, never mind getting lost. But then I remembered.

"Sure," I said, "he's been lost," and watched while McDonald's hawk-like pirate's face looked surprised, even a little offended. In good flights, the four pilots that made up a flight have total loyalty, probably unequaled in life. So much of what you do daily is dependent upon utter confidence, reliance and faith in each other and in your leader. McDonald was kidding around with Jimmy while we waited for Bobby Harms, the usual stuff between the two of them, and he hadn't expected what I said. He was upset.

"What?" he said half angrily, "Where, how?"

"Tokyo," I laughed openly, "R and R last month with me. Conlin put us and two beautiful Japanese ladies on the wrong train for the seaside and got us totally lost."

"Ha!" McDonald laughed, greatly relieved. "I knew it. I did the same thing trying to get to Nogoya one time," and it was right about then someone called attention and the brass came out with Bobby Harms, a two star major general leading, followed by two bird colonels. Harms looked worried and definitely outgunned with his pale silver first lieutenant's bars.

We stood stiffly at attention with the rest of the pilots in the room while the major general spoke briefly with our commander and operations officer who had followed them out of the room. Then they were gone to their waiting transport. Jamie, our Ops officer, waved a hand at us and told us to stand at ease. He put a hand on Harms' shoulder and said a few quiet words to him. Then he patted him on the back and disappeared into the commanding officer's office with our commander.

Jimmy Conlin crooked a finger at Harms and with the two of them leading, we all filed into operation's ready room. We seated ourselves on the folding chairs and the two rump-sprung easy chairs. Jaans, Jimmy Conlin, McDonald and Patton, flight leader of the fourth flight in our squadron, sat on the edge of the sturdy Ping-Pong table and motioned for Harms to take a seat.

All of us knew what this meeting was about. Well, all of us with the possible exception of Bobby Harms. It was an unofficial meeting of pilots in our squadron, a meeting not to point fingers, not to assign blame, but to find out what had happened quickly, on our own, before whatever judgment came down later from the official investigation.

We all flew the same aircraft, the F-86 Sabre, and one way or another, sooner or later, we all performed the same missions. Anything that happened we needed to know, needed to be prepared for, needed to find a solution for in case the same thing should ever happen to us. Meetings like this were often held as a post mortem when the pilot didn't make it. Those were tougher as we tried to piece together what little we knew. The nightly beer calls were meetings in a way, as much for shared information as for the drinking camaraderie.

"Relax, Harms," Jimmy said, "there's nobody here but us chickens. We just need to know what in hell happened," and waited. Somebody got Bobby a cup of coffee and we waited some more.

Finally Bobby spoke. "Jesus, Jimmy, I got lost! You guys know that!"

Conlin was patient. "We know that, Bobby. What we need to know is how and why. Now relax," he ordered again, "this is off the record. Start at the beginning."

"It was so unbelievably dark," Bobby began. "I couldn't believe it. I couldn't even find a horizon line. Jesus, does the brass ever consider waiting until there's a full moon, even half a moon? This is new country to me. I don't want to sound like a complete idiot, but I barely have an idea where I am in daylight, never mind in the blackest night I've ever seen."

"Point," Conlin remarked with a look at McDonald. "Go on."

"I figured I get to altitude—maybe 35 or 40,000 feet—over the base and stay there. Fly instruments, go out on my radio compass over the field for ten minutes or so, then reverse and fly back until I could burn off fuel and come down.

"Makes sense," Jaans acknowledged, "why didn't that work?"

"My goddamned radio compass went out when I was headed in, south to north. I kept flying the needle pointed at 0 degrees. It never swung. It had gone out. What happened then was pretty weird. I still don't understand it." We all waited for him to continue.

"I must have locked on to my instruments. I just doped off, like I was hypnotized and I kept on boring north, flying the radio compass pointed at zero degrees, waiting until I got over base."

"How long before you realized something was wrong?" McDonald asked. "How long did you fly north?"

"That's just it," Bobby said, "I don't know. Maybe twenty minutes, maybe more. When I came to, when I realized what I was doing, Jesus, the shock was like I had put my finger in a light socket. I was flying at

98 percent power, about .9 Mach. I knew I had to be over the thirty-eighth parallel into North Korea, way over, maybe a hundred miles."

"What did you do?" Jimmy Conlin prodded. "What then?"

Bobby was into his story, reliving it. "I bent it around my magnetic compass south like a shot, pushed the power up to 100 percent and put it into a shallow dive, trying for maximum speed even though I was getting low on fuel. I figured they might have scrambled MiGs, though to tell you the truth, I didn't hear much about their radar capabilities when I got my briefing here."

"Point," McDonald said this time.

"The rest of it was touch and go. I got south all right, I was sure of that, but by then I was down to 10,000 feet, damned near out of fuel, my radio compass out and still couldn't recognize a damned thing. I called in Channel D, called a Mayday. When they did that Red Fox thing, I saw our field and made it in with nothing to spare. I'll always wonder if they put MiGs up."

Jimmy Conlin sighed and got to his feet. "They did, so they say," and he looked at Jaans, McDonald and Patton. "Check me on this," he said to them.

"One, we don't send any new guys up unless we've got a moon and clear weather. Two, we make sure of our intelligence briefing on their radar and scramble system. Three, Bobby, you screwed up. You always crosscheck any instrument with some other instrument. Be aware that what you call 'doping off' can happen on instruments, particularly at night," he finished.

"Anything else?" he asked of the other flight leaders.

"Other than saying he was damned lucky," McDonald said, "only one other thing. He waited far too long to call in a Mayday. No altitude, barely any fuel when he called. He was plain lucky," he repeated.

"That's it," Jaans said to the rest of us listening. "Make notes and remember."

"What do you think Wing will do?" Bobby Harms asked as we all got up to go.

"Hard to say," Jimmy Conlin said. "Probably slap your wrist. But Harms, this 'Harm's Way' stuff has got to go. You hear me?"

"I hear you," Bobby said fervently and went on to become one of the most knowledgeable, dependable pilots in the squadron.

Escape and Evade

The Ops room was half full of pilots, some batting the Ping-Pong ball back and forth across the table, some drinking coffee or Coca-Colas, and all talking and laughing in the usual fashion. This was a normal operations day with pilots waiting for a flight and others just down from one. Bobby Harms was laughing about the briefing he had with Squadron Intelligence when he first got to K-55.

"They wanted ten things about me that only I would know the answer to. What kind of crazy idea is that?" he asked the small group of us around the coffee area.

Zulu flight leader Tim Jaans fixed him with a stern look. Bobby Harms was a new pilot in the squadron and had already distinguished himself by having two in-flight emergencies and getting lost on a night flight. He had been fine since then but all the flight leaders were still keeping a watchful eye on him

"Nothing crazy about the idea," he told Bobby. "We all had to do it. True, in your case they have signed the cease-fire, but that doesn't mean all the problems are over. You, for instance, got way beyond the 38th parallel the night you got yourself lost. If you had gone down, had to eject over North Korea and had to try to escape and evade, the ten things were to identify you with."

"To whom?" Bobby Harms asked, ready for a debate. "Okay, I'm shot down or one way or another had to eject and I make it. Now I'm spooking through the North Korean woods and I see a Korean. Why would I speak to him to begin with? And if I do, which would classify me as a complete idiot in my opinion, he's supposed to ask me what my sister's boyfriend's name is, to make sure I am me? C'mon Tim, this makes sense to you?"

Tim looked uncomfortable, glancing at the rest of us for support. None of us answered immediately, having long ago wondered the same thing.

Jimmy Conlin, leader of Tango flight and Bobby's flight leader, came to the rescue. We had been playing chess and Jimmy had stopped his long thought on his next move when Bobby Harms had raised the question of the identifiers.

"Did they give you Morse code when you went through cadets?" he asked Bobby.

Bobby looked surprised. "They did, as a matter of fact. Had to receive forty-five words a minute, I think. Funny you should bring that up. I've always wondered why we had to learn code. It seemed to me the last time that was important was before the Indians cut the telegraph line to headquarters, or the French Foreign Legion was surrounded in some fort in the desert."

Jimmy leaned back in his chair and moved his queen, startling me and putting my king in jeopardy.

"A lot of the intelligence stuff is left over from other wars, World War II, World War I or, you're right, the Indian wars in the West. The military is slow to throw something away that made sense," he said.

"Take swords," he continued, warming to his argument, "they still issue them to some officers. I think they are still given with commissioning in the Marine Corps, although it's hard to see how they can visualize a sword fight. Anyway, this identifier business is probably left over from the war in Europe, when there were a lot of resistance fighters in various countries. If they found a shot-down flyer and wanted to make sure he wasn't a German spy pretending to be American or English to break up the escape routes, they would need to know you are who you claim to be. Maybe Intelligence has South Koreans over in the North who can help us escape."

Bobby looked skeptical. "Really?" he wondered.

"Maybe not," Conlin conceded. "But there is the possibility of spies in prison camps. Rumor has it they have turned some captured troops, then put them back in prison camps to see what they can find out, break up escapes."

"Christ!" Bobby breathed, "that's all it would take to send me around the bend. There I am on some dark night in a bamboo cage, the rain dripping down on me and my rats and somebody whispers through the bars, 'What's your sister's boyfriend's name?' Jesus!" he exclaimed with a shudder, "that would do it."

I moved my castle, taking my king out of trouble and putting Jimmy Conlin's queen in jeopardy. He could take my castle, but my king would then wipe out his queen. I pointed this out to him.

"I wouldn't worry about escapes," a tall, lanky major from Wing said. He had been hanging around operations for a couple of days, usually in conference with our commander. He wasn't on flying status, but from what we had heard he had been a first-class fighter pilot in the last war. When he had arrived in uniform, he had a number of campaign ribbons, including the Silver Star and Distinguished Flying Medal on his chest.

"There have been very few successful escapes over here; in fact, there have not been many even tried."

"Why's that, Major?" Bobby Harms asked.

"Kind of obvious, if you think about it," the major answered. "It's difficult to escape and evade over here. We don't look like them, is the main problem, never mind the language barrier. It's hard enough to do if you speak the language and look alike."

There was something in the way the major said this that caught our attention. Tim Jaan's asked the question.

"You have any experience with escape, Major? It sounds as if you might have some first-hand knowledge."

The major settled into a chair alongside our chess table and stretched out his long legs. He looked at Jaans and then to our utter surprise barked out a long string of words in German. The language was unmistakable.

He grinned at our surprised faces. "I was lucky. I speak German, German with a Berlin accent. I went to school in Berlin for six years as a boy, before the war. When I was shot down in 1943 and put in a stalag, a prison camp, I didn't let them know I knew the language. It was helpful. When I decided to try an escape, it was critical."

"How did you do it?" Bobby asked eagerly. "How did you escape?"

"You'll like this, Lieutenant," the major smiled at him. "There were just two of us and it was on the spur of the moment. We were on a painting detail with two buckets of white paint, a wheelbarrow and brushes. We had been painting buildings until one day they told us to paint white lines down the middle of the streets in the stalag. We did this for awhile and then we were on the street leading through the main gate to the outside."

The major had a distant look in his eyes. "I remember the moment we decided," he continued. "We didn't say a word to each other as we got closer to the gate, which was opening and closing often with traffic; we just both realized at the same time we might be able to paint our way right out through it. That's what happened. The guards opened the gate for us. The guy I was with did something fantastic then. He bummed a couple of cigarettes from the gate guards and then we painted our way slowly out and over a hill before we started running. We kept our wheelbarrow and paint. We went through a lot of Germany with them. We would stop now and again and paint something white. Think about it, who would think a couple of painters with a wheelbarrow could be escaped prisoners?"

Bobby looked ecstatic, pleased beyond measure with the story. We all were.

"That's wonderful!" Jaans said. "You made it back, I gather?"

The major got to his feet. "Yes. We met a resistance group in France who got us over the Channel in a fishing boat. Flew twenty more missions."

Jimmy Conlin swooped a bishop from the far side of the board where it had been lurking. "Check," he said to me and then—looking closer—added, "Checkmate, come to think of it." He was right and I tipped my king over.

"Are you down here for any particular reason, Major? Something to do with escape and evasion?" he asked.

The major put a friendly hand on Bobby Harms shoulder. "I'm here because of this guy. He has had a problem or two."

"Used to," Jimmy Conlin said. "No more," he warned Bobby. "But how is it you're here about Bobby?" he asked as I set up the chessboard for another game.

"Because he got lost on the night flight. It started a whole series of events, not the least being a look at our intelligence briefings. Part of the report claims he didn't know much about North Korea MiG scramble capabilities, wasn't told much of anything. Is that right, Lieutenant?" he asked Bobby.

Bobby was embarrassed. He had taken a lot of kidding about the night flight, as well as a number of de-briefings at squadron and Wing. He had been cleared of everything except poor night instrument procedure.

"Not that I could remember, Sir," Bobby answered formally.

"Well," the major said, "don't worry about it. I'm taking you back up to Wing with me in a couple of weeks. We're reviewing our whole Intelligence set-up, particularly in regards to pilots. You will have caused a lot of good in the end. We've needed to bring the whole thing up to date for quite awhile. What it comes down to is what is the use of our knowing what your sister's boyfriend's name is, when you don't have any idea about their radar-scramble option?"

Bobby looked nervous. "I'm to go to Wing with you, sir?"

"You bet," the major said, "you're going to be our number one case, something of a celebrity," and he started out the door or our ready room. He stopped short at the doorway and turned.

"By the way, Harms, what is your sister's boyfriend's name?"

Bobby was bright red. "Trouble, sir," he finally got out. "That's not really his name, but it's what we called him after she got pregnant."

The major was grinning from ear to ear. "Figures," he said and flapped a hand at us in good-bye.

Pausing for a moment, the major asked, "How did the problem of your sister and Trouble work out?"

"Fine, sir," Bobby replied. "Married happily and had a boy."

The major was stopped now. "His name?" he asked suspiciously.

"Bobby," Bobby said.

"Figures," the major said as he left and he was once again smiling from ear to ear.

The New Guy

The new guy was trim, fit and sporting a well-groomed brown moustache. He was also pretty much ridiculously handsome, enough to snap a second look from man or woman. His eyes were a light brown and seemed a little wary, maybe from a lifetime of quick re-looks or, just as possibly, the fact that he was black, an African-American pilot in, as far as any of us knew, an all-white officer aviator Air Force.

We talked about it, we guys of Tango flight, shortly after our Ops officer had introduced him around our table at the early-morning coffee and rolls in the Quonset officer's bar and mess.

Our number four, Bobby Harms, the guy who flew off my wing in our Tango flight of four, single-seat Sabre fighters, had been ordered over to Japan to Wing for a couple of weeks to an intelligence review. We needed a temporary replacement and Ops, Captain Jamison, had come up with this guy, Jason Dupre, to fill the slot.

As Jamison and our new temporary number four, 1st Lt. Dupre, walked away to fill out some paperwork, there was a long silence around our table. I'm pretty sure we all had very much the same thoughts, but as usual our esteemed flight leader, Jimmy Conlin, put words to it first.

"I will be damned," he said quietly. "That's the first black guy commissioned fighter pilot I've ever seen, from cadets right up to now. All right!" he finished with a sharp look at us around the table.

"Right here, right now!" he continued with a rare show of force of his command authority coming full bore. "Do any of you for any

70

reason have a single problem with bunking, drinking or flying with this guy?"

Bobby One (Bobby Summer), our number two, was laughing at Jimmy. "None, Jimmy, zero, nada, zip. Only worry I ever had was you."

I shook my head. "Never, Jimmy, not once since I signed up to fly until now. He's the first! And never a problem," I said. "The only black fighter pilots I ever heard of were those very good pilots out of Tuskeegee in Europe in World War II."

"Well, okay," Jimmy said, mollified. "You," and he pointed his long index finger at me, "you take him out for the familiarization ride, the usual, show him the countryside, the check points, the usual," he repeated.

The unsaid was "the usual." What Jimmy wanted me to do, besides the look-see of our terrain, was to check Jason out, dog-fight with him, put him ahead and behind me, see if he could lose me, see if I could lose him. It was something done to every new pilot in every flight in the squadron and as I nodded my head okay to Jimmy, I could only hope that Jason knew of this procedure and would not think he was being singled out.

Bobby One got up to leave. He gave me a long look, quizzical, amused and interested. Bobby One was a bright guy, an outspoken guy and a guy about to say exactly what was on his mind. I waited.

"Listen, Jim, you tell First Lieutenant Jason Dupre that all of us, me particularly, don't have an ounce of prejudice aboard. Hell," he chuckled, "tell him I'm a quarter Apache Indian and I haven't scalped any of you yet." And he walked off into the early morning sun.

Jimmy Conlin was staring out the Quonset at the departing figure of Bobby One.

"You know about that Apache stuff, goddammit?" he asked me.

"Yep," I said, "known it from day one."

"How come you didn't tell me?" he asked. I had his full attention.

"Didn't think it mattered," I said, enjoying this hugely. "Does it?"

Jimmy looked at me accusingly then grinned. "No, of course not. But listen, number three, don't mess around with me, you hear?"

I finished my coffee, gave it a half-hour or so then drifted down to squadron operations. I saw Jamison and gave him a lifted eyebrow of inquiry.

Captain Jamie smiled and pointed toward O'Rourke's. "I figured Jimmy C. would send you. Dupre is in O'Rourke's waiting for one of you Tango guys. I told your bar-guy, Joe-san, to give him some coffee and give you some space. I've got the crew chiefs readying two Sabres when you're ready. Luck . . ." he finished with a pat on my shoulder. Jamison was a good guy and an exceptional operations officer. He pretty much ran the squadron for our seldom-seen squadron commander, Lt. Colonel Birthright, and that was exactly the way a well-oiled and well-commanded squadron should run, in our opinions.

I walked into O'Rourke's and joined 1st. Lt. Jason Dupre at a table. Joe-san, our bartender, gave me a coffee. The place had that nice early-morning feeling of a well-liked bar, cleaned up and resting. Joe-san stood off a ways to see if we wanted anything else.

I sat, looked straight at Jason. "You're black, a Negro, colored," I said, having decided to not mess around with this thing. "We don't have any others, not in our squadron, not even in our wing. We, none of us, give a damn. You're a fighter pilot and not one of us in Tango gives one small damn about that race thing."

I sat and pretty much held my breath for a long, long moment. Then Jason smiled hugely. "I'll be a son-of-a-bitch," he said. "Cut to the chase! Call a spade a spade! Okay, okay, okay," he laughed and held out his hand. I shook it firmly.

"Okay right back at you," I said, "We're all set if it turns out you can fly."

"What's your name again?" Jason asked and I told him. "Listen," he went on, "You think I didn't have to be pretty much better than most to survive? You think the whole nineteen 1950's Air Force Officer Corps aviators are as cool as you Tango guys seem to be?"

I took out some topographical terrain maps and spread them out on our table. We sat for a time, smiling at each other, drinking some coffee. Sometimes things just work. By God, it felt good.

Could he fly? Could he? Let me tell you, I'm flat out good and I couldn't lose him. To be fair, he couldn't lose me either. Then he called to me on our squadron frequency and asked if I would go in-trail behind him. I figured he was going to give me some fancy acrobatics and why not. He knew—as I knew—that we both had each other's regard. So again, why not?

But what he then did I had never seen before and—in fact—had somebody suggested it to me, I believe I would have doubted it could be done.

Jason took me into a split-S, diving down to about Mach 1, then pulled up into a half-loop, rolling out on top into an Immelman and then—unbelievably—pulled up into another half-loop to roll out on top into a second Immelman!

Following him, of course I didn't make the second Immelman. I got about two-thirds of the way up in the second half loop, with my airspeed dropping like rock, my Sabre controls getting mushy and let my F-86 fall off on a wing, then over and down. I'm not sure you can stall a Sabre, I never had, but I didn't want to find out this way.

Jason came diving down to join on my wing and called to me.

"Tango lead, Tango two. Sorry."

"Nice maneuver, Tango two," I replied, "now tighten up and hold the chatter. Welcome to Tango flight."

Flight Leaders

Jimmy Conlin shut Bobby Harms (Bobby Two) down quickly and severely.

"No Bobby, no more. Be quiet." And he held his hand up like a traffic cop. We had just heard that Jimmy was to be replaced as our Tango flight leader and Bobby had cursed long and violently.

We sat around a small wooden trestle table in the far end of the Quonset hut that housed the officer's mess and bar at our fighter base.

We were Tango flight, Jimmy Conlin leader, Bobby Harms now flying at number four and I flew at number three. We were, in our strong opinion, the best flight in our 325th Interceptor Squadron. We were missing our number two pilot, Bobby Summer, gone stateside on a temporary emergency leave. That's pretty much the thing that caused it.

Thirty minutes ago, our CO had called us to his quarters and as apologetically as he was ever likely to be, asked Jimmy to step down as Tango flight leader.

A senior captain had been re-assigned to our squadron out of Japan and our CO had to put him on flight status somewhere. Apparently the guy was jet qualified and had rank over the three of us.

Still, Jimmy was very good, seasoned, with great judgment and natural leadership. We had all flown together for most of our Korean tour and we felt unhappy. We had the interdependency and absolute trust in each other that happened in good four single-seat fighters that make up a flight. Flying that way creates a faith in each other that is hard to compare. The phrase, "I've got your back," was true literally and day after day.

Our CO added, "I'm putting him with you guys because you're all as good as I've got and you, Jimmy, may be the best. I'll consider it a personal favor, Jimmy, if you'll check this guy out; see if he's got his chops."

There was never any question with Jimmy. His blood ran red, white and blue and had our CO asked him to swim the Yalu, Jimmy would have done it without hesitation.

When a new aviator is assigned to a squadron and put into a four-aircraft flight, it creates certain real tensions. Number one is his qualifications. Is he any good? Can he fly? A strange question in a way since an aviator is by definition a flyer. He can fly. But the difference between fighter flying and any other sort of piloting is night and day.

Fighter flying is hard, physically hard and intensely acrobatic. Dog-fighting, hassling, air-to-air combat for real or in practice is continual in a fighter squadron. In a tight vertical turn you create many times the effect of normal gravity, as many Gs as you can stand and remain conscious. At five to six Gs you begin to grey out; at seven or eight you black out, which means you become unconscious.

Bobby Harms put it well one night over dinner. He sat back reflectively with a cup of coffee and said, "I had three flights today, went grey out two or three times, blacked out once. I've been doing that practically daily for the last couple of years. I doubt even my mother would believe me."

The new captain went by the name of Donald Sharp. We met him when we left the officer's mess and crossed to the small Quonset housing our Tango flight. Sharp was an angular, raw-boned, stringy-muscled guy in a burr haircut over a lantern jaw. He was half into a flight suit. As Bobby Two remarked later, Sharp looked like a hillbilly just in from a bear hunt.

Jimmy bounced Bobby Harms again but he was half-laughing: "Cut it out, goddammit, Bobby! We give him a chance. I don't give a damn what he looks like if the son-of-a-bitch can fly!"

Jimmy snorted with laughter, frowning at Bobby who was ridiculously handsome in a teen-age way for a 26-year-old. "If we gauged by looks, you'd be in a B surfing movie with Sandra Dee, tops! So shut the hell up!"

Jimmy took Sharp up on his orientation flight that afternoon. This first flight was to show new pilots terrain features, rivers, mountains and where the enemy lived. Jimmy did that but, more importantly, he put Sharp into dog-fights.

You do that two ways. You put the new guy on your tail and see if he can stay there while you try to lose him. The other way is the reverse. We were very interested in the results when we sat with Jimmy after the flight. "Okay, Okay," he began, holding up both his hands in warning, "He's rusty. He's been in Japan for a year running an officer's club. Before that he was stateside as an instructor in a weather outfit. He doesn't have much time in interceptors, in a Sabre."

He frowned and signaled Jo-San, the barman, for another round of beers.

"Look, we're going to have to bring him up to speed fast!"

It was Bobby Two again questioning. "Rusty, well okay, but Jimmy, did he seem on top of it?"

It was a pretty important question. Early in our training in the Sabre, particularly in the advanced fighter-weapons programs in Nevada, our combat-seasoned instructor made this critical statement: "You don't get in the cockpit of the Sabre and fly it; you strap it onto your ass and go!"

It may have sounded a little silly, but it wasn't. It was at the heart of the front-line interceptor flying. The Sabre was the best fighter in the world, a beautiful aircraft, absolutely incredible performance range, the first line fighter to go supersonic, could take more G forces without losing its wings. Sleek, silver and every aviator's dream, it had only one fault.

It could scare you. It was the Nevada instructor again: "Strap it on your ass means just one thing; you have to be in charge. You have to dominate it. You get it?"

If you didn't get it, they washed you out of the program. They sort of patted you on the head and bid you good-bye. Gone to fly transports, weather recon or whatever else suited you.

That's what Bobby Harms meant when he asked Jimmy if Sharp was "on top" of the Sabre. If he wasn't, if this high performance aircraft pushed him out of his envelope of comfort and competence, he could be dangerous to himself and to the other members of the flight.

We all worked hard, hard, after that with Sharp. We flew two, three, even four flights a day. We flew scrambles to ground-controlled intercepts, air-to-ground firing with 50-calibers and rockets. We had dog-fighting on every flight.

We worked Sharp over in solo, in two-and-four-ship formations. We sweated, we punished and we knew as much as we were ever going to know after a week.

Sharp was marginal at best. And marginal wasn't going to cut it. But what happened, happened much quicker than any of us could have guessed.

Jimmy had put Sharp on Tango lead after a few days, putting himself at number two on Sharp's wing. Jimmy shepherded Sharp as much as he could but our flights were a little off-center, not the smooth functioning that we knew so well with Jimmy on lead when it was like four aircraft with one mind.

It was on a night flight on the tenth day after Sharp joined Tango flight. It was Sharp's first night flight as leader.

He had been up twice before on a night flight, once on Jimmy's wing and once on mine. Sharp was okay on formation flying and that's what night flying was all about. Only as number one, the lead aircraft had to know where, when and how while the other three aircraft simply flew on his wing. If a leader should fly into a mountain, so would the other three. It was as simple as that. Absolute trust.

Korea at night is darker than you would believe. The country was in a total blackout, not a light anywhere. Not a glimmer at any of the many airfields, army units, cities.

We got airborne at ten-thirty, a slight mistake as it turned out, as moonrise wasn't until midnight. We had a little starlight but nothing to write home about. As lead, Sharp was going to have to be on instruments as much as anything. The three of us on wing spent the next hour and twenty minutes in close formation. That's hard flying with total concentration as the wing tip and belly lights were blinking hypnotically as usual.

When Sharp put us into echelon and took us into our airfield for landing, he had already made his first mistake. Not until then did he call for a fuel check and we were all very low; Bobby Two at number four was critical. You always use more fuel on wing than lead.

What happened next, happened fast. Sharp made a second serious mistake. Our airfield was 240 feet above sea level and we should enter for landing at 1,240 feet. Sharp brought us in at 2,240 feet. The first time you see your instruments since take-off is after you make your individual pitch-out to land. As each aircraft banks hard vertically left and turns quickly and steeply 180 degrees, your airspeed drops from 300 knots to 200. You level wings for an instant and throw your landing gear lever down and put in full flaps. Immediately you bank again left in a steep 180-degree diving drop to the field. While all this is happening your gaze sweeps over your instruments: gear down, green light on, flaps full, airspeed to hold at 180 knots.

Not one of us caught the thousand foot altitude problem right away. It would never occur to us given the confidence and trust we had in our leader. As number one, as a flight leader, you cannot make this sort of mistake. As lead, it is never about your life. It is always about the terrific responsibility for three other men and their aircrafts.

Jimmy caught it first. His voice crackled into our helmets: "One thousand feet too high, Tango flight. Go around or spike it."

He knew we were all too low on fuel. His "heads up" to all of us was precise. At a thousand feet too high we were all going to be hot and long in the landing. Whether to abort the landing, take it around or not he left up to us individually. If we chose to get down, his instruction was simple: "Spike it" meant to get our wheels down on the runway as fast as possible to help kill off speed.

Sharp went off the end of the runway into the over-run of sand and gravel and collapsed his nose gear. With smoking brakes and locked tires the rest of us managed to stop just short of the end of the runway.

The fire trucks and ambulance were out fast for Sharp who had bashed his head and helmet into the instrument panel. Jimmy, Bobby Two and I left our Sabres with their still smoking brakes and pretty much flattened tires where we had stopped. The ground crew jeeped us back to operations and our serious and grim-faced CO for a debriefing.

Barely in the small briefing room, Jimmy made a hard left to right motion with the palm of his hand while we were still standing in front of our CO.

"Sharp's through, sir," he said flatly. Bobby Harms, looking more and more like the seasoned 26-year-old aviator than a teenager, underlined Jimmy's pronouncement.

"Dump him, sir, before he gets somebody killed." Our CO glanced at me. I held my gloved hand out with my thumb down.

"Right, gentlemen. Sharp's grounded as of now." He gestured toward the telephone, "He's in a neck brace, a little whiplash they tell me and a little bruising around the eyes from smacking his head. Listen," he said again pointing to the phone, "to his credit he said he was completely at fault, brought you guys in low on fuel and a thousand feet high. Asked I apologize to Tango flight."

Our CO, a good guy, a lieutenant colonel nearing retirement age, straightened up and spoke again softly.

"Apologies all around are in order. Things happen, good men survive. I have all I need to know for the moment. You guys clean up and meet for drinks in the mess. Oh," and he met Jimmy's eyes, "Jimmy you, of course, are back on Tango lead, and until your number two gets back, I'll fly your wing."

And with that we closed the chapter on Sharp with the ridiculous and incorrect name.

Rain Scramble

Out on the black and rain-silvered tarmac, the water pooled under our 16 jets until they looked like swept-winged birds hunkered down on a lake, waiting out the storm. The storm cover was low, below minimums for flying, the bottom of the heavy clouds not more than 100 feet above the runway, the base of the cloud cover ragged, like grey and torn bedsheets draped over the land. Everything was wet, battered by the days of gusting wind and rain until it nearly felt as though we were living underwater.

In a storm like this we had little flying to do and no operations planned. The one exception was sitting alert, four Sabres pulled into position off the take-off end of the runway next to a small alert building. Each of our squadron's four flights sat alert every 24 hours. It could get hairy in weather like this and you spent your six hours in the shack reading or playing cards, but in the back of every mind was the fervent wish for the scramble horn not to sound. The transition from the peaceful contemplation of a poker hand to action was intense. You had 60 seconds. Sixty seconds to drop your cards, run through the wind and rain to your cockpit, start up with the help of your crew chief and hit the runway in a rolling take-off. The next 50 or 60 minutes could bring anything. But surely, in weather like this, you could count on the storm to make it interesting.

Jimmy Conlin, Tango flight leader, banged through the door to O'Rourke's, letting in a gust of wind and rain. He stood for a moment in his soaking wet poncho. All the pilots in the squadron were in the room, every pilot except the four in McDonald's Bravo flight who had just gone on alert. Danny Patton, leader of Red One flight, stroked his luxurious mustache with one hand, a water glass half-filled with the amber glow of good Jack Daniels whiskey in the other hand, glanced up from his table near the pot-bellied stove and called to him with mock severity.

"Dammit, Jimmy, fix the door. We've only just gotten the miserable chill off this saloon."

Jimmy pointed a long, steady finger at the Jack Daniels resting on Patton's table. "Pour!" he ordered as the rest of us in his flight came through the door. "Pour four," he added. "Jesus, what a scramble!" and crossed the barroom to Patton's table.

We were just coming off a scramble and had landed minutes ago. It had been the worst. There had been no engagement, no enemy stupid enough to try anything in a storm like this, simply a false alarm that had come near killing all of us. The weather was unbelievable. We had been vectored to the north and, at 40,000 feet, we had just cleared the storm. We had had it all on this flight: lightning, rain, wind, enormous up-drafts and downdrafts and, after it all, one of the ultimately tricky let-downs and landings on a field way below minimums. The three of us in Tango flight had only to stay on Jimmy's wing, but Jimmy had flown like the leader he was and gotten us down safely. We needed the Jack Daniels.

Kono Stevens, our part-Hawaiian number four pilot in the flight since Bobby Summers was stateside and Bobby Harms was flying number two, stood by the table as the rest of us pulled up chairs. His flight suit was very wet, only part of it rain. Patton looked at him sympathetically as he handed him a glass of Daniels.

"Tough flight?" he inquired. We all knew that flying number four in bad weather was the hardest. Four flew off number three, who flew off lead. It was the whip-saw effect. Anything lead did, three and four had to do more. If Jimmy's wing went up 15 degrees, number three's had to go up twenty, number four flying off three even more so. Fifty or 60 minutes of this while being slammed around by a storm was enough to age you.

Kono nodded, not answering immediately, taking the hefty shot of whiskey down in one swallow. "Tough enough," he allowed, exhaling gratefully as the Daniels hit bottom. He smiled at Jimmy Conlin. "Nice let-down," he grinned. "I believe I was still flying wing when my wheels touched down. How low was the ceiling, you figure?"

Jimmy looked pensive. He spread a finger and thumb apart. "About a hundred feet, maybe a little less. I'll tell you this, Kono. I don't want it any lower."

Kono looked thoughtful, nodding. He sat at the next table with two of our four K-site nurses, the only non-fighter pilots permitted in O'Rourke's.

Captain Sarah Brown, long, tall and pretty, leaned over to kiss his cheek. "Welcome back, handsome," she said and poured another drink for him from the bottle on her table.

There's nothing quite like a drink in a good place with people you like best after spending an hour with your precious ass on the line. There is nothing like it. Maybe it's something like after really good sex with someone special. After a time, you stroll down the street arm in arm to meet your best friends, share bottles of wine and the warmth and companionship of being alive. But not really. Good or great sex doesn't usually threaten your life and that's a large part of it. You look at the light coming through the golden beauty of your drink, you taste the liquor on your tongue, let it slide down to burn with good heat inside you. There is the welcome warmth of the stove, the murmur of talk, the solidity of the chair beneath you, all with unnamable peace, joy. There is nothing like it.

O'Rourke's wasn't a large place. It was really just one room with the long bar against a wall. In a corner near the upright piano was the center of attraction, an old and blackened, iron pot-bellied stove, its hinged door open so that the red glow was seen as well as felt. The bar was a nice piece of work, good wood sanded and varnished many times, a copper foot-rail scrounged from somewhere beneath it. Behind the bar was a propeller, an old wooden prop from some forgotten era. Above that was a picture of a P-51 Mustang in flight with fleecy clouds behind it. Pictures ranged on each side of the propeller and below, bottles of scotch, bourbon, gin, winked with shards of reflected light. The barroom had six tables, round and sturdy, and overhead was a fan for the heat of the summer. Next to the piano was a low surface with a turntable on it and a rack of 78 rpm records. Most of the records were inherited and were mainly jazz and blues. A record was playing, an old and scratchy blues sung by the great Bessie Smith. It was perfect in the rain that crashed in torrents on the roof of O'Rourke's.

Jimmy Conlin was finishing up the story of the flight to Patton. "And after all that chasing around," he said, "the let-down was the worst. I'll tell you, Danny, it's no day to be flying."

Patton nodded in agreement. This sort of conversation with Jimmy was really an unofficial briefing. Patton's Red One flight was up for alert in another 12 hours, just before dawn. He would have night as well as storm to contend with if they were scrambled. The three others who made up Red One flight had listened closely as the two leaders talked.

Now it all broke loose. The two other nurses on the base, good-looking Major Sally and slim Lieutenant Winona, entered in a swirl of wind and rain to a cheer of welcome. Someone changed the record and Sarah pulled Kono to his feet for a dance. Bottles and glasses clinked, the sound of laughter came over the rising hum of talk, argument and debate. O'Rourke's was doing its thing. Then we heard it.

Unmistakably, the sound came over the music, the downpour of the rain on the roof, the talk and laughter of us safe and sound. One after another we heard the thundering of the jet engines start up. It was a scramble for McDonald's Bravo flight. Patton went to the door, holding it open as the rain came at him, letting the wind gust through the room.

Jimmy Conlin was by his side. "Damn!" Patton swore over the sound of wind, rain and jet engines and except for this it was quiet in O'Rourke's. Kono and Sarah stopped in mid-dance, glasses at tables paused in mid-air.

Then the roar of the jets on take-off roll was loud in the room.

"Silly bastards, going up on a night like this," Patton said.

Standing by Patton, Jimmy Conlin grinned without humor. "It's not as if they have a choice, Danny."

Patton raised his glass into the storm, the rain beating strongly on the liquor in his glass.

"Right," Danny agreed. "Well, cheers then, Mac," he said, "drive carefully," and with Jimmy's hand on his shoulder, closed the door and they walked back through the room to their table.

The Chicago Rat

He was known as the Chicago Rat although nobody knew why and it made no sense. His name was Bobby Summer and he was as far from a Chicago Rat as you could imagine. He looked like a damned movie star when you came right down to it. He had flowing blond hair that always looked just casually mussed by a gentle breeze, perfect white teeth in a face so handsome that it strained credulity. He gambled mildly most nights and lost consistently with amazing grace and good humor. He was just a little over the edge of being goofy and you couldn't help liking him. He was also one hell of a fighter pilot.

That's what Jimmy Conlin was saying to the six of us around the table in the far end of the Quonset housing the officer's bar and mess. Jimmy repeated it, "One hell of an aviator, I'll tell you. If he didn't do exactly the right things at exactly the right moments, he would be stone dead right now."

Jimmy Conlin was the flight leader of Tango flight and Bobby Summer (Bobby One) flew number two for him. Conlin was the only one who had seen what happened that day, the wild and completely unexpected incident resulting in a crashed Sabre jet and the grounding of every Sabre jet interceptor in all of Korea.

The six of us around the table could not have been more intent on Jimmy's recounting of Bobby Summer's crashed Sabre and his near miraculous survival. One thing we all knew as single-seat fighter pilots was that things happen and if you hadn't pre-thought them so you could act and react pretty near instantly, you could buy the farm, cash in your chips. Bobby One's survival that day had been near perfect with little or no margin for error. It had been a question of making a series of just the right moves at exactly the right moments.

Jimmy held up his hands to show what happened. Flying with hands was something we all did in illustrating whatever flying experience we were discussing. Talk of flying for interceptor aviators was all-engrossing, the only topic worth the telling. To have as an occupation fighter flying, to repeat two, three, even four times a day work that you knew somewhere deep inside could fry you in an instant, blow you into your original atoms, obliterate you totally in a split second, had a tendency to be all-engrossing. You didn't think about all those sudden endings consciously, but you were always willing to learn that one more thing so the abrupt endings couldn't get you.

Jimmy was again holding the flat of one hand just back from his other hand. "I was flying control on him while he shot instrument approaches under the hood. He had made a near-perfect let-down and approach and was about 20 feet off the runway when I called him with a four point zero grade for his approach and he put the power to his Sabre." Jimmy paused in remembering, "We had no more than 180, maybe 200 knots of airspeed."

His hands had been still as he talked. Now, shockingly, without warning, he pitched his left hand into a vertical climb. You could hear our intake of breath around the table. In the quiet of that moment somebody breathed the word: "Jesus!"

That was it. We all immediately knew the problem, the life-and-death equation shown by that horribly vertical left hand. With little or no airspeed and that Sabre standing on its tail, there was no way on God's green earth for the Sabre to recover. We stared at Jimmy's hand.

Jimmy again: "I was on the horn, saying over and over; 'Eject, eject, eject' but I knew if Bobby had any chance, and I honestly didn't think he had any, it would have to be beyond perfect timing."

Jimmy put his hands down and took a long swallow of his beer. We all did much the same.

"Remember," Jimmy said, "I was okay watching him. Bobby, well now, what was he thinking? He knew he needed every last foot of height, of altitude, he could get before he went out and even then, he had to know he must open his parachute the second he was out. It was his only chance."

Jimmy paused, remembering. His left hand suddenly shot up and out. "He blew his canopy off while he was still going up. I was watching him wondering if he would wait too long to fire the ejection seat. I swear he was stone still in the sky at the very top, just before his Sabre dropped off on a wing and started for the ground. Then he fired that ejection seat out of the cockpit. I don't know what altitude he got—maybe 200 feet. Whatever he got, I didn't think it would be enough."

Jimmy was leaning tensely forward in his chair. "He must have had the cool and sense to undo his seat belt and shoulder harness before he pulled the trigger for his ejection seat because he separated from his seat immediately after ejecting and pulled his ripcord. He was falling right for the earth and then, wham, suddenly, his chute opened, gave him one big upward bounce and he was standing on the ground as cool as a goddamn cucumber. The son-of-a-bitch even waved to me," Jimmy finished in astonishment.

There was a long moment of silence around the table as we absorbed it all. Finally the question: "What happened to his Sabre?" Jimmy answered, "Crashed. Blew apart about 100 yards from him. Lucky there too . . . "

"What was the reason for the pitch-up? They know yet?"

Jimmy looked discouraged, "Jammed control column. They pulled the coverings at the bottom of the control column. They're finding everything. Pliers, wrenches, screwdrivers, hell, pocketbooks, even Coke bottles! The brass is sending a real rocket to all the maintenance heads, the crew chiefs in-country. They're inspecting all Sabres before we fly again."

There was a long silence while we all rolled this new information around in our memory banks. Somebody asked: "You ask Bobby One how he knew to do it all, the timing, the details?"

Jimmy nodded. "Of course," and he paused to let this next sink in, "He said he had thought about it all before."

We had listened. We had heard. There was a silence around the table as if we might have been in church.

Then Bobby Summer himself walked up to our table, blond hair a little mussed, handsome face smiling. "Hi guys," he said. We all stood up. It wasn't awkward at all.

Scramble

Off the end of the airstrip in Korea was a small building, a place known as the scramble hut. Inside there was some worn furniture, a clapped-out refrigerator for soft drinks, a coffee maker and heaps of magazines and books of all descriptions. The crew chiefs on duty spent the hours of scramble alert there, drinking endless cups of coffee, picking through the old magazines or napping in corners. Just yards from the hut were the Sabres. Four of them were lined up ready to fly if the scramble Klaxon sounded the alarm that an unidentified aircraft had appeared on control's radar screen.

The scramble horn was an amazing thing. It sounded like an old Model A car horn amplified 50 times. It would blast a peacefully snoring crew chief with a magazine loosely on his chest into the middle of next week. Out of whatever reverie he might be experiencing, there was sudden explosive sound, then movement, the horn continuing its gut-wrenching alarm, the auxiliary power units kicking into life outside, the sound of running feet, coffee cups clattering to the floor and the synchronized ballet of four crew chiefs helping four interceptors and four pilots as they attempted to get airborne in 30 seconds.

Inside the cockpits of the jets, the sound was explosive. Strapped comfortably and loosely into the seats, we went from quiet enjoyment of a Mickey Spillane thriller to a full-scale adrenaline rush, tossing our pocket book over the side, tightening our seat belt and harness, while the crew chiefs held our helmets at the ready. Then it was switches on, hands on the throttles as the auxiliary units roared to full power, the crew chiefs plugging in oxygen lines to our suits as we tested the communications.

As we tasted the faintly rubberized sweetness of 100 percent oxygen through our masks, we would hear our flight leader: "Check in Scramble Alert!" he would call and back would come, "Two, Three, Four," as we acknowledged our positions and readiness. Our Sabres howled up into power and it dimmed the still-sounding alert horn. Then we would see our leader's tailpipe flame as he went to his throttle and moved the short yards onto the airstrip. Without hesitation he would put the throttle to 100 percent and his tailpipe would torch and burn brightly as he made a rolling take-off.

Over the frequency he would call in the low-keyed, calm and measured style adopted by most all fighter pilots, "Let's get it going, Scramble Alert, leader on the roll," and we other three would follow. Thirty seconds and four aircraft would be wheels-up and airborne from the first sound of the Klaxon.

Back on the ground in front of the scramble hut would be the four crew chiefs, eyes a little wild, hair here and there standing on end from the comfortable snooze before the damned horn went off. The auxiliary power units would be brought to idle and then off and after a brief look at the departing jets, the crew chiefs would meander back to the hut. One crew chief might give the departing Sabres a final look, a shake of his head and a comment for his interrupted nap. "Luck, gentlemen!" he would yawn, going back to the hut and his magazine.

In the air, it was always different. In close formation we would barrel away, listening to our leader check in with radar control, the people who had galvanized the whole process into action.

"Take a heading of 270 degrees," they ordered one day and we obediently headed west on that vector as we waited for more complete instructions. With Jimmy Conlin leading our flight, this scramble produced some remarkable flying.

Two hundred seventy degrees had us heading out over the Yellow Sea at a couple of thousand feet while Jimmy called for more specific direction as to heading and altitude. This made for a bumpy ride holding formation as the weather was lousy. There were low cumulus clouds over the ocean with rainsqualls spotted all over the place. Radar control was having a problem and despite Jimmy's repeated calls for an altitude, they delayed. We were forced lower and lower toward the sea by the descending clouds. Jimmy finally took charge. Even the three of us on his wing, flying with our eyes fixed on Jimmy, could see with peripheral vision the white caps on the ocean a scant 50 feet below us.

"Going to altitude on heading 270," he called finally and without further comment he headed us into the base of the clouds. The next 10 or 15 minutes, none of us on his wing would likely ever forget.

What happened, Jimmy told us later, was the instant the four of us went into the weather at near sea level, all his electrical instruments went out. This meant most specifically the instrument showing a little image of an airplane superimposed on an artificial horizon line that was his real source of being able to fly in weather, to fly blind, became useless. Jimmy was down to basics, to flying with only the aid of altimeter, rate of ascent and descent gauge, and airspeed to determine whether we were going up or down. He had one other aid, a primitive—near useless—system in weather called "needle and ball" to figure whether we were in level flight, 90 from it, or even upside down.

As Jimmy told us later back on the ground at debriefing, "Guys, if for any couple of seconds I had any idea if I was right side up or upside down, I would have called for the assistant flight leader to take over. I pity you guys on my wing!"

So true! Forget the acrobatic teams doing wonderful things in formation on a beautiful day with admiring citizens below watching. We were trying to stay on our badly handicapped leader's wing in rotten weather as we clawed our way through 25,000 feet of solid storm clouds. We could have been doing continuous rolls, loops, for all we knew. But one thing we did know was that to lose our wing position, to lose Jimmy, would have us attempting to make a very, very quick transition to our instruments with little or no altitude to play with. Worst of all was the real possibility of a mid-air collision if we were to lose contact on the wing. We all knew the dependency of each aircraft on one another while flying formation in weather is as complete as it gets.

Undoubtedly, the worst position to be in was Bobby Harms (Bobby Two) in number four. In formation, number two aircraft flies off the leader's left wing, three off his right and number four flies off number three. Number four is not a favored position. It's like "crack the whip." Whatever the leader does, number three has to do exaggeratedly and when you get to four flying off number three, school's out. You're all over the place. With Jimmy struggling to keep us in the air, Bobby Two was probably doing maneuvers unknown to man. The stress and skill for Bobby Two to stay tight on a wildly gyrating wing in the weather had to nearly pass human limits. But he attempted to be cool after we were down and Jimmy explained what happened.

"A lot rough," he said matter-of-factly. He attempted unsuccessfully to light a cigarette with shaking hands, "Not the smoothest flight I've ever had," all the while looking ready to throw up.

Jimmy took a long appraising look, realizing how close Bobby Two was to the edge. Then he grinned and leaned forward, lighting Bobby's cigarette. "That was a rough one, sure enough, but Bobby, we have also had one of the funniest scrambles, remember?"

"When was that?" Bobby asked in a whisper.

"It was on a sunny afternoon a couple of months ago, just the two of us on alert, mid-afternoon, a sleepy day and the damned horn went off. It was a bogie, sure enough, and we picked it up easily about ten minutes later."

Bobby Two began to smile. "That trainer, those North Koreans that got lost in a prop job? That time?" he laughed, the color starting back into his face.

"That's the one," Jimmy laughed with him, "Guys, this was something left over from I-don't-know-what, the First World War maybe. It was a couple of lost North Koreans with leather helmets and goggles flying about 50 feet off the ground."

Bobby Two leaned forward into the story. "Fifty feet up, maybe, and I swear to God his top airspeed wasn't over 80 miles an hour. We see it and go ripping by at near Mach. Must have scared them blind, because as we pitch up to make another pass, they duck down so low they're into the trees!"

"Now it starts," Bobby Two continued. "We see we have no chance for them unless we slow way down. Hell, we're flying just above stall at a 150 or so and these guys are practically on the ground, dodging around trees and bushes."

Jimmy had leaned back in his chair, relaxed now as Bobby was smoothing out. "It was one of the silliest air shoot-em-ups in the history of flying. You would have to go back to when it all started, when airplanes were for observation only and the Germans used to wave hello to the French and English and somebody, some stupid bastard, pulled out a pistol one day and took a shot instead of waving."

Bobby paused, then continued. "I think we felt sorry for them, tell you the truth. I swear to God, though, one of the damndest sights I've ever seen was old Jimmy here, sailing by me with his gear down, full flaps, nose high, just over stall and squeezing off bursts of his 50-calibers, trying to lob something in their general direction."

"True," Jimmy said. "Funny thing about that scramble. I knew it even while it was happening. We were so low and slow, screwing around trying for a shot, we could have easy bought it. That would have been a real laugh, an old prop job scoring a Sabre jet, wouldn't it?"

There was a silence for a long minute or two while we all gave this some thought.

"Not really all that funny," Bobby Two said and then looked inquiringly at Jimmy.

"By the way, what was this scramble today all about? I didn't get it, too busy trying to unrattle my brains from the trip up to listen. What was it?"

"Nothing," Jimmy sighed after a moment. "Nothing. A mistake, a blip on their radar, a flock of birds or something."

Bobby took a long breath and got up to get another cup of coffee. His flight suit was sweat-stained black, back and front, as if he had stood under a hose. He lit another cigarette with steady hands.

"A flock of birds?" he said slowly, disgustedly, thinking how close it had been for him.

"Wonderful! Just goddamn wonderful!"

Scrambling to the Sound
of the Klaxon

Jimmy Conlin was slightly drunk and definitely angry. But he was our leader and the three of us, who with Jimmy made up the four pilots of Tango flight of Sabre interceptors, would back his play no matter what. Still, Jimmy, like the three of us, was only a first lieutenant and he had just told the stocky major from supply to do something to himself, which was anatomically impossible.

Jimmy repeated the suggestion, modifying the verb slightly, "Go screw yourself, Major. You're in O'Rourke's, the flight line bar here at K-55 open to fighter pilots and women only. You are neither."

The major looked slightly shocked, not helped by the suppressed grins on our faces. This had happened before and it never lost its entertainment value. Jimmy's hand swept in a circle around our table at the three of us in sweat-stained flight suits.

"You're not to tell us we're out of uniform here, sir." Jimmy was less drunk than angry now. The creases over his nose and encircling his face from his oxygen mask were red.

"We four just got down from a hot scramble and intend to relax until we're ready and have had enough." His busy hand pointed at the attentive watching face of Joe-san, our Korean bartender.

"Joe-san will jeep you up off the flight line to the official Officer's Bar and Mess where I'll be happy to buy you a drink at some future point."

Jimmy stood, all 6-foot-4 inches of him and the major without a peep followed Joe-san out into the night.

Sue, our favorite nurse, sitting at the bar with two guys from Zulu flight, laughed and ambled over on her long legs to sit on Jimmy's lap. "You guys have a rough flight?" she asked.

Jimmy grimaced, then grinned and kissed her conveniently nearby neck. "Yeah, Sue, rough it was. Not so much a bad intercept—more some stinking weather out over the sea."

The weather had been bad, no question about it. The ceiling over our airstrip at K-55, the point at which the steady rain turned into the first layer of cloud and turbulence, was low, under 400 feet or, in other words, 15 or 20 seconds from the moment we broke ground.

It was a terrific transition when you think about it. One moment napping in the scramble hut, the next a blur of seconds at a run, into the cockpit, fired up and rolling, the four Sabres in unison wheeling onto the runway at full power, wheels up and closing on our leader. Time passed? Maybe 30 seconds.

It was something we talked about once every so often.

Bobby Summer (Bobby One) our number two had put it pretty well, just before the vanished major joined us.

"I was dreaming," he said reflectively. "One of those great dreams—you know—waist deep in the crystal-clear ocean off Waikiki, sitting on the sand bottom with tiny waves lapping at me while I grinned at Mary Lou also sitting on the bottom in her killer orange bikini. . .Man!

"Then out of some nightmare the sound of the Klaxon scramble horn goes off—Jesus!—slicing into my brain like some maniac with a screaming circular saw. . ." and Bobby One paused for a moment, his eyes wide in remembrance.

Nobody interrupted him. Bobby One was pretty much unique in our cadre of fighter pilots. None of us had every heard anybody talk the way Bobby did. No fighter pilot ever voiced the word scared or admitted to fear. Bobby One never hesitated. But he was a first-class fighter jock for all of that and we appreciated him deeply. Never often, but when he felt the need of it, he called a spade a spade. When some horrendous thing happened in the sky we were likely to say, "Funny thing happened today but with skill and daring I blah, blah, blah. . ." Bobby would have none of that, he would name it. "Scared myself silly this morning. . ." and on he would go, telling it like it was.

Sue comfortably snuggled down on Jimmy Conlin's lap, one arm territorially around his neck, looked at Bobby One quizzically, a half smile on her really pretty blue-eyed face. She had heard the word scramble many times in the six months of her Korean tour, but she had never heard what it was like, what happened after that Klaxon. It seemed if any jock was going to tell her, it would be Bobby Summer, here and now. "Bobby," she said, "what happens after the horn goes off?"

Bobby looked at her for a long time, the smile gone from his handsome face. He seemed to be gauging something. Then he started:

"After the Klaxon! That's it, Sue. The sound itself does something to you. I've wondered about it. I think some evil genius may have tested it, had it installed in all the many scramble pads. I know it—the ripping almost frantic sound—creates a huge surge of adrenaline through your body that causes you not to get to your feet; it makes you catapult into motion." Bobby One paused for a moment, letting his gaze sweep around the table at the rest of us in Tango. What he saw apparently gave him the okay to continue.

"It's all sound, Sue, and everything is in motion. Sound—the Klaxon goes on and on—and people running."

"The crew chiefs out the door on the dead run, the four of us in Tango right behind them."

Bobby paused again, his eyes inward, searching. I think we all understood. How do you describe something pretty near indescribable? Bobby laughed.

"You know, Sue, it may be that after all, the Klaxon is one of those things where you have had to be there."

Bobby Harms, our second Bobby, flying number four in Tango, stepped in. "I played football for UCLA, the year we went to the Rose Bowl. One of my positions was as a receiver on kicks. After the Klaxon sounds is something like standing on some grass in the open, waiting for a football to come down with 11 big and determined guys running straight at you hoping and capable and intending to knock you on your ass. All the while 60, 70,000 people yell and watch in huge enjoyment. It's something like that."

There were appreciative chuckles around the table.

"It's all in the first couple of minutes, Sue." Bobby One went on. "After that is nothing much. We're all good and can handle pretty much anything in the air."

"Here it is, that first few minutes. The APU's, the auxiliary power units, needed to start our jets—roar into action; we're up and into the cockpits, one crew chief throwing our shoulder harness over our shoulders and connecting them to our seat belt, one taking the safety pin out of the ejection seat and holding it before our eyes. All the while you're busy snugging down your helmet, attaching your oxygen mask, doing a sound check on your helmet radio, attaching the unit for your G suit. Half the time a crew chief, seeing you're busy, offers to start the jet. You give him thumbs up, then you're started and you hear Jimmy calling for a radio check-in. You all answer, 'two, three, four.' Then he says, 'Ready to roll,' and you all click in."

Bobby One took a breath, then a long pull on his beer. "That's about it, Sue. A rolling take-off, joining fast on the wing and we are up and gone. A scramble launch in a couple of minutes. After that it's just flying and we all have that under control."

Sue didn't say anything for a moment, just hauled off and gave Jimmy a big kiss. We all watched appreciatively. Then Sue came up for air and called to a returned Joe-san to get us all a round on her tab.

Well, okay. But as good an effort as Bobby One had made, you really can't describe it. You have to do it. You had to be there.

The Power-off Letdown

Dan Hutchison was a first-class pilot and probably the best wingman in the squadron. He flew wing on Tom Casey, assistant flight leader of Zulu flight. The two were very close, not unusual in a leader-wingman relationship, a pairing whose joining, when right, results in greater performance than the sum of the skill of the two. Not every wingman-leader relationship results this way. Because of differences in temperament, skill, even personality, some wings are not as effective as Casey-Hutchison.

Tom "Mac" McDonald and Michael Dunn of Bravo flight were good examples of the wrong leader-wingman situation. Dunn flew McDonald's wing. McDonald was a big guy, at least 6-foot-4, an imposing personality and a terrific leader, but Dunn came close to disliking him. McDonald was a straight Alpha type, used to leading not only in the air, but on the ground. McDonald decided where Bravo flight would drink of an evening, where they would go on R and R. He set the style of Bravo. Dunn's problem was that he, too, was an Alpha, not quite as strong as McDonald, not as sure of himself, but close enough to resent Mac's leadership role. He flew well on the wing and may not have even been aware of his problem with Mac, but while they were good as a pair, they were not as good as they should have been.

A flight of four pilots in a squadron is set up by the operations officer and it is usually determined by the luck of the draw. Older, more experienced pilots are normally leaders, while the less experienced are on the wing. It's an important joining, like being assigned to a two-man fraternity whose point and reason can amount to life or death. It is a tough thing to leave to chance.

Good operations officers know this and take some pains to balance pilots in flights as best they can. Putting four Alpha types into the same flight, for example, would not be a smart thing to do. But one of the problems with fighter pilots and adjusting them into a flight was the fact that to even want to fly fighters, to have a desire for single-seat fighter flying more often than not attracts Alpha personalities. A flight of four Alpha personality pilots is not a good idea, but sometimes there isn't much choice.

Jamison, or Jamie, our operations officer, responsible for assigning pilots to flights, was good and had set up our squadron well. He probably knew that McDonald and Dunn were not the greatest pairing in the world, but they were a case of having run out of options. He had too many Alphas in the squadron.

Jamie was a little unusual. Most officers in the command structure don't associate too freely with pilots in a squadron. Certainly this is true of commanding officers, who in order to hold a tight rein of command and authority hold a distance from those commanded. Smart operations officers do the same thing, if only to a lesser degree. Some manage to mingle with ease and still maintain their authority. Jamie was like that.

He kept a sharp eye on McDonald and Dunn, undoubtedly waiting until he had a chance with new incoming pilots to rearrange Bravo flight. It wasn't as though they were inefficient or less than capable; it was their basic personality clash. But it all changed when McDonald lost his electrical instruments on a bad weather flight into K-2; after Dunn took over the lead, McDonald's troubles got suddenly worse when his jet flamed out.

This was a tough situation. In bad weather, on instruments, the lead aircraft forgets visual flight and flies solely on the cockpit display of radio-directional indicator, altitude-horizon display, altimeter and airspeed as shown on his gauges. A wingman flies only on the leader's aircraft, paying no attention to his own instruments. When electrical instruments go out, you are left with a primitive device called needle and ball for flight altitude, altimeter, magnetic compass and airspeed.

It's not impossible to fly on this. Lindberg did it on his solo crossing of the Atlantic, but it is not easy. Mac didn't hesitate when he lost his instruments. He called to Dunn to take over the lead. It wasn't five minutes later as they were approaching K-2 to begin their instrument letdown that McDonald's Sabre quit.

Flamed-out, having no power to stay on Dunn's wing in the soup, Mac was in big trouble. Dunn also had a problem. He could let McDonald break off from his wing and try a power-off instrument landing on his own, the obvious answer if you forgot the fact that Mac didn't have much in the way of instruments. It could be done, but the odds on it being successful with no power were not good.

It happened fast, the way most emergencies happen. The main problem Mac would have—besides the difficult job of holding level flight and turns with the needle-ball, would be the lack of his directional radio-compass to find and fly precisely the letdown glide path to K-2. Mac's situation, in the soup at 25,000 feet, no electrical instruments and finally, a flame-out, strongly suggested ejection. It ran through the minds of both men. But as fast as it all was happening, Dunn made his choice.

He called to McDonald to resume the lead, lower his landing gear and flaps and to set up a 165 mile an hour glide. He was going to fly McDonald's wing again, holding his wing position as usual by flying off McDonald's aircraft, but telling McDonald what to do as he cross-checked his own instruments for all the necessary flight information. It was a very tricky thing to try. It was not the sort of thing you would practice.

He told Mac he would tell him right turns, left turns, correction on flight path and anything else needed to make the landing. Mac realized instantly what Dunn had in mind and as difficult as it would be for Dunn, to Mac's credit he did as he was told, realizing it was the best chance he had if Dunn could pull it off.

They made it fine, landing smoothly at K-2 as the fire and emergency vehicles lined the runway. All the way down, Dunn's eyes had flicked rapidly between Mac's Sabre and his own instruments, holding his wing position and advising Mac to pick up a wing, turn right, a little left, a tremendous piece of flying. They broke out of the weather at 600 feet in perfect position for landing and made it without a hitch.

Back from K-2, it was a good night, one of those nights that occur after a close one turns out okay. Most of the squadron was in O'Rourke's. With the weather worsening and heavy rain making any flying the next day a stand down, we caroused, talked and generally let it all hang out. Hutchinson and Casey were shoulder to shoulder at the bar as usual and McDonald and Dunn were next to them when McDonald banged his hand on the bar for attention.

"Gentlemen," he ordered when the room had quieted, "I have something to say. The first thing I have to say is I am buying the best brandy in this saloon for all present," and there was applause and cheers around the room.

"You all have heard of my wingman Michael Dunn's skill and daring at K-2 in which he performed the noble service to God and country of saving my valued ass," he continued and there were more cheers and some hoots.

"Well, I have something else to say. I am proud to be flight leader of Bravo flight, but there might be a misconception about that role. Leader implies follower and while there is a degree of truth in this when flying wing, the greater truth is our wingmen are not followers, not in any true sense of the word. Flying wing is something we all have done and all here know it is no easy task, in many, many ways more difficult than flying lead. But more importantly, what wing and lead do is act together. I believe the word is synergy. Two efforts which together add up to something greater than each of the individual parts," and there were more cheers mixed with boos.

Someone in the back called out, "Get on with it, Mac."

Mac waved the hoots off. "Finally, I ask any and all you so-called leaders in this room to stand and drink to our wingmen," and there was a shuffling of feet for a moment and then they stood; Jimmy Conlin of Tango flight, Danny Patton of Red one, Tim Jaans of Zulu. Then I got to my feet with the three other assistant flight leaders. It was quiet for a moment and in the silence Jamie spoke from the back of the room.

"You too, Dunn, stand up."

Michael Dunn looked startled, glancing from Jamie to McDonald. Mac was grinning.

"He's right, Mike, stand up. You're no longer number two, my wingman. As of today, you're flying number three, assistant flight leader and if Jamie had any sense, you'd be lead and I'd be three.

Cheers, gentlemen," he finished and drank the brandy in his glass in one swallow.

The sound in the room picked up again and in the general conversation I heard Hutchison speak to Casey.

"What about me, Casey?" he grinned, "When do I get off your wing?"

Casey looked at him and smiled back. "Why would you want to do that, Hutch?"

Hutchison signaled the bartender for another drink. "I didn't say I wanted to, I just wondered."

"When I decide to get out of flying," Casey answered with finality.

Dogfight

We left the Quonset hut that housed O'Rourke's. We four of Tango flight—Jimmy Conlin, Bobby One, Bobby Two and I—felt good after a few ice cold beers which followed two intense flight missions that day.

Inside O'Rourke's we had left Captain Jamison—Jamie—our operations officer who had de-briefed us after our last flight, a scramble and intercept of a South Korean transport that had wandered far off the filed flight plan. Instead of the usual de-briefing with Jamie back at operations, we had been jeeped to O'Rourke's where Jamie was having coffee while he did some squadron paperwork in O'Rourke's agreeable surroundings.

We were still outfitted in flight gear, zippered inflatable anti-gravity suits around our abdomens, thighs and calves, shoulder-holstered hand guns, yellow Mae West flotation vests over crotch-to-neck zippered khaki flight suits. Nothing very unusual about our gear except for the miniaturized Japanese samurai swords we carried in a pocket sleeve high up on our left shoulders. Like many things in a flight line fighter squadron, the samurai sword was unofficial and possibly very important.

Old squadron hands passed the knowledge of the wood-scabbarded, wooden-handled, very sharp three-and-a-half-inch steel-blade swords on to new guys joining the outfit.

We flew our single-seat fighters with backpack parachutes fastened to our backs and sat on attached tightly packed, pressurized, instantly inflatable rubber survival rafts.

The old hand over coffee or a beer would explain: "It has happened, you see," he would say, "for one reason or another, the damned raft has very rarely but on occasion expanded in flight. Very, very quickly. There is very little or no room in the cockpit for you and an inflated life raft. Room for you to continue piloting your aircraft, for example."

The old hand might pause for a moment, letting this brand new "red alert" danger sink in, a new "heads up" to add to the longish list of things that could kill you dead.

"But," the old hand would continue in a somewhat weary voice packed with wisdom, "you reach up with your strong right hand and arm, slip your sword out of its scabbard and stab that goddamned killer life raft to death, releasing its air and allowing you to continue your life's work as a fighter aircraft aviator."

Well, you felt like kissing the old hand's hand for giving you the means to dodge yet another red-fanged specter that had been hiding from you in the disguise of a pretty yellow raft that would be perfect for your four-year-old kid to play in if you lived long enough to create that cute little tyke.

For just a few seconds you allowed the movie of you in your wounded Sabre with the inflated life raft plastering you against the Plexiglas canopy at 400 knots, your aircraft completely on its own, unguided by your skilled hand, all over the sky for how long and how must it inevitably end?

The old hand can see the hand-kissing thought in your eyes. After all,s some even older hand had passed the knowledge on to him at one time. He pats you on the shoulder and calls to the Korean barman for another round of beers or coffees. Mission completed.

We finished the de-briefing with Jamie and stepped from O'Rourke's into the late afternoon's bright Korean sunlight. It was Bobby Harms, Bobby Two, who saw the scene first and put a name to it.

"Jesus Christ!" he yelled and repeated, "Jesus *Christ!*" at a loss for further words.

What we all saw was astonishing. It was like a staged scene from a grade B movie. Our pretty and greatly admired chief of nurses, Major Amanda Sally, was backed into a corner made by two buildings, pale as a ghost, terrified, while a big, maybe 60 or 70 pound mongrel dog advanced stiff legged toward her, its snarling, tooth-bared mouth foaming.

Just off to the side but definitely between Sally and the rabid dog stood Tommy Hayden from Zulu flight. Tommy was holding his left arm defensively, his khaki shirt ripped to the shoulder and a long gash on his forearm bleeding.

Jimmy Conlin acted, shouting, "Guns!" and in the same breath added, "Don't shoot until I say so."

We watched Tommy take the dog's leaping, snarling charge and go down with him to the ground in front of Major Sally.

Tommy and the cur rolled over and over on the packed dirt, the dog slinging his head back and forth, tearing at Tommy with each swing.

Tommy had his strong hands around the dog's neck, holding him away from his face and eyes. They were so joined in the violent struggle that we could not chance a shot for fear of hitting Tommy.

Tommy was taking a beating from what we could see. He had both forearms ripped, a big gash looking to be just below his rib cage, a wicked tear below his left ear going toward his neck.

But Tommy was attacking as he was attacked. In all the wild rolling and teeth snapping of the dog, Tommy kept his hands around the dog's neck; the strength of his hands squeezing was so strong that even in the melee we could see his forearm muscles standing out, his hands white-knuckled.

The dog abruptly howled a long, snarling baleful moan and was still. Tommy had strangled the dog. It was dead.

It had all happened in seconds and I don't believe any of us really saw what happened next.

What we finally saw was Sally sitting on the ground next to a very still and very dead dog, her pristine white military nurse's blouse streaked and smeared with blood. It was Tommy's blood. He lay in Sally's lap, his head cradled by her arms and body. She just held him.

"Ambulance! Now! Move!" she shouted at us in a voice so full of urgency and command that we all jerked and moved instantly, in unison. It was Jimmy in full stride for O'Rourke's telephone who moved best, snapping over his shoulder as he ran, "Put those damn guns away and go help her."

None of us really knew what happened from that point on. Oh, we knew and saw our airfield ambulance arrive fast, in no more than a couple of minutes. Before that Sally asked for a blanket and a clean bar towel from O'Rourke's, pressing the folded towel up against the badly bleeding slash on Tommy's neck, then leaving with him in the ambulance.

The airvac helicopter flew him to a transport airfield 20 minutes away. Within the hour he had been flown out of Korea to Japan's hospitals, Major Amanda Sally with him the entire way.

What we heard was that Sally had called our squadron commanding officer from the transport airfield, told our bird colonel she was going and suggested he cut temporary duty orders for her as long as Tommy was going to be in Japan. The colonel had the whole story by this time and complied without a murmur.

They were in Japan for about three weeks, Tommy needing some plastic surgery as well as the series of serum injections used in the case of a rabid dog bite.

Back at our airbase, Tommy returned to flight status, but when he wasn't flying or Sally working, they were together, dinners up at the nurses' quarters, drinks in the officer's club, long walks in the late afternoons.

Their togetherness pleased all of us in Tango flight, really pleased everyone on the base who knew of Tommy, Sally and the dog. After all, Sally was very pretty and Tommy a little scarred up but still acceptable. Major Sally was 29 and Tommy 25, both career officers.

It's hard to say what we all expected, hoped for. It—the expectations—probably had a lot to do with our isolation in a very foreign country, away from wives, girlfriends and family, doing an intrinsically dangerous job that made you reflect on your life and ultimate possibilities.

It was possible we all hoped for a happy ending, hearts and flowers, to marry and live happily ever after.

Of course it didn't happen that way. But they had a very nice time together before Tommy's tour ended and he returned to the States. We all admired their very apparent pleasure together.

Bobby Harms, a realist to the core, put it well. "I believe," he announced over drinks one night, "I would take a few bites from that cur for a couple of months of Miss Amanda Sally's company. Besides," he finished, "Tommy told me that the major told him that she was there for him as long as he lived."

"Now that," Bobby said as he upended his drink, "that's a happy ending."

Practice Combat

As air-to-air interceptors we were polished at the three-dimensional, high-speed, constantly changing combination acrobatics needed in aerial combat. If an enemy broke right in a sudden vertical 90-degree bank pulling six or seven Gs to the right, you have to consider what happens to you attempting to stay on his tail.

Everything the enemy does, you must do and, since he initiated the process, you are always a split second behind.

If he is any good, the second he sees you coming up on his vulnerable rear end, his tail, he throws his MiG into evasive action. To stay with him, again if he is good, is like jumping into a maelstrom at 500 knots.

From the right vertical at say seven Gs, he snaps his MiG over the top and into a similar seven G left vertical and you follow.

Several things now occur. If you can pull more Gs than he can, you might pull your nose ahead of his aircraft and get your 65-caliber machine guns into action. One thing you don't have to worry about is pulling the wings off your Sabre from the G load. Can't be done in either the Sabre or the MiG as far as I know.

If he were to speed-roll his aircraft under from the left vertical so that he is upside down, then without hesitation completes the roll-under so that he is vertical again but pulling in the opposite direction, then snaps under to the right once again and finally over onto his belly diving out and down into a split-S toward the earth, all the while pulling

6, 7, 8 G forces, he is very probably off and gone to fight another day. You don't have a split second to think about that old-fashioned word 'acrobatics,' you simply fly your aircraft in combinations of maneuvers to stay on his tail.

If you don't he may gain the rear position and terminate you and your Sabre. You can't be fairly good at all this, you have to be really good at it, because when you examine it, think about it, it's no game you're playing, it's real and the stakes are high.

There were several things in our favor. One was the practice of air-to-air simulated combat against each other. After a 45-minute flight going up against our Tango flight leader, Jimmy Conlin, for example, trying near desperately to lose him from his tail position on your aircraft, to land and have him come over and whack you on the shoulder, saying, "Nice going Jim, I never got a decent shot at you, had trouble staying anywhere near on your tail. I buy the beer tonight," and you'd feel so righteous, like being short listed for a Nobel Prize might feel.

Other times, other flights, you would be on the tail position against Jimmy and you'd fly so hard and a bit crazy to stay there, that there is no language to describe it, to speak of your maneuvers. And remember, as far as your experience goes, as far as your many practice engagements against other pilots is concerned, Jimmy Conlin was as good as or better than any of them.

There was another guy, a Jimmy Brown, in the fighter weapons school in Nevada. He had exactly five kills in Korea and we all saw his gun camera films for the shoots. Everyone was insane. We figured he ran up against a Red Chinese ace or even some Russian because of the terrific flying engagements. Both the Chinese and the Russians had miles more training than the North Koreans.

Conlin against Brown? Who knows? You had to figure and be thankful that hopefully the other guys didn't have comparables.

Air-to-air combat is all about Gs. A G or one force of gravity is 14.7 pounds per square inch at sea level on a normal temperature day. Two, three, four, five, six, seven Gs is that number times 14.7 per square inch. At eight Gs you have over 113 pounds per square inch on your quaking body. You grey out at around six, seven Gs, your vision telescoping down to a small circle surrounded by grayness. At eight or so you black out.

At five, six on up you can't raise your hand against the forces of gravity. At six, seven, eight, your face is contorted, your lips sagging, same with your jowls, and eyelids. You know this because they were kind enough to show you film in training, film of some poor sap who signed up for the part. Once in awhile in an unguarded moment you muse at what exactly those G forces are doing to your internal organs. Many fighter pilots had hemorrhoids from day after day of pulling large Gs and routinely flew with Tampax or some similar device.

Why G's in air-to-air? Take a for instance: you spot the other guy coming up on your tail so you dive down at top speed, then pull it up into a pretty acrobatic maneuver called a loop. Okay and sure enough that takes some skill but the enemy is also skilled and right behind you and quickly fires off his 20-millimeter cannons and you are history.

No, no. What you have to do is one, see him first; two, turn into him pulling maximum Gs. In order for him to press his trigger on his 20-millimeters with success, he has to pull his nose, his gun platform, harder than you in order to counter the effects of gravity on his 20-millimeter cannon.

So all the while you two are in this aerial dance you never stop the G forces. Sure, in a split second transferring from a 90-degree right bank over into a left 90-degree vertical, there is a moment of zero Gs. Not enough time to matter.

All the while you are pulling those Gs and sincerely hoping to not take his cannon fire, you keep in the back of your active mind the notion of getting behind him, of reversing the pursued and the pursuer.

There is a classic maneuver called scissors. As usual you turn into him pulling all the Gs you can. Then you instantly reverse from a right vertical into a left extreme vertical. You pull all the Gs possible and in the flipping from one vertical to another, you are a split second ahead of him. A combination of things has happened. Your airspeed has fallen, bleed off. Done right, you find yourself in a right vertical while he is still momentarily in a left vertical. You will have him in a move or two more.

The best thing for this enemy to do—or even you if you have had the bad luck to run up against somebody that good—is to cut and run without hesitation. But a couple of seconds of dismay and hesitation at this turn of events may cost you or him dearly.

Jimmy Conlin was hot, pissed. "You son of a bitch," he hissed at me as we sat over a post-flight beer in O'Rourke's.

"I have never in my whole life been so goddamned, had my clock so completely cleaned! Tell!" he ordered and took a long pull on his beer.

I was enormously pleased. To go one up on Jimmy Conlin in flying stuff was as good as life gets. But Jimmy wasn't fooling around. "I said tell, goddammit!"

Bobby Harms and Bobby Summer were quiet and attentive, gazing at me out of the sides of their eyes with respect as we sat under the soft whoosh of the overhead fan in O'Rourke's barroom.

"Listen, Jimmy, we all know where we learned most of the things we know," I said and I trailed off as his eyes were unrelenting.

"Tell! Dammit. Don't mess around."

I quickly added, "I was thinking about it, the scissors thing you taught us," and I rushed on before his set face.

"It's simple. From a right vertical instead of flipping up and over into a left vertical, I went from a 90-degree right bank pulling somewhere around seven Gs, then rolling under into a left vertical and never stopped pulling all the Gs I had. As soon as you recovered and went after me, I did it again. Simple as that Jimmy and I got on your tail."

There was a long silence around our table, then a start of a smile from Tango leader.

"You hear that?" he ordered Harms and Summer. "You hear that? It's what I told you, there is always another damned thing to learn if you're in Tango flight," and he smiled broadly at me. "You hear me, Jim, always, always, always another thing to learn," and clicked the neck of his beer bottle against mine.

Harms and Summer looked at me pleased and interested. I had crossed some unspoken barrier, some benchmark with them. It felt good.

Towing

We saw it all. I don't think either of us had ever felt so helpless. To see the beginning, watch it unfold, to have the time to speak of the dangers, and then to watch it happen was to be forever in our minds, both the bad and the good.

Jimmy Conlin and I were standing on the wing of a T-33 preparing to go on an instrument flight on a hazy, calm day in Korea, while out on the runway lined up for take-off was a guy from Bravo flight. This was a pilot we knew just slightly and who carried with him a reputation for trouble. He was Randy Creed, an experienced pilot recently transferred from the 242nd Fighter Interceptor Squadron when they became over-allotted in pilots.

Creed had been involved in two losses of aircraft, one in fighter-weapons training and one with the 242nd. We heard of this unofficially, by the usual method, word-of-mouth from someone who had known him or a chance remark heard at another base. Despite his being cleared of responsibility in both crashes, guys who seemed too often connected to accidents were regarded suspiciously, close to superstitiously.

On top of that, Creed was only temporarily with our squadron and Bravo flight, only with us for a month until Bravo's number four pilot recovered from an emergency appendectomy in Japan. We were less inclined to give the benefit of doubt to a pilot who wasn't a real part of the squadron.

Conlin and I paused on the wing of the T-33 and looked at the Sabre out on the runway. Behind the fighter was a long line attached to a target banner. We were training in aerial work by firing on a towed cloth target, as well as gun camera air engagements within our own squadron. We were experienced pilots and knew constant training was necessary, but it was difficult, like being back in fighter-weapons school. It felt like going back to take a refresher course in high school. But when the true leaders in the squadron, the flight leaders like Jimmy Conlin of Tango flight, Tom 'Mac' McDonald of Bravo, Tim Jaans of Zulu and Danny Patton of Red One did it without complaint, so did the rest of us.

Jimmy peered at Creed's Sabre as the ground crew stretched the target, the rag, as it is called. "I hope he has towed a banner before," he said quietly.

"Why?" I questioned. I had fired on cloth targets in fighter-weapons school, but I had never towed one.

"It's not as easy as you might think," he said, leaning now against the fuselage of the 33. "For one thing, target towing is usually done with a twin engine prop job, a B-25 or 26."

"We don't have any," I objected.

"I know," Jimmy replied, "and towing with a fighter is tougher. For one thing, you have to keep the airspeed down. If you get going too fast, you rip the rag up. But the main problem is getting it up fast and clean. You have to pop it off the runway as quickly as you can. If you drag it, more often than not you shred it."

I looked again at the runway where the ground crew was having some trouble laying the banner out. We all fly Sabres only, except for training missions in a 33, and I knew the Sabre took a pretty good run to get to lift-off. But the main thing about towing that always amused me, amused all of us who had fired on towed targets in fighter-weapons school, was the idea of flying the tow plane. The line to the rag wasn't excessively long and to have to sit still flying along at 285 miles an hour while pilots just out of cadets made live ammunition firing runs on a banner just behind you was not something any of us would volunteer for.

Runs on a rag were difficult enough in the flying alone. To begin with, a flight of four Sabres would fly a half mile off to the side and parallel or slightly ahead of the towing plane 5,000 feet higher in altitude.

Then, one by one, the four would peel off in a wing-over, basically a split-S, turn back in a high G turn toward the target at pretty much a right angle, fix the gun sight on the target and when close enough to be effective, trigger the six 50-caliber machine guns. While doing this, the rate of close on the target is very rapid and the thought of hitting the target with your jet instead of bullets occurs to you.

But they score the damned thing. In training, all the Sabres have bullets painted in different colors and once down on the ground, the banner is stretched out and the number of hits by each aircraft written up in a log by the duty officer. Say you're firing red and the enlisted guy inspecting the rag looks up laconically and says, "Two red," when purple and yellow and black have all had 30 or 40 hits scored and you realize the necessity of getting close as you fire.

The time from your wing-over to coming in on the banner is so short! Suddenly, you're right on top of the banner firing and at the last possible split second you roll under or over, praying slightly that you miss the rag. Then you power on up the 5,000 feet for another run, wondering what would have happened if indeed you had hit the rag, pulled it into your intake, for example.

Or what it might do to the towing aircraft? Surely the tow line would break easily; still, it would seem that it would give the tow plane a mighty jerk. But the main thing you are concerned with is getting hits. Nothing is more competitive than single-seat, high-performance fighter flying and the notion of coming limply in before your peers with a couple of lucky hits is out of the question.

The problem is easy to solve. You know the extreme right angle of approach, a deflection shot, makes accuracy very difficult. Also the high speed of closure gives you only a second or two to fire. The solution is in your mind as you begin a second run. Make your run to come up almost behind the tow plane and much slower. That way you can creep up on the target and blast the hell out of it. Your angle of fire will come close to the tow plane, but you probably won't hit it, at least you hope not.

You do it. You riddle the target but the tow plane has apparently watched your angle because the radio is suddenly loud with a strident voice. "Watch your goddamn angle, number three! You nearly shot our left wing off. Another run like that and you're reported!"

No problem. You've made your run and shot the holy hell out of the banner. True, because of your low angle when you fired, your scored shots added up on the ground will be long rips instead of neat bullet holes and the duty officer will give you a look. But it will go in the books as 120 hits and top score.

Back on the runway, Creed is set and runs up to power. Jimmy Conlin is quiet as he watches Creed release his brakes and begin his take-off run.

"This is where he has to be careful," he murmured, watching. "He has to get rolling pretty well before attempting to pop the rag up. Too soon and he has a problem."

Conlin had no sooner said this then he exploded in anger and fear. "Jesus Christ! He's got the nose too high too soon. If he doesn't get it down, he won't get it flying!"

He is suddenly quiet as the Sabre continues down the runway, faster all the time, its nose's high altitude never varying

We watch, the two of us, turning as the Sabre careens down the runway, growing smaller as the end of the runway approaches and then, in a shocking, mind-numbing second, we see the Sabre leave the end of the runway, start to roll right and simultaneously explode in a huge ball of flame and fire.

"Oh, shit," Conlin said helplessly," he bought it. "Oh, Christ!" and we stood silently on the wing of the 33.

Conlin was suddenly in motion, off the wing of the 33, yelling for me to come. We got into our jeep and drove fast to the end of the runway, racing with the fire trucks and ambulance. The wind of our passage blew Jimmy's straight blond hair back from his face.

"There's no chance," he shouted over the wind, "the stupid bastard," and we continued to the crash, despite everything, hoping.

It was unbelievable. There was nothing left of the fully fuel-loaded jet. We braked to a halt close to the remains of the exploded Sabre. "Blown to Kingdom come," Jimmy said and then looked suddenly to his right.

There are rice paddies off the end of the runway. Small squares of water-filled rice plots, edged by 18-inch dikes of earth. There is a long furrow like an arrow from the crash site, scoring through the paddies in a straight line, one dike after another neatly holed through.

And then we see what has caused this. At the end, some 100 yards away through the rice is the ejection seat of the Sabre, apparently fired free when the Sabre rolled right and exploded.

We watched speechlessly as the form of Creed slowly detached himself from the seat and stood uncertainly by his ejection seat. He was covered with the human excrement that is used to fertilize the fields. He had a small cut on his forehead. He was otherwise unharmed. Somehow, a not so small miracle, the Sabre in exploding had fired the ejection seat at precisely the right moment and at the only correct horizontal angle across the fields.

Jimmy Conlin looked away, up at the sky, raising his fist and then starting to smile. "What a joker you are!" he exclaimed to the heavens.

After a moment, we started forward to the odor-covered, stupid bastard who was walking slowly toward the stunned group of us here to pronounce final rites.

A Difficult Practice Run

It had been shocking, totally unexpected, and it showed on the faces of the new guys. We wondered what had gotten into McDonald, Bravo flight leader. It was not at all unusual to make a practice run, with or without live ammunition, but it was always on a target in some deserted place in the Korean landscape. This had been a real village, with real houses and, most inescapably, real people.

I couldn't get out of my mind the snapshot memory of a figure running away along an earthen dike between rice paddies as I made a high-speed, earth-hugging, strafing pass. It, he or she, had fallen into the water-filled field in slow motion as I blasted overhead not 20 feet above the ground in a consuming scream of sound. McDonald's face was serious, set and stern, as he began our de-briefing. He knew we were bothered.

Of course, we hadn't really machine-gunned the village, taken out the town square with rockets and bombs. Our attack was simulated, practice, doing everything we would have done on a real mission except firing live ordinance.

McDonald led the flight of our four Sabres on this morning, a flight scheduled with two new pilots from the rotation pool in Japan. There hadn't been much to it from the pre-flight briefing. It was to be a normal orientation hop for the new guys, part to give them a look at the countryside and part to get a line on the new pilots flying capabilities.

Even though I flew assistant flight leader in Jimmy Conlin's Tango flight, Mac had asked me to fly assistant lead for him. Two new guys, Mac had told me, and he wanted somebody experienced and good to lead the second element. Next to Jimmy Conlin, I considered McDonald very highly and was pleased with his compliment. Of course I said yes without hesitation.

It had been normal to start with, the four of us in our single-seat Sabres flying close formation in the crisp, clean air of springtime Korea, tranquil under the recent umbrella of a shaky cease-fire. It had been normal until we saw the small South Korean village off our wing and McDonald had put us into attack formation. We had worked the town over fiercely for a full 15 minutes, using fence-hopping strafing runs, rocket passes and bomb runs. It had been as close to wartime as it is possible to get, the only thing different was the lack of return fire from this friendly village.

There was something wrong with what we had done; it felt strange. It had been like strafing your hometown, shocking badly your family, friends and neighbors. Even without firing our weapons, we all knew the effect on the nervous system of low-level flying for people on the ground. The combination of the mass of the eight-ton Sabre scant feet overhead at 450 miles an hour creates a mass-momentum-speed impact outside human experience, the huge sound of passage hitting all at once in a brutal crack of explosion. It is near paralyzing, like an immense, non-focused blow. It has been known to kill.

"Jesus, Mac . . ." I got out and couldn't finish. I was having trouble putting into words what I felt.

I took a long sip from my cup of hot coffee. "Those were our guys, Mac, South Koreans," I finally got out.

"Jesus," I said again, "the damned war's supposed to be over."

We were de-briefing in the ready room, deserted now as McDonald had asked the two pilots who had been drinking coffee to give us some space. They had sensed something in McDonald's voice and quietly left. Mac was sitting backwards on one of the many cane chairs as the three of us sat facing him on a long, old couch against a wall.

Mac held up a warning hand. "Quiet," he ordered.

We were all lieutenants, the two new guys second lieutenants and Mac and I firsts, but Mac was senior to me and in the mood he was in was not above pulling rank. Probably more importantly, Mac had a special leadership quality that you run into now and again, something in his character that commanded. In our squadron, Mac had it; my flight leader, Jimmy Conlin, had it; maybe Patton of Red One flight; all first lieutenants had it. They were junior in rank but, in many ways, more in control of the squadron than our squadron commander.

Mac got up and got a refill from the coffee maker. Back, he settled into his chair and resumed.

"Either of you two ever target a town before?" he asked the two new guys.

Barnes, one of the new guys, interrupted. "I was wondering, sir, does command okay target runs like the one we made today?"

"No," McDonald answered coldly. "You're bothered by beating up a South Korean village, aren't you?"

Without waiting for an answer, he went on, "Well, so am I. Those people in that village have just been through a war and before that the Japanese invasion and occupation. It's a tough country for a moment of peace."

He was up out of his chair now, prowling restlessly. "The thing is, this is their country and we are not over here having exactly a picnic. It's for them. What we had today is exactly what you guys would have run into a few months back if a North Korean or Chinese battalion had been holed up there. The only difference was they weren't firing back at us," and he chopped at the air with his hand for emphasis.

"I'm going to tell you a big secret. The difference between today and somebody firing back at us is nothing. Nothing," he repeated.

"You would make the same passes," he continued, "the same runs and the only difference would be the muzzle blasts from the ground. It wouldn't change a thing. You would jink all over the sky coming off target just as you did today, come out of the sun, use every trick in the book and ignore the ground fire."

He was back seated again, his finger pointed at the new guys.

"Listen, you ignore it because there's not a damn thing you can do about it! You might get blown out of the sky and that's what happens, or maybe you get hit and pull out of the pattern. It has a lot to do with luck. But during this, there is no way you are going to call in that you don't like these guys shooting back at you and go home. The guys who would do that are long ago out of this business, or never got in it in the first place. You ignore the return fire because there is not one damned thing you can do about it."

He smiled tightly at me, at the three of us. "I don't like scaring those people any more than you do. We all have to do our part. Today was their part. We hit that village because of all the practice runs you've made before in fighter weapons training, nothing told you what it would be like to do it on an actual town, with power lines, one-two-and three-story buildings, real people, dogs, cats, horses and cows. It's different and you needed to know."

Mac got up to end the de-briefing. I still wanted my say. "Maybe, Mac, still I think it was pretty rough," I said.

Mac grinned at me. "Of course it was. But you should know better than to say that. This isn't a game we're playing. Fighter flying is all about being a gun platform, for gunning down other aircraft if you're lucky and if you're not, for the enemy on the ground. Don't shy away from it. Our job is to shoot down the enemy, shoot up the ground people. Just because you don't always see them in an aircraft, a tank or whatever, doesn't change a thing. There are people in the plane, people in the tank, in the bunker."

"Your job, all of our jobs," he said with a long look at the new guys, "is to wipe them out. That's our job. It's why we fly."

Barnes shook his head. "I hear you, Lieutenant, but it's not why I fly."

"Oh?" McDonald questioned, "how's that?"

"I fly because I love flying."

McDonald smiled. "Of course. No question. That's true for all of us. But flying the ultimate in aircraft fighters can be done in only one way: in the military. There's no other way to fly a many million-dollar supersonic aircraft that can do anything and costs over a thousand dollars an hour to fly in fuel alone."

"You're right," Barnes said. "It's a tough trade-off though, isn't it?"

"For some," McDonald agreed, "but not for me."

"How come?" the other new guy asked.

"I'm military all the way," McDonald answered. "If I weren't in flying, I'd be in something else, the artillery or the ground troops, something. You guys, I suspect," he finished with a grin, "are basically civilians at heart."

"One hundred percent," Barnes agreed, "but I'll do my job while I'm here."

McDonald got up. The briefing was over. "You bet you will," he said succinctly and with that, we all went to lunch.

Fighter Pilots and O'Rourke's

It was pretty much as usual, a bunch of us sitting around O'Rourke's on a very stormy night, the airfield socked in with bad weather, the ceiling non-existent, clouds right down to the tarmac, the rain pouring down.

If you had to be in a completely strange country with an incomprehensible language, you could do a lot worse than hanging out with a bunch of friends and comrades with a totally engrossing occupation in common. Add to that a place with a pot-bellied stove toasting the room nicely, an upright piano against one wall being softly played by a pretty girl in a nurse's uniform. The walls were almost entirely covered with pictures and photographs, all of aircraft and women. In fact over and in back of the polished wood of the bar was a large photo of a P-51 Mustang against a background of fleecy white clouds against blue sky. The pilot visible in a crash helmet and oxygen mask. You couldn't really see the aviator's features, but the legend had that it was O'Rourke himself, back in the early days of piston-powered P-51 Mustang fighters, a South African aviator and the first fatality of our airbase and our squadron. Many a toast had been offered to him, to the photo, in the course of an evening.

O'Rourke's was completely unofficial, given that it was inside the perimeter of barbed wire and armed guards of the jets and airstrip itself. It also had very unofficial rules, which were zealously enforced. You had to be a fighter pilot or a nurse, a woman, to be welcomed. All others were firmly asked to leave.

All new pilots arriving for a tour of flying duty were given an extra duty assignment. O'Rourke's had such a slot and in the magical way the military had of putting round pegs in square holes, it, once in a long while, made a perfect fit.

Bobby Summer, Bobby One, in our Tango flight, had drawn O'Rourke's as his collateral assignment after Michael Doud's tour ended. A perfect fit. Bobby was an excellent aviator and the fact that to ply his trade he had to be a military officer was a minor annoyance to him. Bobby was greatly amused by the fact that all the fighting in the Air Force was done by basically young military officers. He had affection for the hundreds and hundreds of necessary support guys, mechanics, supply cooks and so forth, but he would tap a visiting fighter pilot on the shoulder and smile saying: "One in a thousand!"

To watch him ever so politely, but firmly and as inexorable as a thousand year old glacier making its way to the sea at Port Arthur, to watch him ushering to the door a bird colonel was quite a sight relished by all the pilots of the 325th. To see him standing, his head ever so slightly bowed, all tall 6-foot-2 of him at near attention, his right arm pointed rigidly at the door out of O'Rourke's, his first lieutenant's silver bars in nice contrast to the offender's out-stretched silver wings showing the rank of full colonel, was heartwarming.

Later, say at a de-briefing of Tango flight where Bobby One flew off Jimmy Conlin's wing at number two, Jimmy, wrapping up the de-brief, would grin and remark, "Nice job on that bird colonel last night, Bobby. Now if you could fly as well as you handle rank, it would be great." And Bobby would accept the backhanded compliment with a modest grin.

Bobby was very popular, right up there next to a young aviator in Zulu flight, oddly named Jackson Peek. Jackson had the collateral duty of morale officer, which he mainly fulfilled by scrounging up old hard-to-find B movies to show amid the boxes and cartons of the supply room. He would rate the movies by a simple sign on the bar that would suggest one, two or three, referring to beers or drinks to bring with an attendee. He, Jackson, as morale officer, was also asked pretty much constantly during his tour to say something funny. He took it well and remarkably often would do it, say it. Something. Funny.

What happened this one night in O'Rourke's was hard to say. We all indirectly watched Bobby One standing, talking to this bird colonel wearing wings sure enough, but his jacket had the insignia of a transport group out of Seoul. But Bobby's arm had not risen to indicate the direction to O'Rourke's exit.

The next thing we all knew, Bobby and the colonel joined our loosely joined tables and Bobby introduced him.

Bobby did an odd thing in introducing the colonel. He directly named Jimmy Conlin in his introduction. Jimmy was probably the best flight leader in the squadron and a short-timer, due to rotate back to the States in a month.

"Jimmy," Bobby said as he and the colonel seated themselves and got drinks, "The colonel here has something real interesting to say."

The colonel didn't hesitate and we all realized that he was fairly drunk.

In just a few sentences we all recognized the colonel as a type of brass we all knew and detested. The best of senior ranks hardly ever let their rank show except through their actions. The worst, like this colonel, demanded respect and recognition. It is hard to pin down. It's an attitude more than anything, the way he leaned on pronouncing "lieutenant" when speaking to Jimmy, for example. The good brass— particularly in this setting—would immediately shed rank by referring to Jimmy as Jimmy or perhaps Conlin. It was an understanding that underneath it all, rank had little or nothing to do with flying qualifications, particularly in fighters, and that was what the part of the Air Force called fighter interceptors was all about.

The colonel started right in on Jimmy for whatever reason.

"I know of you, Lieutenant, two confirmed MiG kills and your C.O. tells me you're due to go stateside in a month and not sure about a career in the Air Force."

Jimmy nodded noncommittally and that seemed to anger the colonel. The rest of us, Tango and most of Zulu watched the non-exchange with interest.

"Let me tell you what you'll be missing, Lieutenant. Headquarters is considering making a high speed launch vehicle out of your Sabres!" and here he smiled in a ferocious sort of way.

"With a low yield atomic bomb under your fuselage, you will approach at near Mach 1, pick your nose up approximately 30 degrees 10 miles from target, and toggle off your weapon in a parabolic throw to target. You will continue up into a halt loop, an Immelmann, fly directly out on reverse course. Your speed and time should be enough to avoid the blast and shock wave of the atomic explosion!"

There was pretty much a dead silence as we all assimilated this undoubtedly classified information. Then it was Jimmy speaking softly but penetratingly. "What's your definition of a low yield atomic bomb, Colonel?"

The colonel was red-faced. "Depends on the topography, the density of the population . . .", he trailed off into silence as we, Tango, Zulu, Jimmy waited for an answer.

The colonel finally said with angry emphasis and satisfaction. "A million, give or take."

Jimmy stood after a long silence. It was a strange moment as I realized all of our Tango flight was standing with Jimmy and most of Zulu beginning to join us.

"Listen Colonel, let me be clear. Not you, not anyone on earth can order me to be prepared to kill a million people."

"You will if you're ordered to, Lieutenant!" the colonel said, now white-faced.

"Well," Jimmy answered, "I'll have to fix that, won't I," and without another word all of us in Tango left O'Rourke's with Jimmy and jeeped back to our Quonset hut.

We never discussed it further and when Jimmy returned to the States after his tour ended, we heard he resigned his commission and left the flying service.

A Hard Loss

The hole he dug was enormous. It was at least 15 feet deep and wide, a crater created by such violence that it shocked the mind. All that was left of what had been Jack Englander and his Sabre were pieces of unrecognizable metal, twisted and scarred.

We didn't know what had happened to him, other than this silent testimony of the result. Jack had gone up on a night flight, a flight of no real importance, and when he had come down, it was straight down like an arrow, like a falling star, a meteor, to dig his final resting place in the earth. There was nothing of Jack remaining, no vestige of what had been a wonderful guy, a pilot who loved nothing more than flying. Jack Englander was special, something we all had known without words, but felt deeply now. We had to speculate on what had taken him.

Our best guess was lack of oxygen. In jet fighter interceptors, you fly on 100 percent oxygen from the ground up. With all the equipment necessary to fly a fighter at altitudes up to more than nine miles above the earth, nothing is more critical than the demand oxygen system. And there is nothing more deadly in a sly way than to have the system malfunction.

Unlike most other emergencies in flight, oxygen starvation gives no warning. In a terrible way, it is even kind. It's like getting very rapidly drunk without being aware of the process. Like drinking, it produces an initial sense of euphoria, a high, but then it is followed by almost immediate loss of motor control, then a daze and quickly, unconsciousness. All in 30 to 60 seconds. It's like sitting down to serious drinking to the point of passing out, all taking place in nearly the blink of an eye. You rarely have time to realize what is happening, to dump the stick forward and dive with full power down to lower altitude and breathable air.

We hoped this is not what had happened to Jack. We hoped there was no time for a few breaths of air and consciousness before he met the earth.

Jack was the sort of guy your parents were crazy about when you brought him home for the Thanksgiving holiday from college. If there was a downside to Jack, he seemed to cause your parents to look again at you with a thoughtful, re-appraising expression. Your emerging beauty of a little sister took 24 hours to name him Uncle Jack while the family Labrador retriever made it plain she would as soon hit the road with Jack as hang around with the family.

Jack was a first-rate aviator, superior in a quiet way. He made the number three slot in his four-aircraft flight, number three being assistant flight leader, and he made that jump from wingman to assistant lead very quickly.

There was plenty of ego, too, around in a squadron of single-seat fighters, probably as necessary as 20-20 vision for the demands of the daily job at hand, but it didn't come out in the sometimes bad ways it might have in your former life.

Jack had none of these qualities to shake off. Jack just became more of what he had always been, one of life's naturals. The squadron was not the same after Jack dug his hole. One way or another, we all had lost friends and people we had known, from the beginning of training to now and we shrugged it off, knowing it was part of what we did. But Jack, now this was different.

We sat around the large, plain wooden table in the middle of the Quonset hut that was the home of Tango and Bravo flights, three of us who had flown the missing man formation that afternoon for Jack. Missing man was usually done at the services for a pilot who had gone in, bought the farm, crashed. There were no services here. That would be done later back in the States, at whatever place Jack would end up, to be marked by a granite headstone and his family and friends. But after a brief conversation with our commander, our flight leader,

Jimmy Conlin, had told us that we would do an unofficial fly-by at four o'clock for Jack and we had done it.

Our missing man fly-by was simple. We came over our K-site low and very fast in a normal four-ship formation. Just over the flight line with the loosely gathered pilots and crew chiefs watching, the number three jet flying just off the leader's right wing suddenly, almost shockingly, pitched straight up in a vertical climb leaving a gaping space between leader and number four. Missing man this way was silent and eloquent.

Jimmy uncorked three beers and handed them around. He frowned, looking at Tim Ruger, one of the pilots in Jack's flight, who was more or less in charge of the scratchy turntable playing a real bluesy Sarah Vaughn record.

"Change it, will you Tim?" he asked and took a long drink of beer, settling back in his chair.

"What I liked about old Jack was the way he could talk to anyone, even the Koreans and Japanese and he didn't have a word of their language."

Tim, back comfortably in his chair with the record changed, laughed. "He didn't really talk. He did it all with his hands, body and face. He was a great mime. One time in Nagoya on a five-day REMCO flight, we wound up in a little Japanese inn having a glass or two of sake. A couple of huge sumo wrestlers came in to drink beer. You know they have to drink something like two or three gallons a day?" he questioned us and we nodded.

"Well," he continued, "they weren't too excited about having us in their place. We were getting a lot of heavy frowns and looks. Jack went into his sign and body language. It was funny, but it made me nervous, because he could look somehow very Japanese, something they might not be thrilled by."

"What happened?" I asked, amused as Jimmy was by this story about Jack, doing what we all had seen him do in one form or another.

Tim laughed again. "First thing I knew, we were sitting with these guys while they bought us some sake. We had a great time."

The door slammed at the far end of the Quonset and three members of Bravo flight came in. They took some beers out of the old refrigerator, noting them on the scratch sheet under Bravo flight's running tally. They sat down with us.

"Nice fly-by, Jimmy. Good missing man formation."

"It was unofficial," Jimmy explained. "We thought Jack would like it."

"Right as rain on that," Roger Aspin, assistant flight lead of Bravo, said. "Jack was a flying fool. As they say, he probably had more time upside down than a lot of us have in the air. He was the most volunteering guy I have ever known."

"That's what got him," Tim said as the record ended and the silent night filled the Quonset. "That flight was for a returned REMCO bird just back from Japan. I was there when Ops asked for someone to fly it that night for a quick equipment check and Jack was halfway out the door before he finished."

"What do you figure?" Aspin asked in the quiet.

"Oxygen," Jimmy said. "For an impact like that, he had to be at full power, had to be unconscious.

"Jesus!" another of the Bravo guys said. "Better than Mach 1, right in."

Nobody spoke for minutes. Then it was Jimmy again. "Doesn't make much difference, does it? One way or another. I just wish it hadn't been old Jack."

Under the single overhead light, in the cool silence of that place, the six of us sat, each of us locked in own private thoughts.

Not Jack? Who then?

Major Louise

Major Louise Longstreet was chief of nurses and the second highest-ranking officer attached to our squadron. Nobody knew her age, or at least no one was willing to admit to it, but our best guess was somewhere around the mid-30s. This wasn't because she looked it, not at all. In fact, she appeared to be, at most, in her late 20s. The only reason we figured her to be in her thirties was the knowledge that she had served as a military nurse in Europe in World War II, some nine or 10 years before the police action here in Korea. Louise was serving a second tour in Korea and had been here long before us when the going was hot, before the Inchon Invasion, and had the Distinguished Service Medal to prove her worth.

Whatever her age, she was our one and only outstanding nurse from a purely objective point of view. She was great looking. She was easily one of the most attractive women we had ever seen here on our small fighter base near Osan, Korea, or in the wider world we had left behind. She had short blonde hair of the type that can appear the result of hours in a beauty shop by ruffling one hand casually through it a time or two, a lovely wide full mouth, large clear blue eyes and a figure that no amount of disguising by a uniform could hide. She looked enough like a wonderfully popular singer-actress named Doris Day to be her twin. There was not a one of us who was not halfway in love with Major Longstreet.

But there was more. Her skills as a nurse, gained through advanced degrees and intense practical experience under wartime conditions, made her the object of complete confidence by us. We trusted her completely, more confidence than we had in the young and usually recently commissioned medical officers that were attached to our wing in Seoul. Louise had a rare combination of knowledge and common sense that made you know she could either fix it or know quickly what expert in Korea or Japan she should send you to.

With all of that, her smashing good looks and the professionalism in her work, it was her intelligence, wit and sense of humor that elevated her to a special place in our world.

The three times a week movies in an old unused supply tent were her special stage.

Our movies were pitiful. For whatever reason, all we ever had were the worst of old B pictures and not many of them at that. If we hadn't received anything new, the normal problem, the projectionist would run something we had seen many times before. Often the film would break or, more often, the sound would go off, leaving the actors posturing around silently in grainy black and white on the screen. This didn't really bother us as the movies were just a chance to sit around on odd bits of furniture and boxes with our several drinks stockpiled from the squadron club and to hoot, boo and cheer the performance.

Our favorite moviemaker was a guy with two names, at least so the information went in our squadron. For some reason this guy made a lot of B pictures and we probably had most of them. But he also made a few A pictures, often remarkably good ones. On the A pictures his name would be credited as producer, Sam Speigel. On the B movies, it would be the same guy but in a sensitive acknowledgment of the poor quality of the B, he would list himself as S. P. Eagle. We loved this guy, appreciated his effort to disguise himself when forced by the economics of life to make a less than Oscar-winning picture and cheered when the credits named our favorite, S. P. Eagle. It was during one of the sound blackouts of a S. P. Eagle B drama that Major Louise made her star quality known.

Louise was sitting next to Tango flight leader, Jimmy Conlin, up front near the screen. The movie featured a typical leading lady from one of S. P. Eagles's pay-the-rent ventures named Lola and a guy named Biff. They were playing roles similar to the sort of turgid drama that Greta Garbo and John Barrymore used to enjoy, a steamy scenario with lots of flickering candles and long, long close-up head shots of the two, Barrymore-Biff leaning over Greta-Lola on a chaise. In this take, Biff was in the midst of some nostril flaring speech when the sound in our little screening room went out.

Jimmy Conlin didn't hesitate. His lip-synching was almost perfect as he filled in for the absent sound on the screen.

"Are you really from Cincinnati?" he inquired as Biff leaned forward inches from Lola's face.

Lola's mouth on screen went slack with passion in answer to this question and as she spoke in mime, Louise filled in for her.

"God, I love it when you talk dirty!"

Biff, on screen, twisted his mouth in desire. His lips moved. Jimmy Conlin spoke.

"Oh yeah, you liked that? Then listen to this: Toledo, Peoria, Detroit, Sacramento, Daly City!"

Now it was Louise answering with thrilling emotion in the electrified quiet of our little movie theater as Lola mouthed her lines before flinging herself forward for an environmentally unsafe kiss. "Oh, Biff, you ace, take me, take me, take me!"

Well, the house came down. The cheers and yells of appreciation and applause brought more wondering viewers into our supply tent. The lights went on as Louise and Jimmy Conlin took bow after bow. Someone rushed up to Louise with a bouquet of dandelions wrenched from the ground outside the door. It was the end of any semblance of normal movie watching. After that, at least 50 percent of the time the sound was turned off on purpose and one of us tried our hand at lip synching, but the star was always Louise in any role.

She went flying. Not the quite normal ride in a transport plane or some many engine aircraft, but in a T-33, a two-seat jet trainer, a larger version of our first fighter-interceptor, the F-80 Shooting Star.

Not many women ever rode in this sort of aircraft, but that wasn't enough for Louise. Jimmy Conlin was her favorite pilot and told us about her once she was in the air.

" 'Give me a loop,' she would say," he told us over beers in the squadron mess, "and I would give her one, slow and easy."

" 'C'mon, Lieutenant, put some muscle into it!' she would demand and I'd do it. Then she wanted slow rolls, split S's, Immelmanns, all of it. She wanted it all. Then she wants to fly it."

"You let her?" somebody asked.

"Damn right," Jimmy said. "Major Longsteet wants, I give. Hell, I believe with a few hours she could solo, a little more and she could fly with us, better than some of you clowns."

We knew Major Longstreet's year tour of duty in Korea was nearly up and it was about then we got her invitations. They were very nicely done on heavy stock, printed expensively and formally.

"Major Louise Longstreet requests your presence for dinner at eight o'clock on June the 10th at the nurse's quarters at K site number 55, Osan, Korea," it said and went on to say the attire would be uniform formal, RSVP.

It was obvious Louise had gone to a great deal of trouble to send to Japan for the invitations and those of us who received them were honored and impressed. She had asked each of our flight leaders, Jimmy Conlin of Tango, Tom 'Mac' McDonald of Bravo, Tim Jaans of Zulu, Danny Patton of Red One and one pilot each from the flights, with the rest of the gathering, we heard, to be filled by the other five nurses of our base.

We chosen few had the immediate problem of uniform formal. A formal uniform in the Air Force is nothing more than class A drill, beige in the summer and blue in the winter, with a white shirt and black bow tie. We hurriedly arranged for someone to go to Japan for the shirts and bow ties and appeared the evening of the tenth in these pressed and sharply creased outfits, the first time in Korea we had any reason to wear a class A uniform.

It was a magnificent dinner. The nurse's quarters had, as a central meeting area, a large recreation, reading and relaxing main room with a fireplace on one wall. Louise had had most of the furniture removed and a linen-covered dining table made that was in a U shape, seating all 14 of us. She had the squadron emblem, a fighting cock, stitched on cloth over the lit fireplace on this cool June night and at each place there was a metal cigarette lighter with the squadron's fighting cock enameled on its surface. There were flowers in the corners of the room, candles on the table, the silverware heavy and good, the serving done by three young Korean men. The meal was extraordinary and we had to wonder what miracle she had performed as course after course arrived, each with an appropriate imported wine.

It wasn't until the last course had been served and champagne opened and poured that Louise in her sweeping white formal gown rose to her feet. She tapped on her wineglass and gradually the murmur of conversation quieted and then stopped. Louise was feeling the wine. She swayed a little as she stood silently for a moment. Then she spoke. She didn't have a lot to say, but what she said I doubt that any of us would ever forget.

"I'm leaving for the States day after tomorrow. This is my farewell party, the end of my tour," she said and smiled.

"This is the third time I have been with a squadron of fighter pilots and it will be the last time. I was in England with the first one in 1943. I married one of them, a P-47 fighter pilot, a guy just like any one of you, except he didn't make it," and she paused for a second in the silence and drank some champagne.

"I wouldn't trade any bit of the time for anything in the world. But now it is over. I'm going back to the States, retiring," and she laughed briefly at the expressions on our faces.

"I appreciate that. But you should know now, I'm 39 and will have my 20 twenty years of service in another few months. I'm going to get out and then I'm going to enter medical school. Now listen," she said with a sudden intensity, "here is what I want you to hear."

"No matter what I do, no matter what kind of a doctor I become, no matter how rich or famous or successful I may become, nothing will ever be like what I have lived through with the fighter squadrons with which I have been privileged to serve. And that is what I want you to know. This life of yours, this fighter-squadron flying you do, the people you are and the people you are with, will never be the same again no matter what you do in the future. You are very lucky to have this experience in life. Nothing else will ever be like it, nothing else will come up to it in the need for things like skill, courage, camaraderie and utter faith and need in those who are alongside of you. Here's to all of you, all of us," and she raised her champagne glass up in a toast as we all stood and drank with her.

Dixie

We all tried to avoid the Escape and Evasion school in Korea. Not only had we heard it was more than tough, the notion of learning how to escape or evade was contrary to our basic thinking. Primarily, our thinking was simple: Don't get into a position where such training would be handy, or in other words, stay airborne, do not get afoot.

It was much the same thinking we had for the practice ejection seat available to us while we were still cadet pilots. The idea of strapping into a dummy cockpit bolted to the floor of an unused hanger and letting an explosion fire the seat up 60 feet of rails like an artillery shell seemed ridiculous. It would be somewhat like firing a bullet through your foot to make sure the gun would work when you put it to your head.

Nevertheless, Wing had ordered all squadron pilots to take the course of E and E and sooner or later you had to go. Jimmy Conlin, my flight leader, and I had avoided it for six months, but now we were ordered for the 10 days of training. A new pilot, a stocky, chubby Southerner named Robert E. Tillingham was to accompany us. He was nicknamed Dixie, undoubtedly due to his incessant humming or singing of the song. Dixie was a funny guy, a natural, the sort of human who started you smiling for no obvious reason when you saw him, his round, cherubic face friendly and eager.

Jimmy put it well. "Dixie always seems to have heard a good joke a couple of minutes ago. Check it out, he wakes up that way," he finished and we all agreed, having seen it.

131

If the sun was shining, Dixie would cock his face to the warm rays, pleased. "Vitamin D," he would explain and if it was raining, he would express his pleasure with an affectionate glance at the plants and shrubs. Robert E. Tillingham, Dixie, had this to say when he heard about the school: "I get to go with you-all? Wonderful! When do we go?" and Jimmy patted him on the shoulder, shaking his head in wonder.

We flew down to the E and E school in a noisy, drafty, old DC 3, which Dixie admired extravagantly to its pilot. Dixie asked him if he could fly co-pilot and, when the pilot said sure, went forward whistling. "This guy real?" the pilot inquired. "Jet fighter pilot and he really wants to fly this bucket of bolts?"

"You bet," Jimmy said. "Go sit with him. Guarantee you'll have a good time. He goes by the name of Dixie," and pulled his hat down over his eyes.

We landed fine and sure enough, Dixie and the pilot shook hands and did everything but exchange pictures as we left the DC 3. We checked in and the school started bright and early at seven the next morning.

Right away Dixie made his presence known. When the instructor asked what squadron we were from, old Dixie stood at attention and would only give his name, rank and serial number. The instructor, a grizzled Australian by the name of Hall looking to be a little overage to still be a captain, cocked an interested eye at this display of accord with the recently reaffirmed Code of Military Conduct.

"Ease up, Lieutenant," he advised. "Although you would be absolutely correct if you were now my prisoner; one, you are not one as yet, and, two, you'll never get away with name, rank and serial number no matter what your code of conduct tells you."

This got our attention. There had been well-reported, high-level discussions about the effects of brain washing, what captured military could and could not say if the enemy got you. It was widely recognized that the old name, rank and serial number simply didn't work with new methods of interrogation. The powers that be decided to ignore this and once again said: Name, rank and serial number only and tough if you or they don't like it. We questioned Hall on this.

"Well," said the Aussie, "that's what they say, true enough, but if you hold to it, likely as not they will put a bullet through your head for your pains."

This E and E school was official, staffed by a bunch of Army ex-POWs and here was this unusual Australian guy telling us to forget what our Commander-in-Chief had instructed. He not only had our attention, he had our respect. During our first coffee break there was a lot of chatter about him and we learned he had been a crocodile hunter in Australia, a former highly-decorated Aussie officer in World War II who had prison camp experience. He had accepted a year's assignment to teach after some bad stories had come out of North Korea concerning captives.

"Look," he explained, "they catch you alongside your shot-down aircraft, your Sabrejet. They ask you what you were flying and you give them name, rank and serial number. It won't work. The trick is to talk, but not say anything that matters and I'm going to tell you how to do this."

He was good, very good. We all wondered how the Army, Air Force and Marines had been bright enough to hire him. Dixie was immensely impressed, hero worship in his eyes. Jimmy watched Dixie talking to the captain after class and remarked that he just hoped Captain Hall wouldn't ask Dixie to jump out a window. "Sure as hell, he'd jump!" he said.

Captain Hall used a lot of student participation in his classroom. "Tillingham," he said one day, "you're standing alongside your Sabre which you just crash-landed and here comes a staff car with officers to take you away from the troops that have you at gunpoint. The head guy speaks perfect English and says he's glad you weren't hurt. He offers you a cigarette and asks how long you've been flying the Sabre. What do you say?"

Dixie stood quiet for a second, looking pleased that Hall had asked him the question, while the rest of us squirmed, happy we had not been asked. "I don't smoke, sir," Dixie said, "but nice of you to ask. You really ought to quit, you know, it's not good for you."

Hall regarded Dixie for a long moment, then started to smile. "Not bad, Tillingham. A little weird, but not bad at all. You see," he said to the rest of us, "he talked but he didn't say anything, except for his thoughtful health advisory," and smiling broadly now, turned to the desk behind him and stubbed out his cigarette.

We had five days of classroom lectures and it was all good stuff. What we mainly learned was it was not a good idea to be captured.

The lectures also left us with a great deal of sympathy for those who were in prison camps.

The classroom over, our next stage was an attempt at evasion. We were to be dropped in groups of three, 10 miles from the base across a low range of mountains and we had to try to make it back to our base. There would be all kinds of troops simulating the enemy out to capture us. If we were caught, they had a prison camp for us in which we would spend a couple of days. A lot of the military pretending to be the enemy were ex-prisoners of war and mostly enlisted men. Our class was all officers and we could be sure we would not be treated gently by them if we were caught, given this opportunity. Captain Hall's words were that it would all be as realistic as he could make it. We had learned to believe him.

They loaded us into several trucks and drove for a couple of hours, dropping our classmates off at intervals. When the truck dropped the three of us off, Dixie went immediately into the woods by the side of the road and rolled over a small log. He picked up some grubs on a piece of bark and, consulting an E and E book we had been issued, exclaimed happily, "Grubs! Good to eat. Taste a little like figs, they say." He frowned a little, reading on in the book. "It would be better if we could grill them," he finished.

Jimmy sighed deeply with a hand on Dixie's shoulder. "Let's save them for dinner, Dixie. In the meantime," he continued checking his compass, "let's get hiking."

We hiked for about three hours until our first breather, a fairly steep climb up the side of a good-sized hill, staying away from roads and paths as we had been advised. Twice we had to backtrack when we hit a ravine or a steep drop. We were determined to reach the main road, the road that marked the line between enemy terrain and safety, sometime that night and attempt a crossing under cover of dark. Ten miles doesn't sound like much, but staying away from paths in completely unknown country, backtracking often, up and down the hills, made it more like 20 miles.

Jimmy was reading the compass for our general direction, but more and more it was Dixie who had good ideas. About two we came to the top of a ridge overlooking a valley and Dixie asked us to take a break for a few minutes. He unzipped a pocket on his flight suit and brought out a flat, compact pair of binoculars. With that he shinned up a tree and carefully looked the valley over while we munched candy bars underneath the tree.

Back on the ground he absently rubbed charcoal on his face from the remains of an old campfire. "There are at least two patrols down there." He pointed north and south along the ridge. "Anywhere you come over this ridge, you almost have to go down to this valley. That's why Hall put the patrols there. Look," he said and handed me the binoculars, "look closely under that grove of trees about a third of the way up. See the jeep? I think there's another further up on the right. We had better swing south a ways and find another route."

Jimmy gave him a long look. "Where'd you get the binocs? You have other stuff in that suit?"

Dixie grinned his engaging smile. "Sure. Food packs, sewing kit, a good knife, money, a Korean-English dictionary, all kinds of things."

"Wait a second," I protested, "this is supposed to be what we have on us if we went down while flying."

"I fly with this all the time," Dixie said, "don't you?"

Jimmy looked at me, laughing. "Don't answer that," he said. "C'mon, let's get going!" and we dropped off the top of the ridge to stay off the skyline—more from Dixie and the E and E book—and went south for a while.

It was 2:30 in the morning when we finally found the road across from freedom. It was on a steep side mountain and we found guards patrolling up and down and trucks passing quite often. We hit the road where a ravine ran down the slope of the mountain. The road itself was built on fill so that it was 20 or 25 feet above us. There was a good-sized culvert underneath the road for water run-off from the ravine, a pipe about five feet in diameter. We scouted a little up and down from the culvert and then huddled in the cold night at the head of our ravine.

"Nothing doing up from here," Jimmy reported. "Steep mountain above and looks to be a real drop-off on the other side." I said the lower side was much the same. Dixie had been left to watch the road traffic and now he spoke up.

"Guys, the foot patrol goes by every five minutes and a truck or trucks go by in between shining searchlights on this side of the road. Far as I can tell, there is about a minute-and-a-half when the road is clear and even then they could maybe see someone crossing."

We lay back in the brush thinking it over. "You know something," Dixie whispered after a time, "I know this is all fake, a school, we're not going to get shot and all that, but still, I'd really like to make it."

Jimmy rolled over on his side to rest his head on his hand regarding Dixie. Jimmy and I had blackened our faces with charcoal from burnt wood as Dixie had and it worked pretty well. Jimmy, only three feet away, was part of the light and shadow from the moon.

"You're right, Dixie. This whole exercise has been almost too real, those patrols that just missed us, the choppers flying around. Now we're scrunched here in the woods with God only knows what sort of things crawling around and what would we really do?" he whispered urgently.

"The culvert, the pipe," Dixie said. "If we can get into there without getting caught, we have a chance on the other side."

I agreed with Dixie, but pointed out that we had to get down the ravine to the pipe and there wasn't much brush in the ravine for concealment.

"Let me go first," Dixie said. "I've already tried it while you two were gone. The thing to do is go from bush to bush," and he pointed them out. "When you get to that big stand of brush two-thirds of the way there, you wait until the minute-and-a-half when the road is clear and then go for the pipe. When you get to a bush, lie underneath it in an S curve, don't lie straight."

"You already tried it?" Jimmy exploded in a hiss. "And came back? What if you hadn't made it?"

"You guys would have figured it out and tried something else," Dixie said. "Anyway, I didn't go into the pipe, just to the big stand of brush."

"Where did you get that S curve business?" I whispered, still trying to get my mind around his already having risked the run.

"It's in the book," Dixie said softly and was suddenly gone.

It was remarkable. He couldn't be more than 20 feet away under the first bush and disappeared. He made the big stand easily and then was still for minutes. Just as the guard was passing from sight on the down slope, we saw his shadow flee over the ground and pop into the tunnel.

"He made it!" Jimmy breathed. "You think we had Dixie misjudged just a little?"

"Amen!" I said.

"How'd he work out the timing for the pipe after the two-thirds bush?"

"Footsteps," I guessed. "He listened for the guards footsteps," and with that both Jimmy and I, one by one, made it into the culvert pipe the same way.

It was a long pipe and full of spider webs. Breathing heavily, we joined Dixie at the far end of the tunnel. He was looking out the end in thought. There was a very steep drop immediately, a slope covered with what looked to be flat, loose rocks the size of pancakes. From there the grade eased up a little, but was still steep enough until it leveled out in a forest of pine trees.

After some contemplation, Jimmy ventured an opinion. "Bound to make a clatter on that loose rock," and Dixie and I agreed.

"I believe we have to make a run for it," Dixie finally said.

"Hell of a noise," I argued, "plus the real chance of breaking a leg."

"True," Dixie replied, "we'll have to chance the legs. What we need is a diversion, something to get them looking back on the other side. You have any matches?"

"Matches?" Jimmy repeated, not out of surprise yet.

"Matches," Dixie said firmly reaching around in his pockets and pulling our several boxes of wooden matches. All together we had seven boxes and watched in wonder while Dixie made his homemade firebomb, wrapping all the matches tail to tail, tying it all up with thread from his inexhaustible pockets. Then he asked for a cigarette and for me to light it. With this also tied on, he told us the plan.

"I'm going back out to the large bush. This thing should fire off in about two minutes," he said with a critical eye on the glowing end of the cigarette. "That bush is dry and should go up like a torch. When you hear me coming back, make the break," and with that Dixie disappeared back up the gloom of the tunnel.

We saw the sudden bright flash of light at the end of the tunnel and heard the running footsteps of Dixie coming flat out, but the main thing we heard was the guard above us as the bush did indeed explode like a bomb.

"Holy Christ!" he yelled. "What in hell?" and we heard his heavy footsteps running back across the road to the fire.

The three of us blasted out of the tunnel on the dead run, flying down that loose rock like runaway freight trains. In the adrenaline rush of the moment, trying to keep our footing while sprinting on loose rock down a 30-degree slope in the middle of the night, we heard the rebel yell of Dixie's scream into the air.

Christ, we made it! Safe and home free, we hung onto pine trees in the forest, gulping for air and holding our sides with laughter.

"Dixie," Jimmy said between gasps, "you ever scream like that again without warning me and I swear I'll kill you! You damned near gave me a heart attack!"

We got to skip the prison camp due to our escape, the three of us and two Marines. Captain Hall came by our table in the officer's club at dinner the night before we were to leave. He congratulated us on our escape and evasion and then took the lid off a square box he was carrying.

"You three have anything to do with this?" he asked as we peered inside to see the charred remains of Dixie's firebomb. "If you did," he continued before we had a chance to answer, "I'd like you to know you about scared the life out of my guard. Luck gentlemen," and he waved good-bye.

We left at eight the next morning. Our ride was on the same old worn out DC 3, even the same pilot. Dixie and this guy shook hands like they hadn't seen each other in years. Dixie came over to us and said, "I'm going to fly co-pilot, okay?"

"Of course," Jimmy said and then: "Say Dixie, we are going to be needing a new number four in our flight when we get back. You want to join us?"

"Terrific!" Dixie smiled with that eager, happy face, "You bet!" and went forward to the DC 3's cockpit.

"Smart move," I approved.

"Don't I know it," Jimmy said and pulled his hat down over his eyes as the plane started up.

Cease-fire

It changed some after the cease-fire. The North Korean pilots in their very excellent Russian MiG-15's had almost entirely stopped in their desire to come up and engage our also excellent F-86 Sabre jet fighters.

The reason was simple: despite the near equality of our fighter aircraft, we American aviators were better. It's hard to say exactly why.

It had nothing to do with race, although, for example, good as the occasional Red Chinese were flying with the Koreans, for the action, we figured they had the sometimes problem of face. Face or the fear of inability to perform in front of peers had nothing to do with courage. They had plenty of that. But they disliked leading weather flights, for example, not for any personal fear, but because of the regard and responsibility of the other pilots in their flight. It was an interesting problem and one that affected us as well, although to a much lesser degree.

Our superiority as fighter pilots had very much to do with our training before we got to Korea and joined a line squadron.

Jimmy Conlin, Tango flight leader, put it well one night in a lull in our Quonset hut poker game.

Bobby Harms, Bobby Two, had almost breached unstated decorum by hugely complimenting Jimmy after a dangerous and strenuous day of flying.

"Man, Jimmy, I learned a lot today, particularly on that low-level pass in the mountains!"

There was an embarrassed silence around the table at this, not because it wasn't true; we had all learned terrific stuff that day because of Jimmy, but because Bobby Two had said it aloud. He might as well have said "I love you," which we all did in a way, but to say it in so many words was something like the taboo of admitting fear, that you had been frightened, which, of course, happened from time to time.

Jimmy, as usual, took up the slack quickly. "The learning thing," he said, "that's the key. The fighter weapons school in Nevada we all went through was something else. It was such a fast-track, high-speed, completely hairy training time, that it was a relief to get here in action in a line squadron!"

There were appreciative nods and murmurs around the table. Bobby Two spoke up again. "Man, the fighter weapons school had an attitude! I was more worried about not hacking it than I was about buying the farm, eating it."

Jimmy laughed. "There's a great story out of World War II, a Navy fighter pilot involved in a giant melee, a dogfight, in the battle of the Coral Sea. You know how it's—then and now—bad form to chatter on the radio, and this guy starts calling for help, saying he had three zeros on his tail and wouldn't somebody come over and bail him out."

Jimmy took a last look at his poker hand and tossed his cards away.

"Anyway, everybody is very busy shooting and being shot at and this guy again and again on the radio, for the third, fourth or fifth time, 'zeros on my tail, I need help!' " Here Jimmy stopped for a moment reflectively, his deep-set pale blue eyes sharpening. Then he continued, "A voice crackled out on the radios, saying, 'Shut up and die like a naval aviator!' " and we all laughed. It was a good story.

"True or not, it's all about an attitude," Jimmy finished and started shuffling the cards for the next hand. He glanced around the table at all of us in his Tango flight.

"You're all good," he said, "but all of us, me included, are always learning. We all keep looking for that one more thing to learn and that looking never stops." He dealt the cards, saying "Jacks or better to open, sports, and I'm gonna win this hand."

With the cease-fire, things did change to some degree. We made more sweeps, more patrols, more so-called proficiency flights, which meant nothing much more than going up and flying around for the fun of it, so to speak.

Bobby Summer, Bobby One in our Tango flight, got pretty lyrical about an operational pre-dawn look-see flight down the west coast of the Korean peninsula.

We put up with Bobby One's talk; one, because he was a very good aviator at number two off our leader Jimmy Conlin's wing, and two, because no one was going to stop him from saying exactly how he felt anyway. This day was now in the early evening in our Quonset hut quarters, Bobby One relaxed, showered and changed from flight suit into open necked khaki shirt with silver wings and collar insignia of his rank.

He was stretched out on his bed, hands folded together behind his head, eyes reflective and dreamy. We had learned to be quiet when he took off, started to speak, as he, as often as not, put words to what we all felt at one time or another.

"It was what I'd always dreamed about when I was a kid," he started, "in the dark just before dawn, the air crisp and clean, the runway light dimly on down the airfield. I took off, the sound of my Sabre going from roar to whisper as I picked up speed and retracted my wheels. Very quickly as I climbed out from the dark, sleeping earth, I went into that terrific early light of the morning sun. I held it at about 2,000 feet or so and I was moving, 98 percent of power. You know it's funny. We spend so much time at altitude where the sensation of speed pretty much doesn't happen. We have to be low, to have the speed relative to the unmoving earth. At 98 or 99 percent of power I was cooking around five hundred to six hundred knots—as you all know—just below the Mach. I was low and lovin' it! I was right on the edge of the morning light. Man, it felt so clean and good."

We were all quiet, pretending to be busy about something or other, but listening to the words, reliving that experience that we all had had one time or another as Bobby One went on.

"I flew out over the sea and dropped down to maybe 200 feet over the ocean and went north, flying the shoreline, swinging in and out over the beaches and peninsulas. I probably went a little too far north, a little into North Korea maybe, it was so terrific so I pulled up into a steep chandelle and turned back along the same coast, staying still fast and even lower maybe 50 feet off the ocean, popping up when a stretch of land went burrowing off into the sea, slow rolling for the hell of it, it all felt so good!" He paused for a moment, probably realizing how he was carrying on to all of us.

"One guy," he continued anyway, "putting out in a sail fishing boat looked up and waved to me."

Jimmy was smiling broadly, we all were.

"I'll bet you rocked your wings back at him," I said.

Bobby One, with a sheepish grin, said, "Yep. You bet I did. I wished him luck!"

We were all quiet again. Then Bobby Two spoke, "C'mon, Bobby, get your ass up. I believe I owe you a drink or two."

And we all strolled out of the Quonset to the official officer's bar and mess Quonset and had several nice, reflective cool drinks to Tango and the cease-fire.

Suzie

The usual nightly poker game was on, our group of pilots sitting around the smoky Quonset hut, the scratchy turntable playing music softly in the background, the clink of chips pitched into the growing stack on the table. Tommy Rowles and Danny Patton were the last left in this biggest pot of the night.

Tommy was doing what he did best, staying in the hand to the end. It was hard to figure what he thought he was doing. The game was five card stud, one down card and the next four dealt up one at a time as the bets were made. Danny had bet heavily since his first card up was dealt, a king of spades, and later on the fourth card, another king, the king of hearts. You had to believe he had another king as his hidden card the way he had bet and, in any case, he surely had the two kings showing.

Tommy had junk. He had been dealt a six, a ten, and a four plus his down card when Danny got his second king. The best he could have, we figured, was another six as his hole card and he had been staying in because he didn't believe Danny had his original king paired with another in the hole. Now, of course, all that changed as Danny had two kings showing. Danny bet fifty dollars, digging into his pocket for the military script ten- dollar notes that had replaced our dollars here in Korea. Tommy just grinned and matched the bet. The last card was dealt, a three of clubs for Tommy and a ten for Danny. No way could Tommy win, even if his hole card matched any of his other cards.

Danny waited for Tommy to fold and when he didn't said, "Fifty more, Tommy. For Christ's sake, fold, I've got you beat." With nothing but a smile, Tommy chucked fifty more into the pot and called. The cards were turned and sure enough, Danny had his third unneeded king. As Tommy started to fold his hand, Danny spoke again.

"Hold it, Tommy, it's a called hand. Let me see your hole card." Tommy turned his hidden card over and it was a seven of diamonds. Tommy had nothing, a complete bust.

"Why in God's name did you stay?" Danny asked.

Tommy grinned. "I wanted to see your hole card. Nice hand," he laughed and the game went on.

It was typical of Tommy. He was kind of a human non sequitur. He got to conclusions by some independent means not known to ordinary humans. He was a good pilot, steady and reliable, but only if he was on the wing. On the lead, it had been found, he was prone to his own reasoning. Our interceptor fighters were being tried as ground attack aircraft, for instance, and early in his tour Tommy had been put on lead to drop bombs. They were round shaped bombs and after one not too successful run from overhead, Tommy had put us down just over the sea on our second run on the little island target. He told us to toggle off short of the island, flying just off the water. We did and plastered the island with direct hits as the bombs skipped over the sea until they hit and detonated. Asked later why he had gone against the briefing orders, Tommy replied he thought they might skip on the water like a stone, exactly as they had. He said this happily, but our commander was not pleased.

Well, that was Tommy Rowles. Aside from his off-centeredness, Tommy was surpassingly handsome. He was slim and fit, 6-foot tall, blond and blue-eyed with brilliant white, even teeth. We had a number of absolutely beautiful young Korean women working in the squadron mess and with one exception, they were all in love with Tommy. Of course, he didn't seem to be aware of this, although how he could miss it was par for the course for Tommy.

The one exception was Suzie. Of the five women working the squadron mess, Maria was the absolute beauty. The others were not absolutes only in relation to her. Suzie was not beautiful. She was cute and very attractive with a wonderful figure, yes, but she missed beauty.

But she had character far and beyond the others. Naturally, being Tommy, Suzie was the one for him.

It was strictly hands-off as far as these lovely women were concerned, by order of the base commander, but that didn't stop any of us from being enamored. While the rest of us knew how futile our unrequited feelings were, not so Tommy. He would spend hours in the mess, drinking coffee or an occasional beer just to be in Suzie's presence.

We were all there in the mess at the Christmas party that began Tommy's love. Standing at the length of the bar in the long and big Quonset, Suzie had passed by with her bronze serving tray in her hands. Some pilot had reached out to untie the bow holding her apron and Tommy had knocked his hand away. We guessed Tommy must have brushed her in doing this, because without hesitation, Suzie wheeled and brought her tray down on Tommy's head.

It made a wonderful sound, a great ringing bong by the meeting of head and bronze tray like a call to prayers. While the entire room of pilots rocked with laughter, Tommy appeared stunned as he sat there with one hand to his head, but he was smiling and looking at Suzie with adoring eyes.

Suzie, Maria and the other women lived on a hill overlooking the airfield, a hill guarded by fencing and forbidden to us. After work, the women would walk a short distance to where a bus would pick them up to drive up the hill. Not long after the bronze tray incident, Tommy had asked permission of Suzie to walk her to the bus stop and every evening when he wasn't flying, we would see the two walking sedately behind the other women to the stop. There was a marked difference in their attitude toward each other. Suzie was in complete command, seeming not to take Tommy seriously, while Tommy couldn't have been more sincere. We appreciated Suzie's feelings, as it was near impossible that anything could result from a meeting in this distant country. But that was not the way it went.

Tommy wrangled a ride into Seoul toward the end of our tour, not an easy thing to do in those days. He came back five days later and seemed even happier than he usually was. It was Danny Patton who brought it out into the open the night he returned.

"What was that trip all about?" he asked Tommy.

Tommy focused his smiling eyes on Danny. "Suzie," he said simply.

"What do you mean, Suzie?" Danny persisted.

"I met her parents, wonderful people, and I think they will accept me."

"What do you mean, accept you, you fool. You know we are leaving Korea shortly. We go to Okinawa, then Taiwan, then home. We're never coming back, it's the States after that. You'll never get her over there."

"I know," Tommy said, "but I'm coming back." He looked at Danny kindly, knowing that he was about his best friend, knowing he meant well. "Don't worry," he finished.

It was a tough call and hard for us not to worry. We left Korea a few weeks later, spent two months on Okinawa, then we flew over the China Sea to Taiwan. We spent 45 days there flying top cover for the Seventh Fleet pulling Chinese Nationalists out of the Tachen Island group. It wasn't until the day before we were to pull out and fly back to Okinawa that we got the end of the story. Danny Patton told us.

We were in our favorite restaurant in the little town of Taichee next to our airfield on the south end of Taiwan.

"Well," Danny said, "He's done it. Tommy and Suzie are going to be together."

We were amazed. The Air Force was very difficult and wearing and deliberately time consuming in allowing permission for personnel to marry in the Far East.

"How did he do it?" we asked a smiling Danny Patton.

"Look!" Danny said and handed us a letter. It was addressed to Tommy, agreeing to his employment as a transport pilot in Chennault's CAT airline based on Taiwan, flying Taiwan, Hong Kong, Tokyo. "He's signed up," Danny said. "He's back to the States and out in two months. He's coming straight back here to live. Christ, he already rented the best house on the sea you ever saw. Suzie's on her way."

We sat back in stunned silence. Then one of the guys spoke up. "Well, she's going to be one happy lady," he said.

"Not as happy as Tommy," Danny replied and we all drank to that.

Marine Re-enlist

It was a typical slow evening in the early winter in Korea. Like so many other evenings, we drank and talked, sharing our pasts, thinking about the future. The pot-bellied stove in the corner of O'Rourke's glowed with welcome heat and the drinks were cheap and good. Danny Patton had been talking and what he had said surprised us.

Danny Patton with his great handlebar moustache was the leader of Red One flight and the most experienced pilot we had in the squadron. You could get a lot of arguments about who was the best flight leader with each flight voting hands down for their particular leader, but no one could argue about Patton in terms of experience.

There was a reason for this. Danny had an unusual background. Before he became an Air Force fighter pilot, he had been a Marine foot soldier, a combat Marine who had made one of the last and bloodiest island invasions towards the end of World War II, the landing on Tarawa in 1944.

He had been barely 17, he had told us, when he signed up for the Marines and the way fortunes of war sometimes go, he had gone straight out of Marine Corps boot camp into a line outfit that within months was standing off Tarawa waiting to storm ashore. He had taken rifle fire in the second week of heavy fighting, wounded seriously enough to get him a ticket home to recuperate in a stateside Marine hospital. The war against Japan ended in August of 1945 and Danny Patton found himself a civilian again at 18, Purple Heart and Distinguished

Service Medal, a veteran with a long scar down his left arm and not an idea what to do with his life.

We sat and drank for a time and then Jimmy Conlin asked him how that had worked out.

Danny sat back, warming his cognac in his hands, admiring the color through the light. He smiled at Conlin, McDonald and the rest of us.

"I'd never known anything but war. Check it out," he continued, tapping the table with his finger, "I grew up in Malaysia, went over there when I was three with my parents. My father was a petroleum engineer and worked for Royal Dutch. Hell, almost my first memory was looking over my amah's shoulder while she read a newspaper. The headline was *War* in big red letters, war in China by Japan."

"What's an amah?" McDonald asked curiously. "And what were you? Dutch?"

Danny shook his head impatiently. "No, no, my dad worked for Royal Dutch, that's all. Remember this was in what? Nineteen-thirty or so and the Great Depression was on in the States. A job was a job and if we had to live in Malaysia, that's what we did. We were American."

"Too bad," Jimmy Conlin grinned. "You could have been the Flying Dutchman, Danny."

"What's an amah?" McDonald persisted, signaling Joe-san the barman for another round of drinks.

Danny looked uncomfortable. "Sort of a babysitter, Mac, all the Caucasians out in the Pacific had them, amahs, houseboys, servants coming out the ying-yang. Amahs were sort of like a second mother. Free up the grown-ups for cocktails and parties. Hardly any cost to them. Anyway, as I was saying, war was a big news thing out there and when we got back in thirty-seven, thirty-eight, there was Italy and Mussolini and Hitler in Germany. All through grade school and later, high school, all we talked about was the war and what we were going to do in it."

Mac was interested. "But the Marines? Fix bayonets and charge? Were you crazy? What were you thinking?"

"Who thinks at 17?" Danny said. "Probably saw too many John Wayne movies of him holding off battalions of Japs with his bare hands. Who knows? But that wasn't my only mistake."

"You mean because you got shot up?" Conlin asked.

"No. That was all right. They call it a million-dollar wound. Bad enough to get me out of there but no real damage. It's a plus, really. The ladies always ask me about the scar when my shirt comes off. I give them a few humble words about being a hero and I can do no wrong. No, my mistake was when the war ended and I got out."

The Korean came over to our table with the cognac. He asked Mac if he was ready for another. Mac gave him a long look and told him to leave the cognac bottle on the table.

"See," Danny continued, "I didn't have a clue what to do. I'm 18 and all the wars had ended. I mean, I figured what I was all about for most of my life was to be a warrior. And then all of a sudden there weren't any wars."

Jimmy Conlin looked sympathetic. "What a shame, Danny. I'm sure they didn't realize what they were doing to you when they called it off."

Mac was impatient. "What was your second mistake, for Christ's sake."

Danny refused to be rushed. "I had the GI bill and a little back pay so I went to school up in Eugene, Oregon, the University of Oregon."

Mac pounced. "That was it! You found out you were a little light in the brains department, right Danny? I mean after signing up with the Marines, you had to figure you weren't the brightest guy to ever come along. That was your second mistake, right?"

Danny had to smile. Then he looked reflective, even a little sad. "No, Mac, that wasn't it. I got married."

We all looked serious for the first time. All Danny's talk about war and being in it we could understand. But marriage, now this was something else.

"At 18?" Jimmy Conlin asked. "Jesus, Danny, that sounds a little hasty. Someone you had known?"

"Are you kidding?" Danny laughed, but not happily. "I was 19 by then and I had known her for exactly one month."

"One month. Well, she wasn't pregnant anyway," Mac said.

"You're fast with the math," Jimmy Conlin admired. "I take it the marriage didn't work out," he continued to Danny.

"Hell it didn't," Danny growled. "It was the best thing to ever happen to me. I was so in love with her I couldn't see straight. Hell," he repeated, "I still am," and drank off his cognac in one swallow.

We were all uncomfortable. The conversation had started out the way a lot of discussions do in Korea, a bunch of guys pretty much isolated who had mostly not known each other before getting closer to the bone as time went on, finding out more and more about each other. Danny Patton had been in the squadron before we got there and with the aura that comes with being an old hand, we had all been a little distant with him, less inclined to share our pasts and futures. We had not had any idea Danny had been married.

"Sounds tough," Jimmy Conlin said, pouring drinks around and topping up Danny's glass. "Bad divorce?" he questioned gently.

Danny didn't answer right away, playing with the base of his glass. "No. No divorce. I'm still married, sort of. Separation, they call it," and he sat back heavily in his chair and told us the rest.

"She was two years older than I. She was a junior at Oregon when I started. We got married and it was fine for two years, but by then I knew what I wanted to do. I wanted to fly. I dropped out of school and used the GI bill to take flying lessons, then got a job crop dusting. She hated it. She was scared to death all the time. Then this Korean thing came up and I had to give it a try and here I am. She left me when I went into cadets. She said it was either her or flying, not both. I haven't wanted a divorce and she doesn't either, not yet at any rate."

McDonald had his flight leader's face on, frowning as he listened to Danny.

"It's a heavy story, Danny. What do you think you're going to do now that this little war is history? No more wars for you, for awhile anyway. You going back to her? What do you think?"

"I have to fly," Danny said and the way he said it we all heard. It was not something he said offhand. He had thought about it long and hard and this was his conclusion. We could see how hard it was for him to say it.

"Stay in the Air Force?" Jimmy Conlin questioned.

"Nah," Danny half laughed, rolling his shoulders to loosen them, like a boxer after three or four rounds of a workout. "I've had enough of the military. My tour's up in a couple of months and so is my enlistment. I'm going to get out of the service at headquarters in Japan, then do some flying out here in the Far East. I like it out here, maybe I'll stay."

"Who are you thinking of flying for, Danny?" somebody asked.

"Indo-China Air, I think," Danny said. "They're looking for pilots, I hear. They're based in Saigon, Vietnam. I hear it's a nice town, very French. Should be fun."

Annie

Tim Jaans made a sound like the air hissing out of a tire punctured by a nail.

"Look at this, now . . ." he exclaimed under his breath, his head turned, peering back over his shoulder as we stood up to the bar in the Tsuiki Officer's Club.

We were over in Japan from Korea for five days of REMCO, repair and refit of our Sabres, three of us, Tim Jaans, Danny Patton and me. Trips for REMCO were a bonus out of Korea, an add-on to the two R & R's we got in a year's tour. Command tried to hand out REMCO trips impartially, spread them around the squadron, but as often as not gave them to those pilots seeming to be most in need of a break in Korean squadron life. We three apparently qualified on all counts.

Danny Patton and I half-turned to see what had excited Tim. What we saw got our attention all right; it had the attention of about every eye in the place as well. It was Saturday night and the club was nearly full with Japan-stationed American officers and their wives in for a pub dinner and a few drinks. Jaans, Patton and I were the only Korea-based pilots in the place and, as usual, felt like outlaws here among the men and women stationed in Japan.

We not only felt this way, it was apparent that the Japan-side people reacted the same way, with some reason.

More than once, pilots from Korean line squadrons, over for their first R & R after three or four months, hadn't waited to clear the Tsuiki base before getting seriously into drink. It wasn't appreciated. Tsuiki base was a sedate rear-echelon outfit, its style in line with U.S. officer's clubs, where junior pilot-officers were seen but not heard and wives of colonels gained reflected equal rank.

Pilots out of Korea were used to a near rank-less life, a life where flying ability was everything and fighter flying was the epitome. Pilots out of Korea would usually have a drink or two in the club, then hightail it into the town of Tsuiki itself for a night of drinking at the Sabre Dancer, Tsuiki's legendary nightclub and hotel, with or without a lady from the Sabre.

We saw what had caused Tim to exclaim. A fighter pilot named Sutcliffe from a Korean fighter-interceptor squadron had just entered the club arm and arm with the most famous entertainer from the Sabre Dancer, the lead dancer, tall, beautiful Yokosan, or Annie, as she was known. This was taboo, verboten, against the rules and law in the Tsuiki Officer's Club, which would allow none of the recently defeated Japanese nationals in the club. The only Japanese allowed in the club were the bartenders and waitresses.

Yokosan was striking. She was dressed in traditional Japanese style in a figured black-and-white silk kimono, wide white obi and sandals. Her hair was up, carefully done, her face with just a hint of pale rose lipstick on her mouth and eye shadow accentuating the tilt of her eyes. Sutcliffe's face was stern and firm as he led her to the only vacant seats, a couch, two chairs and low table in the center of the room.

Jaans spoke to us in a whisper, out of the side of mouth. "Jesus, he's in for big trouble. Could he possibly not know she, or any Japanese, is not permitted, is against the standing order?"

Danny Patton shook his head. "He knows. I've heard of him. He's angry over the fourth-class citizens we have made of the Japanese. It seems he was over here before, got sick and instead of checking in with the medics, he went to the Sabre Dancer. She took care of him for four days, she and the other women. He damned near got in hot water for that one. He's a stubborn bastard, but he's not dumb. He knows," he repeated in a low voice.

The drama was just beginning. We were watching openly now from our place at the far end of the long bar and saw that someone had instructed the bar not to serve them. Sutcliffe took this for a long minute or two and then he was on his feet.

The dining room and bar murmur of conversation had practically stopped as Sutcliffe stood before the length of the bar. The Japanese barman kept his head down, trying to ignore Sutcliffe standing there. Sutcliffe had his hand raised for attention and he remained that way for a long few seconds. Then he brought his hand down, palm open, flat on the bar. The slap of his hand meeting the wood sounded like a small-caliber pistol shot in the quiet.

"Drinks, now, at our table!" he ordered in a voice that wasn't going to take any argument from anyone. He told the unhappy Japanese bartender what they wanted and went back to their seats. He sat beside Yokosan, who was impassive in the face of the hostility in the room.

Across the room we could see the major in charge of the club being talked to fiercely by his wife. Her face was red with anger and it didn't take a soothsayer to figure she was demanding he do something about this lieutenant and his forbidden Japanese woman. The major got to his feet.

The scene was more serious than it might seem. We were all in the Air Force, in the military, a career where any rank superior to yours carries with it ominous implications. A direct order from a major to a lieutenant could not be disobeyed, at least not without bad consequences. In a battle situation, it could get you shot. You learned to take orders, even orders like this one, dumb as it was.

But Danny Patton had had enough. There was a sharp edge to his voice. "That's it, guys, straighten up," he said to us. "We're going to join him. Let's see what this major will do to the four of us," and with that, we crossed to Sutcliffe and Yokosan.

Danny Patton was all courtesy and formal politeness. He put his hand out for Sutcliffe to shake.

"Hello, Sutcliffe, nice to see you," he murmured. "You remember me, Dan Patton from K-55," and he waved his hand at Tim and me, saying our names while he looked at Yokosan, waiting for Sutcliffe to introduce us.

Sutcliffe's face was beautiful, incredulous, surprised and hopeful, all at the same time. It was obvious he didn't know Danny and couldn't have cared less. He shook hands hard with each of us. He looked at Danny.

"Do you see what is happening, what is about to happen?"

Danny grinned at him. "We do, Sutcliffe, we certainly do. Mind if we join you?"

"Appreciate it," Sutcliffe grinned back at him. "Christ, do I appreciate it!" he repeated and turned and introduced us to Yokosan.

We each in turn gripped her hand, murmuring her name, following Patton's lead with a slight bow and grave politeness. Her eyes were something, fully aware of what was happening, what Sutcliffe had done, what we were doing. I think we all felt from the look she gave us, whatever was going to happen, it was worth it. Tim Jaans and I talked later and wondered if we would have taken the step Patton had taken, if he had not been there. It was hard to say but I know we were glad to be standing there.

We sat in the adjoining chairs to wait for the major, who had stopped when we had crossed to Yokosan and Sutcliffe. Now the major started forward again. We stood to meet him, the four of us, as he was a few steps away. Then it happened, the damnedest, most unexpected thing any of us could have imagined.

Our Korean supreme leader, a legendary pilot ace and a full colonel, appeared out of nowhere, like a genie out of a bottle. He had not been in the club, we were sure of that. He must have been alerted to the situation by someone with better sense than the Tsuiki Officer's Club major. Taking on a club full of non-combat Japan types was one thing for us, but this colonel quite another.

We stiffened to a full brace, came to rigid attention, but the colonel at once told us to stand at ease. He greeted us and said he had not had the pleasure of meeting our lady. Sutcliffe, looking faint, managed to introduce him.

We were stunned. We stood in shock. The colonel asked if he might join us for a cocktail and then sat beside Yokosan and asked if she were enjoying the evening.

Well, the next few minutes passed in a daze, the colonel carrying the conversation. He was the perfect image of an officer and a gentleman. Then Sutcliffe seemed to know his point had been made and a miracle had happened. It was time to go.

Sutcliffe and Yokosan thanked the colonel for the drinks he had bought, said goodbye to us then left the Tsuiki Officer's Club.

The colonel winked at us as he turned to leave, asked when we would be back in Korea and told us to relay his compliments to our squadron commander. We thanked him and stumbled back to the bar for a much-needed final drink.

"Well, we dodged a bullet that time," Danny Patton said in relief. "But I'll tell you two things. One, I'll always wonder where he came from and, two, that colonel is what being an officer and gentlemen is all about."

Tim Jaans had the answer to the question. "He came in answer to my prayers, I think." It was as good an answer as any and, after a bit, we headed off to the Sabre Dancer.

Thirty-Second Decision

These things happen. After almost a year of Quonset huts, armed guards and seven-days-a-week hot and edgy flying, suddenly a cease-fire, a brief hiatus, then out of Korea to the amazing sights, sounds and sand beaches of Okinawa.

But like all good things, it ended. A month later, abruptly within 24 hours, part of our squadron was here at Yon Tan, flying off a mountain top, living in tents, with 20 back-to-back open-air toilets in the middle of a wet, soggy field just behind and off our flight line.

The first I knew of it was when I was ordered into the commanding officer's office with Jamie, Captain Jamison, our operation's officer there and looking serious.

"You lead, Jim," Jamie began, "Bobby Harms is your assistant flight leader at number three, Bobby Summer on your left wing at number two. We'll give you a good number four."

The CO, Lieutenant Colonel Birthright, smiled and cocked one of his bushy eyebrows at me. "All okay with you, number one?" And when I nodded yes, added, "Congratulations."

Jamie spoke again. "Bobby Harms okay as your number three?"

"Absolutely!" I could only say.

"Your flight will be Blue One and you Blue leader," the CO continued. "For your info, Conlin is staying behind. He's on temporary assignment. So the new flight name for this tour."

It all happened very fast. I had just time for a quick meeting with my Blue One flight, a briefing and a hello to Tommy Hayden our new number four from one of the stay-behind flights, and we flew to Yon Tan.

And it kept raining, one heavy tropical burst after another, with the ambient air temperature hovering around 90-degrees Fahrenheit and the humidity a notch higher.

We had flown into Yon Tan early the previous morning and on this, our second day, had already logged two flights before noon.

We were flying in "turn-around" air-to-ground attacks on an innocent little island 20 miles off the west coast of Okinawa. We were sharpening up our somewhat rusty skills in air-to-ground work, different from our official designation as an air-to-air interceptor outfit.

Speed becomes very real, working down close to earth. Barreling in on that island off the ocean at some 50 to 100 feet, at around 500 mph you did some quick calculations as to when to pull up to clear the island's peak at 256 feet. We were good and could fly this air-to-ground fighter-bomber stuff, but none of us liked it.

We had been briefed at noon for an all-squadron takeoff and island attack at four o'clock. Sixteen Sabres to takeoff in 10-second intervals, re-form into four-ship flights and go out and plaster that little island in the western Pacific. It had stopped raining for a moment and except for large pools of rainwater on the runway it was a pretty normal hot midsummer afternoon in Korea.

There was only one problem: my Sabre wouldn't fly. As simple and as true and as nightmarish as it was, the bird simply wouldn't fly.

I was still on the runway with my airspeed passing 180 knots as I flicked a glance at my airspeed indicator.

Bobby Summer, my wingman, was up, powered back to stay with me and he called on our squadron frequency, "Get it up! Blue Leader, get it up!"

The whole squadron was being scrambled, 16 Sabre jets in twos, full fuel, all armaments including a new wrinkle of 12-foot long canisters of jellied gasoline called napalm.

We were to take off in elements of two, on the runway roll after counting 10 seconds before releasing brakes. Counting 10 slowly, counting to 10 legitimately. No one counted 10 that way; to be sharp, to be hot, most had counted to 10 in seven or eight seconds.

I had counted to 10 in maybe five seconds and the two jets ahead of us were still solidly on their takeoff roll and beyond them, two more just breaking ground.

Bobby Summer and I were element number five of the eight elements scrambled. The air was full and twisted, heated and howling with the full-power jet wash of eight powerful jets with ignited JP4 fuel: kerosene, gasoline and air mixtures.

Dimly, very quickly, I realized I was in a high-speed wing-tip stall. The end of the runway was coming up fast, in just seconds more. I was passing through 200 knots and my control column felt like an ingot of iron, no life, no lift.

I was there in that old binary place: hit the big red button on my instrument panel and I would drop everything, two wing tip fuel tanks, two 100-pound bombs and the two napalms. I believed my Sabre would spring into the sky if I punched the red button while all hell would exist down the runway behind me. There were at least two elements of Sabres on the roll after me that would have no chance, no option but to drive into it all.

Ten seconds, seven seconds, 220, 230 knots, the end of the runway there. I squeezed the handgrip of my control column with strength, then with extreme delicacy pulled barely back as I went off the end of the runway.

I wasn't flying and I hadn't crashed. My nose was up and I could see the tops of the pine tree forest coming at me as I fell through them, still for a nanosecond then bending near flat under the fury of my passing jet wash. It seemed forever as my Sabre and I teetered on the edge of eternity then I was up, flying, and the only and final comment came from my wingman above who had stayed with me: "Jesus, Blue Leader, Jesus Christ!"

Bobby Summer and I sat in the late afternoon of that same day in our four-man tent at Yon Tan, drinking beers with Bobby Harms and Tom Hayden, the four of us that made up Blue One flight for this Korea assignment. We'd rejoin Tango when we returned to Okinawa. It had stopped raining for a moment.

We were still in our flight suits, unzipped and pulled off our shoulders in the 85 to 90-degree heat.

Bobby Summer repeated, shaking his head in disbelief, "I was still with you, maybe fifty feet up and the last time I took a snap look of my airspeed, it showed 250 knots and you were still on the damned ground!"

Tommy Hayden and Bobby Harms swiveled their heads in unison to look at me, as if they were watching a tennis match. They didn't say a word, just waited for me to speak. The thought of a Sabre at 250 knots and stuck to the ground was pretty near beyond belief to these two experienced aviators, but they didn't say anything, just looked at me like I was some strange animal in a zoo.

I looked back at them and said again: "It wouldn't goddamn fly!" My voice was a little hoarse. I cleared my throat and took a swig of beer. Tommy opened another and handed it to me, silently crushing the empty with two fingers.

"Listen up, you two jackals! My fault totally. I counted to 10 in maybe four or five seconds. Stupid! I got into a high-speed wing-tip stall and that's the story."

There were two more clicks of beer cans being opened as Bobby Summer took up the story. He eased back on one elbow. "You know how this place sits," he began. "Pretty much a cliff face on the north end and falls off in a pine forest at the other. They carved it out on top of a mountain."

"Not excessively long either," Bobby Harms added thoughtfully.

"Right," Summer continued. "Well here goes Blue Leader off the end of the runway, as near as I could tell, not particularly flying."

He paused reflectively, thoughtfully. He shot an odd look at me. We were pretty good friends. "I thought for a second or two we had lost Blue Leader for sure."

Hayden broke in. "Back up a second. You think you would have jumped clear if you had punched off all that hanging stuff? Did you think you'd be up and gone before it all went off?"

"I had no idea," I said. "Maybe yes, maybe no. One thing I knew for sure was those guys behind me would eat it."

"Hero?" Tommy Hayden suggested quietly.

"Not a chance," I said, surprisingly, angrily, "Do that and get away with it and I get down and the rest of the squadron lines up and shoots me dead. Deserve it, too. You get a choice like that and it's no choice."

"I guess," Bobby Summer mused. "Anyway, off he goes falling through the tops of the pines, nose high, tail low, torching, knocking back the tree tops, singeing them, went quite a distance before he started to come up."

Bobby Summer was talking to Hayden and Harms as if I weren't there, flying his hand down his ribcage, fingers high, palm low, wobbling his hand back and forth for comic effect. Hayden and Harms were grinning.

Bobby Harms swiped at his eyes with the back of his hand. "What did you do, Blue Leader, when you got to flying, punch off that lousy napalm into the forest?"

"No, no," I said. "Nobody knew about all that except Summer with his wing-side seat. We went ahead and bombed the hell out of that little island off the coast just like we were supposed to."

There was a fair silence while we all thought about bombs and this effort to recycle our air-to-air interceptor outfit into an air-to-ground mission.

It was my turn to bring the good news. "I talked with Major Jamie and our CO. They told me to pass the word. We're going from a line outfit to an air-to-air quick response tactical strike squadron. Big meeting tomorrow. You'll be happy to know no more bombs and napalm shit, end of that."

It was raining harder as the day ended. "C'mon," I said, standing up and re-zipping my flight suit, "Let's go over to the mess tent for a steak and a decent drink."

We all stood for a moment before leaving. Bobby Harms said it: "Nice to have you still with us, Blue Leader. Yeah, nice," and we walked out into the rain.

Okinawa

Easy Flying

One of the things that creeps up on you unnoticed during a tour in Korea is the isolation. You're not aware of it at first, as so much life in military flying is the same. Your last base had the same excellent fighter aircraft, the same trained and professional ground support, and with the exception ofs the difference between simulated targets and the real things, much the same flying. And it is true that the business of life in a fighter squadron anywhere is so engrossing it makes whatever else exists: marriage, hometowns, loves and drive-in movies, insignificant in comparison.

At a K site you live in a Quonset hut, but it still has a recognizable bed even if it is steel framed with a thin cotton mattress all covered by mosquito netting instead of a comforting Beautyrest. A steak dinner is to be had with however many gin martinis you think you can handle, even though it is always in the same large Quonset that passes for a squadron officer's club. What you do is fly and the fact that where you do this—as well as everything else—is enclosed with a barbed wire perimeter doesn't immediately register.

But the fact of the matter is you don't meet friends for a dinner at a new and hot restaurant in an adjoining town; you don't have dates with some pretty lady; you don't play tennis or golf on a Saturday or Sunday. Except for two or three quick week-long trips across to Japan for Rest and Recuperation, this K site is where you live, eat, sleep and drink for your tour.

You don't see it happening right away, but things start to change. You live in a flight suit or simple khakis without a tie, only silver wings on your chest and legends of rank on your collar to identify you. You can't remember the last time you had on full uniform, wings, brass, jacket, tie, shirt and polished shoes. You wear paratrooper boots—recommended in case you have to eject and walk out—at all times unless you're asleep. And perhaps most importantly, rank, the foundation of military life with its salutes of respect and obedience, almost disappears.

The fighting in the Air Force is done by pilot-officers, unlike other branches of the military where the majority of combat is accomplished by enlisted service people, and especially in a place like Korea, except for necessary orders, the gauge in flying is expertise, how good you are. It's quite a change.

Danny Patton arguing in the big Quonset with our newly arrived commander, a lieutenant colonel re-tread from the last war, got all our attention one evening. Danny was a seasoned first lieutenant a month shy of completing his year's tour and an excellent flight leader. He had a big cigar in his hand and was gesturing with it.

"Colonel," Danny said and his voice carried, "you can't make a vertical overhead rocket run in a Sabre from 10,000 feet. You can't do it and expect to hit anything. By the time you get it pointed down and level winged, you have five, 10 seconds maximum to find your target, line it up, and fire. Even then, you'll pull six or more Gs coming out of the dive, trying to avoid following the rockets into the ground. You could do it in the last war with prop planes and slow airspeed, but not these Sabres!" We saw to our astonishment the colonel nod in agreement and call the waitress over for refills of their drinks.

We didn't know it, but we were gradually and surely changing. Our Quonset housed two flights, eight pilots in all, four of us in Tango flight in the north side and Bravo on the south. We had a small, old refrigerator in the middle of the hut for beers and a long table that usually held a poker game. We were a day fighter squadron, flying two, three or four missions a day, ate and drank at the squadron club, poker at night to the accompaniment of jazz music from a rickety turntable, mixed with a few books and that was our life. Because we were all changing, we didn't notice what was happening.

Patton had a luxurious moustache, a full lip tickler that stretched inches on each side of his mouth. One by one, moustaches grew on the rest of us. A good percentage of us who smoked had taken to cigars, from scotch and soda to straight brandy or cognac, from shoes to boots, uniforms to old faded khakis. None of this would have made much difference if the transfer back to civilization had been gradual and in the normal small groups of two, three or four. But that is not what happened. We went in a group, the whole squadrons.

One sultry evening we were informed both squadrons were to fly out the next morning, to leave Korea en masse and to hop skip to Japan and then our new tactical base on Okinawa. If it was a sudden and welcome shock to us, it was hard to imagine what it would do to the staid, old-line Army regulars that ruled Okinawa. From their comfortable, stiff and formal officer's mess high on a hill overlooking our new base, with white-jacketed servants moving unobtrusively from linen-covered table to table, the wives and full uniformed husbands, they were in for a terrific shock. We didn't realize it, but we were like 16 guys who had spent a year camping out in the bush, like Dan McGrew come out of the hills. The way it began set the tone.

Because of some fuel foul-ups in Japan, we were late flying out over the Sea of Japan to Okinawa and by the time we got there, it was dusk. The weather had been marginal when we left Japan and over the field on Okinawa, black roiling clouds were highlighted by a spectacular sunset.

We came in high, 16 Sabres in flights of four, made one big circle at 40,000 feet to get our landing clearance and then took it down on the deck to make our landings. Our squadron frequencies crackled with the message from our colonel leading us: "Land in flights of four in two-minute intervals."

With 16 fighter aircraft arriving suddenly from across the sea, all to land in 10 to 15 minutes, now this was quite something. You come in flights of four at about 1,000 feet off the ground, straight for the runway holding strong airspeed. Over the end of the runway, one by one in quick sequence, you pitch out in a 90-degree bank, lowering your gear and flaps as soon as you complete the pitch out, then with a final 180-degree reversal, set it on the runway. You can get down in seconds.

Once down, our leader, the nicely adjusted lieutenant colonel re-tread, commandeered three taxis and in sweaty flight suits, G suits and boots, the 16 of us in our squadron drove to the Army officer's club with the idea of having a drink or two.

What we had become came to us gradually as we stood up to the long, polished mahogany bar after ordering drinks. Amid cigar smoke, chatter, and laughter, we became aware of the adjoining dining room. It held tables with ladies and gentlemen in civilized attire, eating dinner to the faint sounds of music. At a central table was one very angry full Army colonel, who, after a few minutes of conversation with other officers, pulled himself up into a stiff walk and came into the bar.

"This," he said menacingly, "is an officer's mess!" and we realized that not one of us in flight suits had any symbol of rank and given our appearance and demeanor, he really couldn't be blamed for not figuring us to be officers and gentlemen. It was a tense moment.

Patton was front and center like a shot. Formally, he introduced our lieutenant colonel leader. It was nip and tuck for a minute, but with our commander back in control, his poise recovered, he asked if we could order champagne for the dining room. The Army colonel was a good guy and accepted. He added that next time here he would expect us to be in correct uniforms. With the Army colonel accepting the champagne, we were all able to leave in peace.

We never were invited back to the Army mess. It didn't make any difference. It was going to take us many months to recover our civilized ways in the free and breezy flying on Okinawa.

In fact, some of us never did.

The Great Water Ski Bet

McDonald ruled Bravo flight with an iron hand. He was tall for a pilot, just a fraction under 6-foot-four with piercing blue eyes set under bushy eyebrows, all commanded by a great beak of a pirate's nose. He was Bravo's flight leader and considered the best in the squadron alongside our Tango flight leader, Jimmy Conlin.

Flight leaders did more than lead our flights of four on missions; they also had a large hand in planning and fighter flying techniques. There were no better pilots than Mac and Jimmy at these jobs and, as a result, Bravo and Tango were friends, natural friendly enemies as well as competitors.

McDonald was a Yale man, Conlin the University of California. McDonald had rowed stroke on the Yale varsity eight-man racing shell that had taken the Ivy League championship, while Jimmy at 5-foot-10 had been a running back for the University of California's Golden Bears football team. McDonald drank scotch and soda and Jimmy bourbon and branch water. About their only merging of interests were women and airplanes.

With the cease-fire more or less signed in Korea, our two squadrons of first-line fighter aircraft had been designated as a tactical strike force and rotated to the island of Okinawa. Our mission was to be combat ready, to be able to fly out to any trouble spot within 24 hours notice. In the meantime, we were to train at the job of fighter flying, jobs we already knew first hand, but the training was necessary to maintain peak levels of skill.

Okinawa was a little bit of paradise after Korea, fun flying, no barbed wire surrounding our base, restaurants and bistros within easy reach as well as the Tea House of the August Moon for late night eating, drinking and romancing. The transition was great, the level of excess considerable. McDonald's flight immediately bought two old World War II jeeps for transportation and our Tango flight struck back with the purchase of four ancient motorcycles, wonderful machines, two spread-handle Indians, a 1938 Harley-Davidson and an improbable BMW two-stroke. As little as we knew of Okinawa, the realization that this island had some of the best beaches in the world was a bonus none of us had imagined. If we weren't flying, eating, drinking, ramming our motorcycles around or romancing, we were on the beach.

Just because we competed with Bravo flight did not mean we failed to like each other. The fact was we saw more of Bravo flight than the rest of the flights in the squadron. A case in point was the Christmas fly-by planned late one night by our leaders, McDonald and Conlin. Our commanding officer had given our flights a free hand in the plans and execution of whatever we thought appropriate. McDonald had put forth the idea late one night in the bar of the Kadena officer's club.

"Let's give the island an eight-plane formation air show, cross-overs, low-speed and high-speed runs, the works. What do you think?" he inquired of Jimmy, who nodded vigorously in agreement.

"Which flight leads?" Jimmy asked, not unexpectedly.

"Gotta coin?" McDonald replied and with the coin toss, they planned the Christmas fly-over.

It worked out fine, the eight of us up early on Christmas morning, airborne by 8:30 on a clear, cold day. We ran two four-ship V flights at first, coming in at speed over Naha at one end of the island, then over Kadena and on to the Army base. We dropped it low over our Army friends, hoping very much we might catch some late sleeping brass still snoozing. After that we did an eight-ship in trails and four-ship crossovers.

On this last run we unveiled our special effect. We had printed bundles of Christmas and New Year's messages on five-by-four-inch sheets of paper and had stuffed these into our speed-brake wells. When we popped our speed brakes open, we showered the island with our holiday greetings. We were all in a good mood that night as we gathered for Christmas dinner in the club. It was hard to say when the bet took place, but it was late, a lot of holiday cheer had been drunk, and it was between McDonald and Conlin.

"What exactly are you saying?" McDonald asked of Jimmy and there was a semblance of quiet around our two tables as we realized the two had been arguing for some minutes.

"I say that you are pitifully ignorant and not only can I water ski on one ski, I will bet you and Bravo flight that I can do it by noon tomorrow off a beach and pulled up by a motorcycle."

McDonald, who had apparently never even heard of water skiing in this early 1950's era, leaned back heavily in his chair, his cigar in one hand, his drink in the other. He pointed the cigar like a pistol at Jimmy.

"You have a bet!" he exclaimed. "Why you dumb cluck, where do you think you're going to find what you call a water ski on this island?" He waved Jimmy off as he started to speak. "Too late," he crowed, "I make the bet a case of scotch, Bravo against Tango, by noon tomorrow!" The bet was on.

Tango flight huddled early the next morning and with aching heads, we considered the bet.

"We'll make a ski," Jimmy said at length. "There's a little carpenter shop in Kadena. Bend a piece of wood up at the tip, shape it a little, make a foot holder out of inner tube rubber. It'll work fine," he urged while we all looked a little dubious. "I'll need a lot of line," he continued, "Has to be lightweight and long. Any ideas?"

"Parachute shop," Bobby Harms, the BMW motorcycle owner answered, "I know the sergeant in charge, get all you want."

Decided, Harms went off to see his sergeant friend and I went with Jimmy to find the carpenter shop. Our first problem immediately presented itself when we found the shop. Language. The two smiling and agreeable carpenters were Okinawan-Japanese and spoke not a word of English. The concept of a water ski itself, even with words to communicate, was an uneasy one for anybody who had never heard of such a notion. Jimmy was equal to the task.

He drew a picture of a speeding boat on a scrap of paper, then a line to a figure standing behind it, apparently following the speedboat on a stick. Then he drew an arrow to the stick and drew another picture of an expanded view of the stick from the side and top. I held up a 5-foot scrap of half-inch-thick, eight-inch-wide board that was lying about and Jimmy with hand gestures showed how the front must be bent in a curve, shaped, where the rubber inner tube should be cut and placed. Admittedly the sketches were not of gallery quality, still we both thought the smothered laughter from the two carpenters was excessive. The fanning out of a bunch of American dollars brought the job back into focus and the two set to work. The ski was heat bent to make the curve and in less than an hour we had a primitive water ski.

It was 11:45 by the time we met on the beach. This beach was critical. The sea was usually as flat as a pancake here, the sand of the beach fine and hard packed and you could walk out 200 yards and only be up to your calves in water.

We of Tango flight gathered above the beach on our motorcycles to check out the scene on the beach below. McDonald and Bravo had their jeeps parked on the sand and, as we looked, we could see they considered this a sporting event they were bound to win. Both jeeps were full of pretty women, chests with beer and other beverages packed in ice. Seeing us, there were loud shouts of joy as they pointed to their wristwatches and the time. We had 15 minutes to win or lose the bet. Jimmy gathered us around him.

"Okay, we're going to have to be fast with this," he said and he had his leader's voice working. "Harms, it'll have to be your BMW to pull, it has the best acceleration. Let's see the line," and Bobby Two showed him the many coiled loops of this parachute cord, light, strong and a lot of it.

"When we get down there, tie it on to the back of your cycle. When I wave to you, set off down the sand. Get it up to about 30 miles an hour and don't watch me. Just try to maintain that speed. Oh," he stopped for a moment, "one other thing. I'll try for a smooth take-off, but to some extent you will feel my weight hit you. Just keep it straight and running." He turned to me. "You come with me," he said, and with that we gunned our motors down to the beach.

We were running out of time. We ignored the hoots and shouts from Bravo, Harms tying off the line to his motorcycle as Jimmy and I waded out into the shallow water with McDonald. There was more line than we had thought, well over 100 feet of it. We were directly out from Bobby Harms and his motorcycle idling on the beach waiting for our signal to start. As far out as we were, the flat water was still only to our mid-calves. Jimmy had the single bar leading from a split in the parachute cord in his hands over his head, his one foot in the rubber of the foot holder of the ski while he stood on the other, my hand on his shoulder for support.

McDonald looked a little concerned. "You sure you know what you're doing? There's only 12 inches of water here and just a film towards the beach. Not so good if you fall. Hell, Jimmy, let's call this thing off and drink some beers."

Jimmy grinned at McDonald. "Nice of you, Mac," and he spoke to me. "Start Harms," and I waved Bobby forward.

Everything seemed to slow down at first. The three of us watched as Bobby Two quickly got his motorcycle going down the beach, the long line to Jimmy gradually moving so the Jimmy had to hop his ski to the right as the angle kept increasing. He had the line handle well over his head waiting for it to tighten and, as Bob continued down the beach, I think the three of us realized what was happening.

It was the parachute cord. Strong, light and immensely resilient, it was doing what it was meant to do. It was stretching and stretching.

Jimmy glanced at me quickly. We both knew what was going to happen. The line would stretch to its limit and then, with all the pent-up kinetic energy stored, would fire Jimmy forward like a rocket. He had only two choices: let the line go and lose the bet, or hold on and hope to ride it out.

Then it happened. The line hit its limit and Jimmy went from standing in the water with McDonald and me, to 30 miles an hour in the blink of an eye. At the same instant, Jimmy's weight hit the back end of Bobby Two's motorcycle, jerking it almost out from under him. The next few seconds were something to behold.

On the beach Bobby fought to bring his motorcycle back up, cranking on the throttle as he tried to straighten out the machine. Jimmy on his ski was catapulting on an angle toward the beach and the sand, struggling to stay up and at the same time to turn the ski parallel to the sand.

By the time Bobby had his cycle running straight, he later told us, he had to be going 50 from the throttle he had given it. Jimmy got the ski turned just barely off the sand and was flying down parallel to the edge in no more than a half inch of water. No more than 10 or 15 seconds had passed and Jimmy held on for another 20 before throwing the line in the air and coasting for what seemed forever. He finally stopped way down the beach and held the ski over his head in victory. Not one single sound had been heard during the whole time except one shriek from a girl in a jeep.

McDonald stood with his hands on his hips staring off down the beach. "That," he said to me, this ace aviator and adventurer, "is the goddamnedest thing I have ever seen!" and as Jimmy rode back up the beach on the back of Bobby's motorcycle to the cheers of Tango and Bravo flights and the pretty ladies, the ski held aloft in triumph, he added, "I've got to do it!"

Well, try though Jimmy did try, there was no stopping McDonald. "Don't even think of it," Jimmy pleaded. "It was a damn miracle I made it and I know what I'm doing," but Mac would have none of it and spent the next few hours taking the worst spills imaginable before finally riding out the catapult start and skiing up onto the sand of the beach.

It was a terrific day, a huge victory for Tango flight, although not the last bet we would make with Bravo and we surely didn't win them all. It was late in the afternoon after McDonald had made his one successful run that we saw Mac uncork a couple of beers and hand one to Jimmy.

"Tell the truth, Jimmy, you ever do that before?"

Jimmy looked serious. "Never! Oh, I've skied before, but I'll tell you McDonald, between the motorcycle and the parachute cord, never. And I'll tell you something else. It will take a lot more than a case of booze to get me to ever try it again."

McDonald smiled at him. "I think I'll go with you on that never-again business. But I had to try it, didn't I?"

Jimmy took a long pull of his beer and shook his head. "No. I wouldn't have."

"The hell you wouldn't," McDonald said and they sat there grinning at each other.

Trouble Breathing

We were in a flight of four flying in tight formation on a beautiful spring morning over the island of Okinawa. It was the kind of day that made you think about your luck. Luck at being a pilot, luck at being with the best tactical strike squadron in the Far East, lucky to be flying the F-86 Sabre, the best fighter aircraft in the world, and lucky to be out of Korea in one piece.

Tim Jaans was leading our flight. Tim was leader of Zulu flight, one of the four flights in our squadron. The rest of us were pilots from other flights who wanted to fly on this early Sunday morning. Our squadron was experienced, all old hands, and we pretty much flew when and how we wanted. Over coffee that morning, Tim had suggested we fly and when we agreed, he had our sleepy Ops officer okay the four aircraft for flight.

Designated a tactical strike force here on Okinawa, our job was to stay sharp if we were needed for some trouble spot in the Far East. So far, it had been a vacation, the flying loose and easy, the opportunities for life other than the squadron's, as in Korea, wonderful. No more barbed wire surrounding our base, restaurants and entertainment everywhere and beaches for fun.

The four flight leaders in the squadron pretty much decided what we needed to stay ready, except for routine instrument flights and perfunctory mock air battles and tactics ordered by our command and operations officers.

Tim was the sort of pilot who couldn't get enough of flight. He was up in the air even if he had to urge others to join him. The three of us hadn't needed any prodding this morning. The weather was gorgeous, a special morning when everything smelled fresh and clean, the blue sky dotted with fluffy white clouds, so perfect they looked like a stage setting. We had gone in trail after we had some altitude, one behind the other, playing follow the leader as Tim took us in huge, lazy loops and wing-overs around the clouds.

Now he had placed us in tight formation and had climbed to 45,000 feet. Below us, the island lay like a jewel in the blue waters of the Pacific, the puffs of clouds like cotton candy between us and the sea. Then, without warning, Tim flipped his Sabre over onto its back and dove straight down out of the formation.

I was flying number two position off Tim's left wing, and Bobby Summer was flying number three, assistant flight leader's slot, off Tim's right wing. Both of us had to abruptly veer away as Tim went over and dove. It happened so suddenly, with no warning from Tim that all Summer, Casey flying number four and I could do was get out of the way.

Bobby didn't hesitate. He immediately took the lead and ordered us to follow him, then put us into a dive to follow Tim, calling to him on our squadron frequency. There was no reply as we dove steeply, trying to catch Tim's Sabre still in a vertical dive below us. None of us had any idea what had happened, but we knew it had to be serious and sudden or else we would have been warned.

As we passed through 20,000 feet, we finally heard Tim on the radio, 10,000 feet below us.

"Sunday flight," he called, using the flight designation we had agreed on, "slight problem here. Fly independently, Sunday leader to land."

Bobby rogered this, putting us back into a three-ship V and circled the field, waiting for Tim to land. Tim's call to us hadn't told us anything. We all knew Tim, knew what a cool and experienced leader he was. Whatever the problem, it was totally unusual, a unique thing he had done, but he seemed to have it under control, if not explained.

We watched as Tim let down to landing pattern altitude of a thousand feet and then put his 86 into a steep climb to 3,000 or 4,000 feet. He did this two, then three times as we circled, watching. Bobby called again.

"Sunday leader, do you have a mechanical problem, an emergency?"

"Negative," Tim came back, "Will land shortly," leaving us still with the mystery of what was happening to him.

On his fourth try, Tim landed smoothly. Our fuel was low, so Bobby put us into landing echelon. When we had landed, taxied, parked and signed off our aircraft, we hurried to squadron operations. Jamison, our Ops officer, met us at the door.

"What happened up there?" he demanded of us. "What kind of maneuvers were you up to?"

Bobby was quick to answer. "Nothing. Nothing at all, Jamie, just an easy fly-around. What did Tim have to say?" he asked impatiently.

"Not a damned word. I wouldn't give him time to talk, tell you the truth. He was bleeding from his ears, Bobby, both ears. I sent him straight to the flight surgeon. What the hell were you guys doing up there?" he asked again.

Bobby shook his head and with the rest of us, was out the door on the run. We grabbed a squadron jeep and drove fast to the flight surgeon's medical station where we cooled our heels for half an hour until Tim came out. He was pale and drawn. Both ears were blocked with cotton. There was blood on his flight suit.

"Jesus, Tim," Bobby Summer exploded, "what in hell happened?"

Tim shook him off with a shrug. "Wait. Let's go someplace, have some coffee. I'll tell you then."

We dressed and drove off base to Hernando's Hideaway, on a cliff overlooking a stretch of sandy beach, our favorite spot for a Sunday breakfast or lunch. We ordered coffees all around, holding up on breakfast until Tim let us know what had happened.

Tim was particularly quiet, withdrawn, looking out to sea with a thoughtful expression.

"I don't know what happened," he began. "We were just flying along and my throat closed off."

"What?" Bobby said. "What do you mean, your throat closed off?"

"What I said," Tim repeated. "One second everything was fine, then, in the middle of a breath, the start of a breath really, my throat closed and I couldn't breathe. Maybe not my throat, but something."

He glanced sharply at me. I think I had an unbelieving expression on my face.

"Try it!" he ordered me and he wasn't kidding. I did. I began to take a breath and stopped it quickly. It was terrible. Even sitting there knowing I could breathe if I wanted to, I felt what it must have been like. It wasn't panic, but it was close. I guess Tim saw this on my face.

"Now think how I felt at 45.000 feet, leading with you guys on my wing. I not only couldn't breathe, I couldn't speak. It wasn't the oxygen mask or the feed. It was me. I had just the start of a breath, hardly any air. I don't know how long I tried to breathe, not long. I didn't have much time. I had to do something, so I split S out of the formation, just dove straight down."

He had our total attention as he went on.

"I started to breathe again at around 20,000 and figured I had better get down and see what was wrong. That's when the next thing happened."

Summer was thoughtful. "The reason you kept getting low and then taking it up again?"

"Right," Tim agreed. "Every time I got below 2,000 feet, there was this terrific pain in my head. It was so bad my eyes would shut, no matter how much I tried to keep them open."

We thought about this. You can do a lot of things if you are an experienced pilot, but landing with your eyes shut is not one of them.

"So, Tim, how'd you work that little problem out?" Bobby asked.

"I tried to drop it down two, three times," Tim said. "No go. Finally, I set up for landing a thousand feet high, throttle back, gear and flaps down and propped my left eye open with the fingers of my throttle hand. The other one closed. Terrific pain. When I got down, I could feel the warm stuff coming out of my ears. Blood, and the pain stopped."

We all looked concerned. It sure didn't sound good.

"What did the flight surgeon say?" Casey asked him.

"He's not sure," Tim said sadly. "I'm to go back Monday, when the full staff is there. Except for a slight cold, nothing he could see. He warned me I might have to go to Japan, the Air Force's Tokyo hospital, if they can't figure it out. He says the ears are all right, didn't break the eardrums, but he has no idea about the throat business. He grounded me."

We all sat back, ordering another round of coffee, looking out the window at the beautiful day, the sea and the beach, thinking. Flying was such a funny business.

One day you're cock of the walk, flight leader, doing what you most want to do. Then anything could happen. A head cold, a sudden pain in your back, the instruments in your cockpit are beginning to be difficult to read. Anything.

You don't get better in your physical self as time goes by in the flying of fighters. It's a very demanding job. Your every corporeal function, all required to be of high order, can blow at any time and your career is over. Maybe Tim would be lucky.

Then again, maybe he wouldn't. It always seemed to happen, most to guys who sincerely love what they are doing. Life is funny. It always seems to get you where it hurts you the most.

Navy

We were really excited. The Navy's aircraft carrier, the USS Princeton, previously at sea in the Pacific, had dropped anchor in the harbor on Okinawa that evening. To our immense pleasure, our free-wheeling commander announced that our squadron of 16 Sabres would buzz the carrier at 6:30, shortly after dawn the next morning.

It was hard to say what rated first in our excitement. A chance to put it to the Navy was too good to be true. Our fighter squadron was recently out of Korea and going up against the Navy fell just slightly below going up against the Russians or Chinese. To say that fighter pilot rivalry between us was heated was to beggar the word.

Then there was the difference between the Navy and the Air Force. The Navy took very seriously the notion of "officers and gentlemen," with heavy emphasis on the gentlemen part. At that point in time, in the early 1950s, the Air Force was only several years old and still had a lot of relatively casual ways of the Army Air Corps of World War II. The Air Force looked primarily at the ability to fly and not so importantly at the notion of gentlemen.

Not the Navy. The Navy had a lot of the stuff the British called for in officers, like the World War I lieutenants out of Oxford and Cambridge who were supposed to lead attacks out of the trenches by strolling out with an umbrella or kicking a soccer ball.

We remembered the story Jimmy Conlin told us in Korea about the Navy flyer calling for help saying that the enemy was all around him. Finally, back came the anonymous growled advice from another Navy flyer, "Shut up and die like an aviator!" That was the Navy, a lot of style for sure.

Navy aviation was full of Ivy League types from Yale, Princeton and Cornell, while the Air Force had a heavy concentration of state university men with a few Stanfords and Ivy Leaguers thrown in for seasoning. It could be safely predicted that a Naval flying officer would be liable to order escargot at dinner, while his Air Force opposite number called for a sirloin rare, or perhaps some barbecued ribs.

None of us would ever question the bravery and courage of naval pilots, or aviators, as they preferred to be called, but it was something like the football played in the Ivy League. Scheduled against powerhouses like Penn State, their 180 pound halfbacks had to go up against 340 pound linemen who were as quick as cats, or their line risked life and limb trying to stop 280 pound fullbacks who could outrun cheetahs. No, there was no question as to Navy courage.

And to top it off, during this era, the Air Force's primary fighter aircraft was the swept-winged F-86 Sabrejet, the best in the world, while the Navy aviators flew definitely second-rate jets, the Cougar and the slightly better Panther, neither of which was any match for the Sabre.

We were eager and ready the next morning, assembled for a 5:30 briefing, every pilot accounted for, even two who had been in hospital for minor ailments. Our commander spoke succinctly:

"We'll come in initially in flights of four, my flight on the lead, followed by Tango, then Bravo and Zulu. I want airspeed and I'll bring us in at around 550 miles an hour. The carrier flight deck is 80 feet above the water. We will come in at 30 feet, below the deck," he noted unnecessarily. "Ten-second spacing between flights. I will order other passes in the air. The weather is perfect. Any questions gentlemen?" he finished and looked inquiringly at the 16 of us.

Jimmy Conlin, leader of Tango flight, spoke up. "You think the Navy will be up at that hour, Commander? They might be having a touch of orange juice and a hot roll or two?"

"Point," our commander grinned. "I'll contact the *Princeton's* air controller before we take off and suggest the viewing from the flight deck might be interesting at 6:30 for their pilots. I mean aviators," he corrected himself. "Anything else?" he finished, and then catching himself, added: "Check your wardrobes. All decorations and service ribbons to be worn. The Navy flashed to me last night they would be pleased to have us for a look at the Princeton and dinner tonight at five in their officer's wardroom. You will look sharp!"

He paused for a moment, grinning at our surprised expressions at this invitation, checked the briefing room for other questions and, when there were none, said he would see us in the air.

Out on the airstrip, strapping into our Sabres, it was that special time just before dawn, the airstrip cool in the faint light of the rising sun barely below the horizon, the crew chiefs moving swiftly in the shadow of the coming day. The auxiliary power units necessary to start our turbines kicked into action, as one after another, our jets came up to power, tailpipes glowing with yellow-white fire. Our commander led the first element of two into the air and two by two we followed, joining into flights of four in V formation.

We flew out of the shadow of the earth up into the bright and glorious sun of the dawn, leaving the quiet land in twilight behind as we took a long, climbing swing out over the blue Pacific, shaking out the kinks as the sun rose in the sky and slowly lit the island below. We took our spacing and prepared to dive on the harbor and the long and serious shape of the USS Princeton at peaceful anchor below us.

We came in from altitude, pushing over from 35,000 feet in a steep dive to level out about five miles from the harbor entrance. We were at more than the briefing speed of 550; we were just below .9 Mach, holding over 600 miles an hour. At that speed, we would be in the harbor entrance in 30 seconds.

Jimmy Conlin came in with our Tango flight higher than the briefing altitude of fifty feet to about seventy feet, to avoid the jet wash of our leader's four aircraft. Flying wing on Jimmy meant holding utter concentration on his Sabre, so that when we flashed past the Princeton at about the level of their flight deck, we had a peripheral snapshot of tiny figures on the deck as we were there and gone. Jimmy pulled us up fast in a four-aircraft chandelle after we passed, leveling off at 10,000 feet on reverse course over the sea and then to dive again for a second pass. There was no sound to us of our passage, but we knew that the speed we had held must have sounded like the first blast of World War III to the Navy watching us.

We made three passes in four-ship V formation, then our commander ordered us in single trail, the 16 Sabres to make a final fly-by, each solo with 10-second spacing. He called a final instruction that we make a ground target exit after passing the carrier. A target exit meant each was to pull up after the run, banking sharply right and left or wing rolling. The idea of this maneuver in practice was to discourage anti-aircraft gunners from getting a smooth track on departing raiding aircraft.

This, like the whole show, was pure and simple hot-dogging, and we couldn't have been more pleased. We came off the Princeton in radical rolls and 90-degree banks, putting our all into the performance and some of us scaring ourselves. It was a morning not to be forgotten for us and, in a way, for the Navy flyers as well. Pilots, or aviators, love airplanes, even the enemies. Wives and family, friends and colleagues think they may be loved by flyers and to an extent it is true. But a pilot's real love is for aircraft and the flying of aircraft.

We spent most of the remaining day getting ready for dinner on the Princeton. The main problem we had was that of service ribbons. None of us had any and we scoured the Army-Navy stores and their display cases for the correct ribbons to tack on our jackets. Jimmy Conlin was the hit of the evening, having found a ribbon that indicated some obscure prior service he had toward the end of World War II. We were all assigned a Navy flyer for this dinner and Jimmy's companion was a droll lieutenant commander. In the wardroom just before being seated, this guy, in a lull of conversation, pointed out that his guest was indeed unusual. He indicated Jimmy's ribbon and expressed surprise that Jimmy was a veteran of the Spanish American War, although he allowed that the Air Force was full of surprises. They got out a service ribbon reference book and the lieutenant commander was right. Jimmy had goofed.

Dinner was excellent, served by white-jacketed mess attendants in the paneled and muted atmosphere of a Navy wardroom. None of us spoke of it, but the difference between this gentlemanly and rich setting so contrasted with the Quonset huts and steel-framed beds of our Far East tour that we were subdued and appreciative. No question, the Navy had style and substance.

It was later on our tour of the flight deck that we had to doff our hats to the Navy. We had been aware of the postage-size view of the Princeton's flight deck from the air, but here on the platform itself, the thought of bringing a jet onto its absurdly small space at a 160 miles an hour at sea on a dark night or stormy day was fearsome. It was probably the single most difficult thing to have to face daily in high-performance fighter flying.

The Navy would get better aircraft, front-line and world class. But while we always had an 8,000 foot runway to come home to, these guys had one of the ultimate challenges of fighter flying: catapult launch and recovery and arrest from a carrier on the high seas.

It had been a day to remember. The Navy was suitably impressed with our air show and after discussion with their aviators about the mechanics of landing their aircraft at sea on a rising and falling flight deck, we had to call it a draw with the aviators of the Princeton.

Fiona

Our job on Okinawa as a tactical strike force was a piece of cake. As best we understood it, it was our mission to be able to fly into any trouble spot on 24 hour's notice, sort of like the Calvary riding over the hill with bugles blowing to the rescue of the settlers. That ego-boosting imagery was the way we saw it, at any rate.

Of course, it was a lot more than that for support personnel, the people responsible for the back-up cargo planes, the logistics of moving everything necessary to put 16 aircraft in the air and keep them there. They had to consider everything from Band-Aids to bombs, bacon and eggs to jet fuel and bullets. But for us pilots, all we had to consider was the ability to climb in and fly to where they pointed us. We were highly trained and combat ready, so, like the prima donnas we were, we rested on our oars and had fun.

Having fun, flying for the sport of it, however, doesn't mean not keeping the edge sharp. There is only one way to keep a high level of skill in the flying of single-seat, high-performance jet fighters: you have to fly a lot and work at those skills that would be required if things ever heated up again in the world. It is very much like what athletes must do in order to hold their ranking. The hundreds of miles a runner puts in before a meet doesn't show, but without them, he has no chance of beating the opposition. Flying is like that, and we went through our versions of a runner's hundreds of miles by gun camera shoot-downs in mock dogfights, simulating weather by flying under a hood, low-level strafing runs and aerial tactics of all sorts. We even sat a two-aircraft alert, two pilots and two jets off the end of the runway, ready to get airborne in 60 seconds.

It seemed a pointless thing to do on this sunny, peaceful island, but in the end, it was part of the hundred miles of training and practice, and we did it, regretting only slightly an afternoon lost to one of Okinawa's beaches. They would scramble us every now and again, not with the pulse-rattling sound effects of a real scramble horn, but with a phone call to the crew chiefs in the nearby truck. We knew either the operations officer or our commander would have a stopwatch on us to time our lift-off, so we worked hard at getting in and off in 60 seconds or less, sometimes spending the afternoon strapped in the cockpits in order to be up in 30 seconds.

The Ops officer was feeling whimsical one afternoon as Tommy Braden and I sat alert, and when the civilian British BOAC DeHaviland airliner was airborne at 5,000 feet and climbing on course, he scrambled us, calling us on the radio and telling us we were free to escort the airliner out to sea. It was a nice thing for him to do, giving us a chance to hot dog it by flying formation alongside the airliner, giving all the passengers staring out the little round windows a close look at airborne jet interceptors. It was definitely a nice break for us, but in the end it changed Tommy Braden's life. It was on that innocent practice scramble that Tommy first met the BOAC stewardess at 10,000 feet over the China Sea.

Tommy was on lead for our scramble and kept us down low over the ocean after we were airborne, building up speed quickly until we were holding over 600 miles per hour. Then he pointed us near straight up so that we popped up to 10,000 in a couple of seconds, jumping alongside the four-engine DeHaviland like two genies out of a bottle. The DeHaviland was a sleek plane, powered by four inline Rolls Royce Merlin engines, wonderful engines to hear. We had admired them when the airliner ran up for take-off back on the ground. They sounded like nothing so much as giant sewing machines, revving ever higher and higher as they were brought up to take-off power. Flying just off the DeHaviland's wing, Tommy gave the startled pilots a friendly wave, pointed to his helmet and held up five fingers for our UHF channel frequency. The Brits came on channel quickly.

"Bloody hell, Air Force, what's happening!"

Tommy was all conciliatory smoothness. "Nothing, nothing BOAC. Sorry about the sudden arrival. Please accept apologies."

The DeHaviland's captain, leaning around his co-pilot's shoulder to see us on the right side of his aircraft, grinned at this. "Apologies accepted, I guess. Hang on while I inform our passengers that we have not gone to war with you colonials. Or have we?"

Tommy shook his helmeted head. "Negative, BOAC. Do we have your permission to escort you out?" he asked. The captain smiled and agreed, taking his headset off and disappearing from view on his way back to the passengers. As quickly as he left, an enormously pretty face under a blonde head appeared and put his microphone headset on. She was wearing a tailored blue blazer over a white blouse and what we could see from our position just off their wing about 25 yards away, was a vision of English beauty in a stewardess.

"Hullo, Air Force. Nice of you to give us a thrill," she said in a rich English accent. "May I have your names for my excited passengers?"

Tommy took his Sabre even closer to the BOAC's wing. "Tommy," he got out after a moment, then perhaps realizing how unofficial, how unmilitary this exchange was, he continued. "First Lieutenant Tommy Braden," he finished, his smoothness a thing of the past and belatedly adding my name.

"Hello, Tommy, I'm Fiona, Fiona Vickers, and thanks again for the fun," she laughed, taking the headset off. I could hear Tommy echo the name, "Fiona," in reply as if he found it to be an almost unbearably nice name.

The captain was back in the cockpit and for the next 20 minutes we escorted them out over the sea. Tommy parked me on the left side of the airliner while he took the right, the side that held Fiona in the window of the attendant's compartment. He did wing rolls away in the few fleecy clouds, dove it down and then in long, swooping loops would come back to his position off the wing. I did much the same on my side, to the evident enjoyment of the passengers, but I saw not a trace of the beautiful Fiona. We had to finally break off as we reached the limit of our fuel range, but not before Tommy announced to Fiona and anybody else who happened to be listening on UHF channel five, that he would greatly appreciate her address. The BOAC captain smiled at this and gave his microphone back to Fiona who unhesitatingly gave it.

Back on the ground at our airbase, Tommy and I had a couple of cold Coca-Colas as the ground crew re-fueled our birds. Tommy was very thoughtful and intent.

"I'm going to marry Fiona," he said at last, dead serious.

I laughed. "What are you talking about? You're crazy," and I searched my mind through all the many reasons this declaration didn't make sense. "For all you know she's already married, you think of that, you dumb cluck?"

Tommy was truly startled and I felt bad as he looked at me in pain. "You think so? No, no, no. Don't stewardesses have to be unmarried to fly?"

"Sure, Tommy, I was just kidding," I replied, having no idea but happy to see the anguish leave his face. "But look here, you don't even know her or she you. You're putting me on, aren't you?"

"The hell I am," Tommy said, back to his serious look and he clutched the clipboard on which he had written Fiona's address.

In the months that followed, Tommy changed. He had always been one of the focal points in the squadron, a guy always ready for a beach party or a night at the Teahouse of the August Moon. He was not exactly a typical pilot with a 'live today, for tomorrow, etc.' attitude, but still, he was well into the holy coordinates of a fighter pilot's life: flying and drinking, flying, drinking and excitement, flying, drinking and romancing.

He changed all right. He wrote constant letters to Fiona in London, haunted the overseas post office for replies. He had sworn me to secrecy about his plan to marry the beautiful Fi and given the seriousness of his plea, I had no choice but to go along with him. One of the ways you could see the change best was the way he now played poker. He had always been in the games, feckless and fearless in the style that came naturally to him, staying in hands he had no business in, losing more often than not, enjoying the play and not particularly interested in winning. No more. He played it close to the vest, smartly and cleverly. He became a big winner overnight.

He talked to me about it. "I've got to think of the future," he muttered aside to me, raking in another big pot. "It's our future," he finished.

Fiona had asked for a picture in one of her early letters. Tommy panicked. As his only confidant in this situation, he came to me.

"What if she doesn't like me?" he moaned. "She's so beautiful! Am I good-looking?" he pleaded.

Tommy wasn't good looking. He looked like a cowboy more than anything. In fact, he was raised on a ranch. He was medium tall and lean-muscle strong, with a face that looked weather-beaten, a face that probably wouldn't change for the next 50 years. He was rugged-looking more than anything, the sort of face they describe in women's magazines for their heroes and he did have the whitest, most perfect teeth you've ever seen. I took him off to a local photography studio and we got a good picture of him, although he wouldn't wear the cowboy hat I thought would look good.

Two-and-a-half months after that fateful scramble, Tommy got the news that Fiona would be coming through again on a flight. Tommy hadn't been idle during this time. In addition to God only knows how many letters to Fiona, Tommy had written to British Overseas Airlines and sent his impressive flying credentials to them. He had been conditionally accepted as a pilot with them pending a personal interview. He was due to rotate back to the States shortly and he planned to resign his Air Force commission and go to England.

I was very nervous. He had made me a part of this and it had gotten way out of hand. "Tommy," I tried to caution him, "you don't know her. Or she you. You're sort of super pen pals, nothing more. You're completely out of hand." He just smiled at me.

Well, Fiona came again to Okinawa and she was even more outstanding than either Tommy or I had imagined, not only smashing looking, but smart and with a great sense of humor. She had five days in Okinawa, five days with Tommy, on the beach, evenings in small candlelit restaurants, dancing at the officer's club. I had dinner with them the last night, Fiona stunning the roomful of pilots with her beauty.

Both Tommy and I finished our tours in the Far East shortly after that and he wrote to me at my new base in Nevada three months later. He was in England. He asked me to take a leave and come to London. He asked me to be best man for him and his Fiona.

It was a great time of the year to be in England and it was a lovely wedding.

Formosa

Crash

Dick Sullivan was down somewhere in the China Sea. He had drawn the assignment of flying a full colonel from Wing on our flight from Okinawa to Formosa and the word was that he'd had engine trouble and had to ditch in the ocean. As far as we knew, it was all open sea on the flight path he had flown. The rest of us in our tactical fighter squadron, flying the same route, hadn't seen anything of the sea since we had taken off, as a solid overcast was socked in over the entire 500 miles of it. It was a low overcast, the cloud cover running up from just off the ocean surface to 10,000 feet.

It was bad enough to hear Dick had gone down, but we were all imagining how it must have been for Dick and the colonel. First ejecting, then drifting down in clear sky until enveloped in the clouds and then—abruptly—to splash down in the unknown sea. It was either that or Dick had dead-sticked his jet through the clouds and crash-landed in the ocean. We didn't know. All we heard was that he was down.

Dick wasn't the only pilot who had trouble. Two Sabres from another squadron had gone down as well. They had made it to Formosa okay, but attempting a critically low-fuel instrument let-down, had flamed out. The two pilots safely ejected. It wasn't a great start to our mission of flying top cover for our Navy's Seventh Fleet.

Steve Forbes, a major on temporary duty from Wing, brought us news shortly after we landed in the late afternoon of the second day.

We had been flying over the Formosa Straits on our mission and, in addition to worrying about Dick, we were interested in the success of a landing in the ocean. Our Sabre's air intakes for our jet engines were right in the nose, large ovals. We figured putting down in the sea would be a disaster the moment the intake dropped and the sea rushed in. It would probably be a real quick and final nosedive. Ejecting was another problem. Even though we flew with inflatable life rafts strapped to our butts and wearing backpack parachutes, the Air Force didn't have any water landing survival training for pilots as the Navy did.

"Dick made it okay," Forbes announced to a group of as he poured himself a cup of coffee. It was great news. We waited expectantly for more.

"He lucked out. He had his boots off, ready for a wet time either ejecting or trying to put it down in the ocean, when he saw a tiny hole in the clouds and right below it an island."

We were surprised. It was true that when we had suddenly been ordered off our home base on Okinawa to fly to Formosa for this top-cover assignment, none of us had much of any idea about the China Sea. But since then, knowing we had to fly back when our job ended, we had checked out maps of the area. None of us had seen any sign of land between Okinawa and Formosa.

"What island?" Kono Stevens from Zulu asked. Kono was part Hawaiian and a real water man from years of surfing in Hawaii. He sounded vaguely disappointed that Dick had found land. "I didn't see any land on a map anywhere near our flight path."

"Pure luck," Forbes repeated. "He was over a radar installation, a postage-stamp bit of an island, just the radar dish, a barracks for four guys and a short grass strip. If it's on the maps, it's a pinpoint. He bellied in, wheels up, and barely stopped short of going off a cliff into the sea. He's still there, waiting for the brass to figure out how to pick them up."

"Luck!" Kono agreed. "Jesus, how important it is. And usually not a damned thing you can do about it. You find a little hole in the clouds and it just happens there is an island below it in 500 miles of open sea. What are the odds?"

Terry Bishop, flying at number two for Bravo, laughed in total agreement. "A million to one, if that, and no takers. Reminds me of a guy who had to bail out over Texas one dark and stormy night."

"Easy, Terry," I cautioned. "Is this another one of your tall tales?"

"Not so," Terry shook his head emphatically. "No. It's a true story. I read about it. I think it was in the Air Force Times."

"Gotta be true if it's in print," Conlin agreed sardonically.

"Anyway," Terry went on, "talk about luck, try this one. This guy tries to fly through a thunderhead and it gets real bad, extra bad when his engine quits on him. He punches out, ready to hit the silk and there he is at 35,000 feet prepared to float down under his parachute."

"Fair enough," Conlin said. "When does the luck come in?"

"There are two kinds of luck," Terry cautioned us, "Dick's good luck and, the other side of it, bum luck. This guy had both."

"How did that work out?" I asked Terry, intrigued despite his known habit of bullshit. We were all interested too; it's hard not to be interested in good and bad luck when what you do has a lot of hazard to it and demands at least your fair share of luck.

Terry wasn't going to rush it. Now that he had us hooked, he was going to take his time. He got the coffeepot from across the room, refilling our cups, going on about thunderheads and their unique problems as if we had never heard of them.

"First of all, as you all know, he realized there wasn't much oxygen at 35,000, so he waited as long as he could before he pulled the ripcord on his chute. The trouble with this is trying not to breathe as you fall like the famous manhole cover at 1,142 feet per second, freezing cold, rain and hail slashing at you and lightning going off every second of two."

He definitely had us now. One of the reasons fighter pilots spend so much time talking to each other and recounting flying stories is not that there is usually anything really new about what's being said; one way or another, most things had happened to all of us. But reliving it peacefully with a coffee or beer in hand somehow makes the incident more human, more capable of being assimilated. It has something to do with sharing, knowing, even if not stated we all had sudden flashes of primal fear. We shared this. It's one of the reasons fighter pilots talk so much to one another.

"In the article I read, he claimed he was holding his nose as he fell, like a guy jumping off a high board," Terry continued and we all had to smile at the image, knowing that it wasn't all that dumb a thing to do. Even falling at terminal velocity of a 180 miles an hour, 1,142 feet per second, it still would take you 20 or 30 seconds or so to reach good, breathable air. At high altitude you can pass out in 30 seconds, get very incapable, drunk is the closest similarity before that. You could pass out or go stupid before you pulled your ripcord and opened your parachute.

"But, okay, he plummets down and finally pulls his D ring and the chute opens, but this is just the start of things. As you may remember, meteorology tells us there are terrific updrafts and downdrafts in a thunderhead, a cumulonimbus," Terry explained in his best professorial style, while we waited impatiently for him to get on with it.

"Right after he pops his chute, and he is fairly low by now, he catches an updraft. Not your everyday updraft. In this one, he goes up like he's in an express elevator. He doesn't know how high. All he can tell is that he goes high enough to run out of breathable oxygen and he passes out. He comes to again later, apparently now in a downdraft, and he's going down like a rocket. He is also covered with frost and ice, like he'd been in the freezer overnight. He gets low again and the same thing happens. Another sensational updraft and up he goes. He figures he passed out at least three times, maybe more. All the time he's being pelted with hail or freezing rain. About the only thing that didn't happen was lightning hitting him and he's not dead sure about that."

"Wait a damn second," the major interrupted, putting his coffee aside. "Who buys this alleged story of his?"

"That's the trick!" Terry crowed triumphantly. "He had his home squadron on the radio just before he ejected and they noted the time he ejected. They had enough time to be there when he finally came down. It took him 33 minutes from when he ejected to making it to earth! Guys," he pleaded with us, "he was frostbitten on his fingers, his nose, covered with frost and he was a basket case, babbling incoherently about being cold, elevators, nightmares."

"Okay," Kono said. "Quite a story, Now where's the good luck?"

Terry looked offended. "Right there in front of you, Kono. I mean, he could have never come down. The thunderhead sat over Texas for days. He could have stayed in it like a yo-yo the whole time."

Forbes took a long breath, sighed. "Terry, if you weren't a pretty fair wingman, if you weren't an okay pilot, I swear . . ." and he broke off as our operations officer came into the room.

"Listen up," Captain Jamison instructed us. "They picked Dick and the colonel up by boat. But there's more. The colonel is so impressed with old Dick, he's putting him in for a citation. Wait," he waved us off as we started to talk, "there's even more. He's going with the colonel to Japan, 10 days full expenses in Tokyo, on the colonel. He thinks Dick is pure luck."

"Luck," Terry said in wonder. "Another guy, another time, and they would be sloshing around in the ocean with sharks circling."

"Luck," I agreed. "Like Creed, the time he was ejected as his plane rolled and blew up on the ground and it ejected him out horizontally, unhurt."

"Luck," Kono chimed in, "Englander happening to walk in when Ops asked a dozen guys for a volunteer for a night test flight. He got it before anyone could say anything and crashed when the oxygen system failed."

The major let the last of his coffee trickle down his throat, looking hard at all of us.

"You want to know what luck is?" he asked after a moment.

We waited, waited for him to tell us some cosmic answer. We were intent. Fighter flying calls for a lot of things. But luck, now here was something skill couldn't make up for, courage had nothing to do with it, knowledge, intelligence, ability, anything you could name, had nothing to do with luck. I doubt if we could be any more interested if he was going to tell us the meaning of life.

"So tell!" Kono finally broke the silence.

"Luck," the major began and the light from the sunset came through the window at that moment and fell on his face, a shaft of light shining on his red hair and keen profile.

"Luck is like a waterfall, like the pure melted snow cascading down the ageless mountains to find the meadows below."

We were moved, quiet at the beauty of the symbolism. Then Kono spoke in a suddenly hoarse voice.

"Jesus, that's beautiful. But why like a waterfall?"

The major grinned then shrugged. "Why not? C'mon you guys, I'll buy dinner."

MiG 15s and F-86 Sabres

We sat around a card table in the shade of a red and yellow striped beach umbrella and contemplated our world on the edge of a Chinese airstrip.

Our world: four swept-winged, sleek and silver, Sabre-jet interceptor aircraft.

The fighters were swarming with Chinese personnel servicing and refueling. As we watched, a Chinese soldier on a ladder ran a cloth over our squadron insignia painted near the fighter's nose. He turned and grinned toothily at the four of us, his cloth swiping at the black and red fighting cock insignia. He shouted something unintelligible in Chinese and threw us a very Chinese half-assed salute. Jimmy Conlin waved cheerily back saying, "And Gung Ho You, pal."

These guys were Chinese Nationalists settled here on the island of Formosa with their leader Chiang Kai-shek when the Red Chinese ran him off the mainland of China.

Everything eventually comes down to one. The Red Chinese didn't like the aging warlord Chiang Kai-shek and our country was pretty much pals with Chiang or at least hated and feared the Communist Reds more. The Reds wanted Chiang's occupied islands of Tachen in the Formosa Straits.

So the wheels turned and the next thing Harry Truman sent our Seventh Fleet down to cover the withdrawal. This was okay as far as it went but at this point in time our U.S. Navy had fighter aircraft that were inferior to the Russian-Chinese MiG 15s.

The Navy flew straight-winged fighter jets, the Panther and Cougar. They were no match for the Red Chinese Russian built MiG 15s.

Our squadron's peaceful sojourn from Korea to Okinawa was abruptly ended. Our orders were to fly out over the South China Sea to Formosa within 24 hours. Our F-86 Sabres were to fly top cover for the Seventh Fleet.

It always comes down to one in the end. This end was the four of us in Tango flight sitting under our beach umbrella on Chiang Kai-shek's airstrip at Hong Chow, Formosa. It always comes down eventually to what a great writer called the sharp end, given enough time.

We had seen our MiGs on our first day. They were sent out of Shanghai, we were out of Formosa, and they cruised parallel to us off the coast of China maybe 15 miles away. They had their version of top cover as well, we figured.

We would fly up the island side of the Straits of Formosa over the Tachen Islands and our U. S. Navy. The Red Chinese would send their MiG 15s out of Shanghai to fly off the coast of China. It was a strange feeling to fly peacefully within sight of each other perhaps 15 miles apart. Nine miles below, the Chinese Nationalist troops abandoned the Tachen Islands under the watchful eyes of our U. S. Navy.

The first few days of this were tense with anticipation of a fight, but then a feeling of camaraderie developed between us and the MiG fighters. After all we were all just pilots, guys who loved to fly.

On the fourth day it happened. The lead MiG pulled forward from his formation as they prepared to leave their station. He rocked his wings at us. He waggled his wings! Wow!

After a few seconds as we all observed this, our leader, Jimmy Conlin, pulled forward and rocked his wings in a return good-bye.

It was strange this near-friendly feeling we had for the Red Chinese in the MiGs. It was all the more awkward because we had a chilly relationship with our Nationalist Chinese pilot-officers at Hong Chow.

We had several problems with them. The fact was we had been ordered here for our top cover mission not because we were better aviators—although of course we thought we were—but because we had better fighter aircraft. The Nationalists flew F-84 Thunder jets, essentially an air-to-ground fighter, while we had the superior F-86

Sabre interceptor. For the Nationalist Chinese, it was a stunning loss of face.

It was a short mission. Our Seventh Fleet ruled the seas and Chang's Nationalist troopers abandoned the Tachen Islands in less than three weeks.

Our top cover flights became routine and after the first few, somewhat tense days, our MiG friends stopped coming out of Shanghai every day to let us know we weren't the only tough guys in the area.

Near the end of our stay, our Tango flight went up for a last patrol. The MiGs had been coming up again and whether Jimmy had planned what we did or just acted spontaneously we never knew. What we did know was we all liked it.

Flying in echelon with the MiGs 10 miles off our left shoulder, we approached the point where we would reverse course. Jimmy came on the radio, his voice low and firm: "Heads up, Tango. Go in-trail for a turn around."

Then as we professionally slid smoothly into in-trail, one close behind another just down from each other's jet wash, Jimmy continued, "Cuban eight coming. Look sharp for our friends," and with that we did it.

A Cuban eight is a pretty maneuver you learn early on in flight school. You slide your aircraft down and to the right, picking up speed. Then with everything done ever so smoothly, you pick your aircraft up, banking left and climbing until you are at the top of your chandelle. At the top with your airspeed down close to stall, you are nearly weightless standing vertically on your left wing. Smoothly, smoothly you follow through to your left, maintaining a past vertical bank as you slide out of the sky. Near the bottom of your half-Cuban you gradually level your wings until you are exactly where you started but on a reverse course.

With four silver jets in unison against the intense blue of a China sky, it is as pretty a bit of flying as you can imagine outside of a dream.

We were good, very good, as pros we had done it as smoothly as it can be done. It was our farewell to Formosa and our MiG friends.

We never did warm up to our Chinese Nationalist hosts or, for that matter, them to us. Maybe it had to do with what Jimmy had called face or maybe they were nervous about their gorgeous Chinese wives with us around.

Bobby Harms our number four had the last word at dinner the night before we left.

"Okay, okay, I can see their reasons. Tell you what though," and he lifted his glass in a toast. "For my money, I'd like to hang out with those MiG guys. Aside from Communism, capitalism, round eyes, slant eyes, white, yellow, east, west and all that bullshit, I bet we could get along fine."

And we all drank to that.

Taichee

McDonald, Jimmy Conlin, Patton and I were told to stay back on Formosa when the squadron left. There were four F-86's down for mechanical problems and not ready to fly when we completed our mission flying top cover for the Seventh Fleet. The fleet had been covering the withdrawal of Chinese Nationalist forces from the Tachen Islands and required our fighters in the unlikely event that MiGs out of Shanghai should think to protest.

The withdrawal had gone smoothly and successfully and now the four of us were to hang out until the mechanics and crew chiefs got our Sabres ready and then we would make the jump together back over the China Sea to Okinawa.

We couldn't have been more pleased. Conlin and Danny Patton were about half in love with the beautiful identical twin Chinese sisters who owned and ran our favorite restaurant in Taichee, The Inn of the Bamboo Forest, while McDonald hugged his lost love for the wife of a Chinese lieutenant colonel to his chest like a miser. I couldn't get enough of the flavor of Taichee and Formosa and was in the midst of a series of interviews with CAT airline, seriously considering a flying job with them when my tour was up. Probably above all, the four of us had become more than a little Asiatic and this chance to spend a few weeks away from normal squadron duties and flying and indulge ourselves with food, drink and the ladies of the Orient was compelling.

Patton brought the subject up. We were in our usual booth on the second floor of the Inn, the large swinging wooden windows propped open with sticks unless there was rain, quietly working our way through many bottles of Chinese rice wine. The secluded booth was walled on two sides with bamboo and the opening for service was strung with lines of glass balls that chimed like the distant sounds of some happy revelry when a waitress entered or left.

Danny sighed happily, leaning on an elbow, watching out the window, enjoying the continual activity on the street below. "I don't know," he said as if picking up the thread of some previous debate, "I think I would be quite happy here for a long, long time."

McDonald looked sadly up from his glass of wine. His dangerous love affair with the wife of one of our host's Chinese wives had ended when their commander, a brigadier general, had complained to our commander and McDonald, not easily told what to do, had been ordered in no uncertain terms to lay off. What our commander had actually said was unknown to us, but whatever it was, it had not gone down easily. Mac was not easy to order around. Just how far the affair had gone was a matter of keen interest in the squadron, but McDonald had stiffly rejected any and all attempts to inquire. There was no doubt, however, that he had fallen hard. He was with us constantly and unlike his normal self, quiet and sorrowful.

"Maybe not," he said in reply to Patton's thought. "This is not just another country, it's a whole different culture, different logic, different value system. It's tough enough with the language problem alone. I was trying to tell Lai Chee something one day . . ." He broke off abruptly as all our heads swiveled to him.

It was the first time he had ever mentioned her name to any of us. He reddened and shook his head as if coming out of water. "If you can't communicate, it's terrible," he amended, warning us off with a look of his intense blue eyes.

Jimmy Conlin, who was probably closer to McDonald than any of the rest of us, was not going to let this opening go by.

"Communicate," he demanded. "Now's the time, Mac. We're all here, just the four of us. Talk to us. Lai Chee? That's her name?"

Mac was silent for a long minute while the street sounds drifted up from below, the street seller of roasted chestnuts with his charcoal fire and his odd, high-pitched two-note advertising warble, the sing-songs of greetings and conversations.

"Lai Chee," he finally agreed and groaned aloud, surprising us all. "She was, is, the most beautiful and sexiest woman I've ever known!"

We sat without a word, all thinking the same thing. We were surprised, shocked. We had wondered, speculated, weighed the chances and mutually decided it was impossible that he had had a full bore, red-toothed love affair with the wife of a senior rank of our Nationalist hosts. We were, after all, here on a full-scale tactical air mission with lots of flying. How had he done it? Where?

The Chinese Nationalists were enormously protective of their unmistakably gorgeous wives, many—if not most—film actresses who had fled from Communist China with Chang Kai-Shek's officers. Mac had met her when newsreel photographers had had a group of us shake hands in mutual admiration on film for the folks back home. It had been painfully obvious to all of us, and that included her lieutenant colonel husband, that McDonald couldn't take his eyes off her and she hadn't seemed to mind it at all.

"I'll be damned!" Danny Patton said admiringly in the lengthening silence that followed McDonald's outburst. "You dirty dog, you did it, didn't you?"

Jimmy Conlin held up a warning hand to Patton, but even he couldn't help smiling. McDonald dying of unrequited lust when we all thought he had a serious case of a broken heart. I started to laugh, I couldn't help it. Big, go-to-hell McDonald, Bravo's esteemed flight leader, all of us worried as hell that he had really fallen for this Lai Chee when what had happened was he had fallen in bed with her and here he was now trying to fight off a grin that was starting to form on his mouth.

Conlin was laughing now, all of us were. "You bastard!" he said in relief, "You let us think you were dying for love, you pig."

McDonald looked offended. "I was sort of in love," he argued to no avail over our hoots of laughter.

Mai and Loa Tai, the twin Chinese sisters, came through the beaded glass curtain, attracted by our laughter. They always sat with us as the evening progressed, between running the restaurant, meeting and seating people. We always ordered much more than we could eat of the best Chinese food any of us had ever had, drank many bottles of the sisters' most expensive wine and tipped heavily in order to justify our evenings at the table. They were sensational looking with their tight sheath dresses slit on the side up to the top of their thighs. It was near impossible to tell them apart, sloe-eyed, full-mouthed beauties that they were.

It was late and the restaurant was near closing. Conlin and Patton would be going off with the sisters to where they would dance to music played by an improbable quartet of Chinese they had discovered. Mac and I would find a quiet bar and hang out for a time, have a drink or two, maybe a dance with a hostess. Conlin had one more question for McDonald.

"What did our commander say to you, Mac? I keep wondering what he could have said to stop you."

McDonald looked thoughtfully at the three of us. Then he spoke simply.

"He said the brigadier general, the lieutenant colonel's commanding officer, told him he didn't care what I did. But he felt he should warn me that the lieutenant colonel said he was going to shoot me dead if I saw his wife one more time. The brigadier said he believed him. Our guy said he believed it, and, guys, so do I. I don't blame him, to tell you the truth. I saw Lai Chee one more time for about two seconds. She went pale as a ghost, put her hand out as if she were holding a gun and pretended to pull the trigger at me. I got the message, language or no language."

Leaving

It felt like autumn. The 16 sleek and silver Sabre jet fighters chocked down and lined up in rows in front of operations looked somehow forlorn. The field at Kadena, Okinawa, the airstrip that had been home to our tactical strike squadron rotated here after the Korean War, already seemed abandoned.

We were going home. Our Sabre jet fighter squadron that had been everything to we 16 pilots in a year at a K site in Korea and for the last four months here on Okinawa was being broken up. We were packed, checked out medically with our last physicals, suited in our class-A uniforms and awaiting transportation to Japan for the beginning of the long Pacific hop to the States.

Eight or nine of us, mostly pilots in Tim Jaans' Zulu, McDonald's Bravo, Jimmy Conlin's Tango, and Danny Patton of Red One sat around tables high over the sea in Hernando's Hideaway, our favorite bistro on Okinawa, each of us with his own private thoughts.

Home. It was hard to grasp. Home had been our fighter squadron for so long another home seemed barely possible. We had shared so much together in the time in Asia, so many memories, so much danger, excitement, fun and sadness. The squadron was our home and the distant place we were headed seemed faint in the past, hard to recognize.

I looked around the tables, at Jimmy Conlin, flight leader and friend, whom I trusted beyond anyone I had ever known and who had proved equal to this trust time and time again. Tom "Mac" McDonald, leader of Bravo, his great hawk-beak of a nose buried in a schooner of beer, who shared with Conlin the ultimate opinion of pilots in a flight: they were the best. Bobby Harms, who'd grown out of "harms way," and Bobby Summer, whose humor always kept us in balance. And all the rest. Fighter pilots. These men were real to me, real as only people who have shared what we had, can be.

Now home. Harry Truman president, supermarkets and gas stations, drive-in movies, the surf at Malibu and the lights of San Francisco. I felt, I think we all felt, a strangeness, like immigrants ready to take ship for a new country and wondering whether we wanted to go.

Some wouldn't go home. Englander, Swaner, Michaels, taken in the sky where we did our job, vanished in the blink of an eye. They wouldn't go home except in our memories. Jack Englander laughing and pouring the champagne when Lacy announced his engagement. Swaner and Michaels, best friends, nearly inseparable, who collided over Yon-Tan, together even in that final moment.

We all knew, imprecisely and vaguely, but we still all knew this had been one of those periods in our lives like no other. It had been one of those times when everything we did would have a great effect on the rest of our days, no matter what twists and turns our lives took. It had been a space in time we would remember with clarity forever, when the people we knew mattered a great deal and the experience was unique.

In a way, we knew how lucky we had been with all of it. The rattling roar of a piston engine in cadets, the magic of the first solo ride, the pride of silver wings pinned on our chests. The eerie whine of the first sound of jets in the world we were to fly, the utter reliance on self and wingmen in flying single-seat fighters.

Then the steel-framed Quonset huts, the mosquito netting, the armed guards around the perimeter of the airfield, the 45s worn in shoulder holsters; the rowdy drinking nights in the flight line bar of O'Rourke's while the upright piano in the corner pounded out another tune; the good-looking nurses and the homely ones, all beautiful. The flights going off in the first rays of sunlight as dawn rose over the hills and mountains of Korea; the night flights over the sleeping island of Okinawa and the South China Sea; the sudden departure to Taiwan and the top-cover patrols in the Formosa Straits.

Most of all, we all knew how lucky we had been to have flown in a line squadron, to have known what it was like to be bonded in that special, isolated way by what we did and where we were, far off from everything familiar and known, flying in strange countries for unknown people.

McDonald heaved a great sigh. "Jesus," he exclaimed, "this is like a wake. Barkeep," he called over his shoulder, "bring more beer for this damned group, cold and chop-chop," always ending with the same admonition no matter in what country we were.

He peered around the two tables, squinting over the head of foam on his beer. "What's the matter with you guys?" he demanded. "We're going home, for Christ's sake. Show a little life."

Patton of the large and luxurious mustache, grinned at this. "Not me. I'm coming back. Pronto. This is where the action is."

Jimmy Conlin raised his white-blond, nearly invisible eyebrows that gave his light blue eyes a special intensity. "Here?" he questioned.

Patton chuckled. "No. Not here, Jimmy. Air Vietiane, that's the place. Fly out of Saigon, get a little French culture, wonderful slim women, good pay. Come with me?" he suggested.

Conlin shook his head, not quite decidedly. "I don't think so. I have a yen to see the mideast, maybe fly for one of the oil companies in Saudi, maybe Iran or Egypt."

Tim Jaans, leader of Zulu flight, broke in excitedly. "Listen, Jimmy. If you're thinking of that part of the globe, check out flying a Sabre down to Israel. They need warplanes. Friend of mine, finished a tour here a year ago, tells me they are paying 1,500 dollars a trip to fly a Sabre there. Or you can fly for them training pilots."

A guy in Zulu flight interrupted. "Isn't anyone staying in? Twenty years and out a light or full colonel, half pay on retirement? What's wrong with that?"

"Boring," Patton said succinctly. "The war's over. You want spit and polish, regular military peacetime life? You know what it's like? 'Yes Sir.' 'No Sir,' 'After you, Sir' for the next 15 years? Lousy airbases out in the desert, PXs and rinky-dink officer's clubs? What kind of life is that?"

The guy in Zulu had an answer: "You get to fly the best aircraft in the world."

There was a silence at this while the cool breeze off the sea below us stirred the air in Hernando's.

"Point," Patton said. "Still, a big price to pay."

There was a longer quiet after this, each with his own thoughts. We were already separating. You could feel it. The close-knit squadron feeling, the bond that came near to making us with one voice, attitude, was changing. Zulu flight, Bravo, Tango and Red One; each had seemed to have one personality, one voice, but now individuals were emerging, each with his own decision to make.

Other voices were heard. Tommy Vespers was engaged to a BOAC stewardess in England and had signed up to fly for the Brits. One guy had checked out Formosa and would go there to fly for Chennault and his Flying Tigers on the run from Hong Kong, Taipei, Toyko. Two quiet pilots and the Zulu guy to stay in the Air Force.

It was over. All that remained was the flight home. A short hop to Japan, then Wake or Midway, then Hawaii and finally to California. Some of us would have short time in some airbase, some would be out as soon as we landed. Flying, sure, that was what it was all about.

From those young days, reading everything on flying we could get our hands on, stories in paperback pulp magazines like *War Aces* and accounts of Rickenbacker and Luke Short, the balloon buster in World War I, Yeager and Boyington in World War II, we had wanted to fly. We made balsa wood models in our rooms, and then growing and yearning until those hazy early days as flying cadets, finally starting the long road to wings. Then solo, transition to jets, picked for fighters and the jolting training in fighter-weapons when we thought we had it all under control. Then Korea and a line squadron, Okinawa and Formosa.

Each one of us, different as we could be, yet underneath we were alike. We wanted to fly, needed to fly. We were lucky. We had flown.

Epilogue

Flying the Clouds

Flying an advanced fighter jet is about as free as you can get. Between your maximum altitude and ground zero below, there is nothing you can't do. Your altitude is around 9 to 10 miles up and that gives you lots of room to play.

A proficiency flight, the term used for going up and doing any fool thing you please, is a flight to keep you current, easy and familiar in an aircraft. You can roll it over from 10 miles up and point it straight for Mother Earth just for the hell of it. Your airspeed indicator jumps immediately and, before you know it, you're over the speed of sound and accelerating.

You don't think about it, but this straight-down ride has to be a short one. For instance, at eight hundred miles per hour you travel over 13 miles in a minute, about 1,200 feet in a second, the length of four football fields in the blink of an eye. In 30 seconds, you have gone around eight miles straight down and it's definitely time to think about pulling it out.

Of course, the altitude you play with is over the ocean or sea-level land and you wouldn't want to make the mistake of diving over 10,000 or 20,000 foot mountains thinking you had 10 miles of space. If you were over mountains and got a dive lower than you should have, fighters have a very handy aid called speed brakes. These are two flat metal plates recessed into the side of the fuselage that are connected to hugely strong hydraulic pistons.

Touch a switch on the side of your throttle and—instantly—the two pistons are activated and thrust tennis racket-sized metal plates out into the airstream. Think about the impact on your hand if you put it in the airstream outside your automobile at 70 or 80 miles an hour and you begin to get the idea of speed brakes. The difference is instead of 80 miles an hour, it's over 800 miles an hour. Trigger the switch and you are slammed forward in your seat harness. You feel as though your aircraft has run into a wall, soft but firm, but with this help, you pull your aircraft out of its dive in time.

Wing roll your aircraft so that you bore holes like a corkscrew; go up, down, or level and watch the earth revolve below you, or the horizon spin before you. Need something to play with? Find some nice fat cumulus clouds and fly in, over or around them, or dive down and fly along a coast just over the surf line, following the contours of the land like a hunting sea bird.

Flying the clouds is a unique experience. The type of cloud is the only thing that varies. On earth we have days of overcast, horizon to horizon covered with low-lying cloud cover, making the days on the surface gloomy and grey. It's a different world just above this overcast. Here the sun always shines, the sky is always blue and brilliant with light. The cloud cover can stretch for a 100 miles in every direction. Sometimes it is a nearly flat surface of white, like an enormous snowfield in some improbable place, without mountains or hills; more often it is gently bumped with mile after mile of connected half bubbles of cloud, like millions of clean, white sheep gathered tight together.

Better to play with is a day with fat, billowing cumulus clouds, growing and rising as you watch. There are clear, blue sky spaces between these giants, breaks of form in a new world that might as well be on another planet. There are a number of ways to play with this universe, but in many ways the best is to imagine them solid, to fly through tunnels or holes you discover, ski-fly just off the surface of long alpine-like runs, take the ski jump and loop before you again touch further down on the snow-cloud mountain.

Cumulus clouds are pillars, rising hot air from surface heating, then cooled to precipitate cloud. They have a vertical form. In a cumulus cloud condition, you find at higher altitudes more cloud structures no longer connected to earth, large, spaced formations with clear air in between. They are in constant motion, growing,